DEN OF THIEVES

VICKI THARP

DEN OF THIEVES

Original Cover Design by Designs EE

Editing by Duli Noted

Proofing by EK Editing

ISBN 978-1-948798-40-2

 Created with Vellum

1

MAXIMILIAN HUFF STOOD OUTSIDE THE ROW OF FADED BLUE doors of the derelict apartment building that looked more like a strip motel from the seventies and wondered if he should have never left ten years ago.

Or if maybe he'd returned just in time.

The sun had barely come up. The complex was deserted except for the bedraggled woman who'd walked through the parking lot from the street—her skirt high, her neckline low, and bags under her make-up smeared eyes.

Max gave her a nod, and she offered a wan smile before letting herself into one of the apartments a couple of doors down. He trudged up the rickety stairs, still uncertain how this would all play out. Would Liberty toss him out on his ass and slam the door in his face, or would his sister sit down and have a civil conversation with him?

He expected the former. Hoped for the latter.

Pulling the cocktail napkin out of his back pocket, he checked the apartment number one last time. He would have knocked on his sister's door six months ago when he'd moved back to the San Fernando Valley, but it had taken him that long to track her down.

He rapped his knuckles on the door.

Huffs, as a whole, weren't well known for getting their shit together early in life. Or ever. But he was trying like hell to fix that.

And if he could spare Liberty all the mistakes he'd made, he would.

If she'd let him.

He knocked again with the meat of his fist, louder this time, the door shaking in the jamb. "Open up, Liberty. I know you're in there."

A muttered voice that Max couldn't even identify as female came through the door. "Fuck off."

Yeah, sounded like her.

"Come on, Libs, I—"

The door swung open, slammed against the wall, and bounced back. Max stuck his foot across the threshold to keep it from smacking into his sister's face.

"No," she said, not even looking surprised to see him at her door. "You don't get to call me *Libs* after all these years. You gave up that right when you left."

"Look..."

Liberty turned and walked away but didn't close the door in his face, so he considered it a win and followed her inside.

To call the apartment a flophouse would be generous. The fact that Liberty hadn't run out the door screaming told him his sister wasn't there against her will... but *damn.*

Several worn mattresses littered the floor, some with rumpled bedding, some with nothing but a dirty oval where an unwashed body had slept. And the smell... let's say he'd been to poorly run animal shelters that had smelled better.

Wearing a pair of faded jeans and a spaghetti strap tank that had seen better days, she walked to the nearly empty refrigerator, pulled out a carton of milk, and gulped straight from the container.

A thump came from down the hall, and a petite woman in panties and a cropped tank walked out. She rubbed at her face and bed-rumpled hair. "What the fuck, man? I'm trying to sleep."

"It's just my brother," Liberty said, with neither affection nor disgust. More of an *inevitable* flavor to her tone. She gathered her bright red hair and put it in a ponytail with the elastic from her wrist. With the dye job, he could have passed her on the street and never recognized her. "Go back to bed, Mina. We'll try to keep it down."

"I'm up now." Mina eyed Max for a moment before shuffling into the kitchen and pulling a bag of generic powdered donuts from the cupboard. She sat on a barstool, her nose in her phone.

Max glanced around, expecting to spot drug paraphernalia, but didn't find any. And though his sister had bags under her eyes that no twenty-two-year-old should have, she didn't look particularly high, or spaced out, or hungover. The knot in his stomach loosened a quarter turn. "What kind of place is this?"

Liberty wiped her mouth with the back of her hand, a stubborn Huff brow raised at him. "Really? That's what you lead with?"

"I—" He considered what he wanted to say next, but there was no good way to ask it, so he lowered his voice and snuck a glance at Mina, who didn't look like she was paying them any attention. "You a prostitute?"

"Sex worker is the preferred term. And what if I am? You riding in on your white horse to save me?"

Maybe. He glanced around the room again. Would that be so bad if he wanted to give her a better option? Not that he had the room in his efficiency apartment over his tattoo shop or the money to put her up in her own place. But he'd figure something out if she'd let him.

"If a hot guy pounded on my door and wanted to rescue me, I'd let him," Mina muttered, not looking up from her phone.

"Ew," Liberty said. "He's not hot. He's my brother. And he's gay, so he wouldn't be into you anyway."

Max's head snapped back to his sister. He hadn't been out when he still lived at home. Admitting that sort of thing would have been hazardous to his health. Liberty couldn't have known.

"How did you know?"

She shrugged and polished off the remainder of the milk and crushed the carton with her hand, leaving it on the counter with all the other empty food wrappers and pizza boxes.

"I walked in on you blowing Ricky Hodges." In air quotes, she added, "Your high school best friend."

"I didn't see—"

"You were a little preoccupied."

"You never told Mom or Dad." It wasn't a question. If she had outed him back then, home life would have gotten much uglier than it already had been.

Again, that maddening shrug, though this time there was a softness to it. "I didn't understand what you were doing back then. But I knew not to tell."

He closed his eyes. Even though he'd left home shortly after, he'd stayed in the valley, and it would have made dealing with his parents that much harder. When he opened his eyes again, the thanks in them, he left unspoken. Liberty gave him a fractional smile. "It wasn't just you looking out for me all the time."

A lump rose in his throat, thinking that his kid sister had felt the need to protect him when she'd been a kid herself.

Fuck, he wasn't here to reminisce about their shitty childhood.

"You didn't answer my question," Max said. "Are you a sex

worker?"

Mina scoffed. Liberty scowled. "What? I'd be a great sex worker."

"You're barely a passable money mule. You're going to get your skinny ass fired if you lose the money again."

Money mule? "For drugs?" As close to the border as they were, it wasn't unusual for people to sneak money back across the border for the cartels. Is that what his sister was caught up with?

Liberty ignored his question, and to Mina said, "It was an accident."

Mina glanced up from her phone. "That's not how they saw it."

"What are you saying?" he and Liberty asked at the same time.

"That you'd better be careful, that's all." Mina went back to her phone as if she hadn't dropped a bomb on Max.

"*Lib—*"

"Why are you here, Max?"

"After I'd heard about Mom and Dad dying, I—"

"The crash was three years ago. What? You thought we could be a family again? Like some over-acted made-for-TV afternoon special?"

"A what?" Mina glanced up from her phone for a second but went back to it when Liberty waved her off.

"Or even *Modern Family*," Liberty continued.

"Then what is it?"

"This is some fucked movie. Something you watch knowing there's a twist you won't see coming. Forgive me if I refuse to buy a ticket. Go back to where you came from, Max. I don't want any part of it."

The front door opened, and a thin man who looked to be in his forties walked in with a black backpack that *thunked* when it hit the floor. His gaze drifted over Max and focused on Liberty. "Time to go."

Max's hackles went up. "Go where?"

The man walked farther into the room, stole a couple of Mina's donuts, and hitched a thumb at Max. "Who's this asshole?"

"Nobody," Liberty said before Max could answer. "He was just leaving."

Max raised his own stubborn brow at her. He hadn't been anywhere close to leaving. He still had way more questions than answers, but Liberty brushed by him.

She picked up her keys off a bare nail by the door and slung the backpack over her shoulder. He stopped her at the door with a hand on her arm. Was that backpack full of money? What would happen if she got caught crossing the border with it? Or worse, what would happen if she lost the money again?

He lowered his voice, even though there was zero chance the guy wouldn't overhear. "Don't do this."

"What are you going to do, Maxie? Drag me back to your tiny apartment above the tattoo shop? What then?"

How had she known where he lived? How had she known about the shop? It had taken him six months to find her, and she'd known where he was that whole time? The shock must have shown on his face.

"I saw the spread the Sunday paper did on your shop when it opened. I can read. Don't act so surprised."

But before he could ask why she hadn't stopped by, she pulled her arm free. "I've been saving up. This is my last run. I'll be back tomorrow. Or the next day. Maybe I'll look you up then."

Max waited the day. Two. A week even. But when Liberty didn't show up at his shop, he went looking for her. Turns out, Mina hadn't seen her either. She hadn't seemed too concerned. But the acid ate away at Max's belly, and when almost two weeks had gone by with still no sign of his sister, Max knew who he needed to go to for help.

But Liberty hadn't been the only person he'd left behind, and he didn't expect a warmer reception from his ex.

DEREK WATTS FLEW JOSS KINCAID'S TWIN OTTER PLANE PAST THE skydiving landing zone and banked into the turn to make his approach to his friend's private airstrip. On the ground below him, Joss and his boyfriend Milo Malone, or was that fiancé now since the letters on the grass in white athletic field chalk clearly said, 'Marry me?'

"Is that... are they..." Foster Torres sat in the co-pilot seat—after promising not to touch a thing—and leaned against his window to get a better look. "Holy fuck, they're—"

"Fucking?"

Foster covered his eyes with his hand. "I can't unsee that. Even from this height."

Derek chuckled. "I guess this means we're going to have to wait a little longer on that cake."

He lined up on the airstrip and decreased his speed as he went in for the landing. Foster had a tight grip on the door handle and the edge of his seat, his eyes squinted nearly closed.

"I have landed this bird before, you know."

"Yeah, but we're coming in awful fast."

Derek shook his head. "It just feels fast this close to the ground."

They touched down, with only a squeak from Foster as Derek decelerated and brought the Otter to a stop near the hanger.

"We're here." Derek shut the engines down and prepped to leave. They'd worry about refueling later.

They climbed out of the plane, chucked the front wheel, and started walking toward the hanger. Foster glanced back at the dirt road that led up to the landing zone. "How long do you think they're going to be?"

"As long as they want. It's not every day you get a marriage propos—"

A man stepped out of the open doors at the rear of the hanger.

Not *a* man. *Maximilian Huff.*

"Oh, hey. Who are you?" Foster asked.

Max didn't answer, and Derek didn't bother to fill Foster in. Hard to do that with the wind knocked out of you, your mouth gaping open like an oxygen-starved fish. Max stood there with his thumbs tucked into the front pockets of his jeans, his worn leather jacket unzipped, and his reflective sunglasses covering his eyes. He'd filled out. Not the twenty-something kid he'd been ten years before. But he was just as fit.

And just as sexy.

Damn him.

Max stepped in front of Derek. When Derek stuck out his hand to push Max away, Max fisted his hands in Derek's T-shirt and swung him around. Derek's back hit the side of the hanger.

Foster held up his hands. "Whoa, hey, um—"

One withering look from Max shut Foster up. Then Max slammed his lips against Derek's, taking the kiss deep when Derek opened his mouth in surprise. Derek didn't fight back. He sank into the kiss, his dick immediately hard.

Max still smelled of tattoo ink and disinfectant. An intoxicating combination that Derek, for some reason, had never been able to resist. Max wasn't only Derek's ex... he was Derek's kryptonite.

His worst mistake.

And his biggest regret.

Max broke the kiss first, a cocky, satisfied smile on his lips as Derek fought to regain his breath and his mental balance.

"So, um, I take it you two know each other." Foster slowly backed into the hanger. "I'll just be in here…"

Whatever else Foster said was lost to Derek as Max raised his sunglasses to the top of his head, revealing dark circles under his piercing blue eyes. "You never could tell me no."

Derek wanted to tell Max to fuck off. Instead, he grabbed Max by his jacket and switched their positions, cutting off Max's arrogant chuckle when he covered Max's mouth with his. A drop of sanity brought Derek back to himself, and he pulled away before the feel of Max's hard-on against his hip had Derek doing things he'd years ago promised himself he never would.

"How did you find me?"

"Google. I stopped in at your office. Your partner told me you were here."

"*Fucking hell.*" Taking on a business partner had seemed like a good idea at the time. Derek was seriously reconsidering that at the moment.

"You know," Max said. That low, sultry voice had always drawn Derek's attention. "I never should have left."

Those words. Derek had dreamt about hearing them in the weeks and months after Max had disappeared. Max's eyes drifted to Derek's lips, then came back up to his eyes.

Before Derek could fall into another ill-advised kiss, he took a step back, needing the distance to give him a modicum of clarity and ask the important question. "Why are you here?"

Max's gaze dropped to the ground before meeting Derek's again. "I need your help."

"Fuck." A rueful laugh escaped him. "I should've known you didn't come back for me."

Derek shut down all those emotions he didn't want to ever feel again, the insecurities, the unmitigated anger, the unconditional love. He shoved a hand to the center of Max's chest, and Max's back thudded against the side of the hangar this time. He leaned in close, eyes locked on Max's. "Lose the address. Lose my number. Forget you were ever here."

He stepped away, determined to put Max in his past where he belonged.

"Need me to call the cops?" Foster met Derek as he strode through the hangar, headed for his Mercedes Roadster. He'd leave Joss, Milo, and Foster to celebrate without him.

"No. Max was just leaving."

The slap of Max's motorcycle boots on the concrete grew closer as Max jogged to catch up.

"*Derek.* Would you wait a goddamn minute?"

Derek stopped, hands on his hips as he stared up at the steel beams overhead. How could Max still have that kind of power over him?

Foster faded away. Whether he'd abandoned them and gone into Joss and Milo's apartment inside the hangar or drifted out the back again, Derek couldn't be certain.

All that he knew was that he was alone with a man he had no defenses against.

Max stopped a step behind him, the draw so strong Derek almost turned around. "If it were just for me, I'd go. But this is about Liberty. She's in trouble."

The gruff concern in Max's voice couldn't be faked, unless in the time he'd been gone, Max had become an Oscar-worthy actor. And it *was* Max's little sister. Derek did the mental math. Liberty wouldn't be a kid anymore. She'd be an adult. But still... Derek turned around, knowing it would be the second biggest mistake of his life.

He crossed his arms and sank into *private investigator* mode. Talking to Max would be much easier if he looked at him as a client and not his long-lost ex.

2

MAX HELD HIS BREATH, WAITING FOR HIS PLEA TO SINK IN. WHEN he'd moved out of his parents' house, he'd stayed in the valley to keep tabs on Liberty until things got too toxic for him to stay.

Derek had met Liberty on a couple of occasions. Occasions where he and Derek had pretended to be just friends. Looked like he hadn't had to pretend where Liberty had been concerned, considering she'd already caught him going down on a guy years before that.

His heart kicked against his sternum, not only waiting for Derek to respond but also because of that kiss.

Fuck. He'd promised himself not to bring their past into this. But all it had taken was one look at Derek, and he hadn't been able to keep his hands or lips to himself. How had his attraction not diminished over the years? How had it only intensified?

And by the way Derek had pinned him against the wall and stuck his tongue down Max's throat, their mutual attraction and explosive chemistry hadn't waned.

But Max had to put a lid on that. Finding Derek wasn't about looking up an old flame. It was about finding Liberty.

Derek's brown eyes narrowed, his voice clearly wary when he said, "What's going on with Liberty?"

From the backside of the hangar came the chug and whine of what sounded like a gas-powered golf cart. Derek glanced out the rear hangar doors and held up his hand. "Is this urgent?"

"I wouldn't have tracked you down, especially on your day off, if it wasn't."

Max almost added that he wouldn't have tracked Derek down, *period,* if it hadn't been for Liberty, but he bit back the words.

This wasn't a personal visit.

And it was some kind of fucked up that he had to keep reminding himself that.

"Wait here." Derek met the two men who climbed out of the golf cart, keeping one eye on Max while he spoke as if he expected Max to disappear on him again.

Fair enough. Max probably deserved that.

Derek hugged the two men, spared Max a glance as he walked by, and grumbled, "Follow me."

Max scrambled to follow. Derek didn't make it easy for Max to keep up. He threw on his helmet, backed his motorcycle out, and popped the clutch on his Harley as Derek's taillights disappeared down the hangar's driveway.

He sped down the winding road leading back to the valley from the San Gabriel foothills, leaning hard into some of the tighter curves that the Roadster hugged like a long-lost lover. He caught up with Derek as they hit the valley floor.

Max followed him through heavy traffic to a potholed parking lot in a seedier part of the city. Derek popped out of his car and headed down the sidewalk without a backward glance.

"Would you wait the hell up?" Max called out as he locked the forks on his bike, not convinced after looking around at some of the boarded-up businesses nearby that his bike would be there when he returned.

But he didn't see where he had a choice, so he jogged down the busted sidewalk after Derek.

He caught up to Derek as he opened a glass door with dark reflective tinting. There was no business name on the door or above, but the sound of canned music hit him as he blindly followed Derek inside.

It took a few seconds for his eyes to adjust. The darkness took mood lighting to a whole new level. Or maybe the dim lighting strategically hid all the flaws and health-code violations of the hole-in-the-wall bar.

That early in the day, Max was surprised it was open for business.

A bartender behind the short length of bar at the back of the room gave Derek a nod.

Derek nodded back and chose a table in the far corner. Max assumed his choice of tables was for the privacy it provided, even though they were the only customers there.

Just like Max remembered, Derek sat with his back to the wall, an aspect of his police training that he'd never lost, even in an establishment where he appeared comfortable and wouldn't be expecting any trouble.

You could tear the man out of the department, but you couldn't tear the department out of the man. Apparently.

Max had to bite his tongue and his sense of urgency as the bartender took their drink and food order. He didn't bother to look at a menu—not that he'd been provided one—and just ordered the same bacon, mushroom swiss burger and fries that Derek had.

When the bartender was out of earshot, before asking about Liberty, Derek said, "No reminiscing. No recriminations. And for fuck's sake, no more kissing." Derek leaned back and glared at Max. "Got me?"

Max held back the hint of a smile that wanted to surface. Derek had always liked being the one in control. Fine. They'd play it his way. Max could keep his body parts to himself.

The fact that he still had a semi from kissing Derek was beside the point.

"Yes, sir."

The corners of Derek's lips twitched, suppressing either a smile or a grimace. "Smartass."

"We can sit here all afternoon talking about my finer qualities, but if it's all the same to you, I'd rather not waste any more time. Liberty could be in danger, and I have to find her before something bad happens."

Derek sobered and accepted his beer from the bartender. When the man was out of earshot again, Derek said, "What makes you think she's in danger?"

Max pulled his beer toward himself, but his stomach had enough of a twist in it that he wasn't sure it would stay down.

What little Max knew, he told Derek. About the cheap apartment where people seemed to live on top of each other like roaches. About Mina's 'money mule' comment. About the black backpack. About Liberty's promise to be back in a couple of days and look him up, but how she'd overshot that time frame by close to two weeks.

As he spoke, Derek drained his beer down to half a glass, the thick head of foam on his dark ale all but gone. "Sounds like she wasn't all too thrilled to see her long-lost brother. Maybe she's avoiding you. The way you busted into her life, I'm not sure I could blame her."

Max raised a brow at the not-so-subtle dig and finally took a sip of his beer. "You said no recriminations."

"That's not a recrimination. It's an opinion."

They wouldn't get any closer to finding Liberty if they spent all day arguing over semantics, so Max mentally moved on but dropped a pin in the topic for later. Maybe Derek wasn't as unaffected by Max as he'd let on. Searing kiss aside.

Or maybe he's still hurt.

A tightness formed in the center of Max's chest, and he tried to swallow it down with beer.

"Have you gone looking for her?"

"Her apartment is the only place I know to look. There's always someone new who answers the door, and they won't let me in. They also refuse to tell me if she's there or not. She could have been in the other room this whole time for all I know. But I haven't seen her coming or going. At least not the few times I've been by."

"You've sat on her apartment?"

"Not all night. A few hours here and there. I've got to work. It's just me, my assistant, and clients who take it badly when their tattooist is so tired the linework goes to shit. Besides, I'm not exactly inconspicuous on my bike. Someone already called the cops on me for sitting outside their complex too long down the street from my sister's."

Did he sound too defensive? As if he weren't doing all that he knew to do?

Derek raised his hands in surrender. Yup, Max had sounded defensive. "I was just asking. It's where I would start if I were looking for her."

The bartender came by with fresh beer and their burgers and made himself scarce again. They both fell silent as they dug into their food. Max couldn't help but watch the play of Derek's jaw muscles as they worked, or the bob of his Adam's apple as he swallowed. Remembering how it had felt to have his lips there, to have full, unfettered access to Derek's entire body.

He reached a hand beneath the table and subtly adjusted

himself, but Derek caught the movement. Derek must have known what Max was doing. That time the slight twitch of Derek's lips definitely looked more like a grimace than a grin.

The burger grease ran down both of Max's wrists. He pushed a bite of food into his cheek. "So, are you? Looking for her, that is."

DEREK SAT BACK AND RAN THROUGH THE RAMIFICATIONS OF agreeing to help Max find Liberty. On the one hand, he'd have continued contact with a man who'd turned his world upside down... twice.

Once when he'd walked into it.

Once when he'd walked out.

On the other hand, Liberty was missing, and as much as Derek assumed Liberty was avoiding Max much in the same way he wished he could, on the off chance that Liberty was in danger, could he ignore that possibility?

No. He couldn't.

His best option? Find her fast, keep Max at a distance, and get back to his ordered, Max-less, sex-less life.

Derek tossed the dregs of his beer into the back of his throat, convinced he would regret his decision when he said, "Yeah, I'll look for her."

Max didn't hide his relief, but he schooled his smile, which was just as well. Derek hadn't forgotten how utterly devastating that smile could be when its full wattage shined on him.

Max pulled out his battered wallet. The burnished leather looked as if it had been in and out of Max's pocket for the last ten years. He thumbed through the bills. More ones and fives than the twenties and hundreds that Derek had in his.

"How much, you know, do you need to get started? A retainer, is it?"

"I don't want your money, Max." Yeah, and the way that came out, it sounded like Derek wanted so much more.

Which was definitely *not* the case.

Not one bit.

Nope.

The bartender came over with the bill and set it between them. Max reached for it first, and Derek let Max pick up the tab, even though Derek could have afforded it much easier. But Derek knew that Max had his pride, and if Derek wasn't going to let Max pay him for his time, then he had to let him pay for *something*.

Derek dreaded Max asking something along the lines of *then what do you want?* Because at that point, Derek didn't have a clue. Maybe to go back to the start of his day and land Joss's plane and not find Max standing in the hangar.

But that kiss... you would have missed that kiss. That kiss that stirred your dick for the first time in a long time—one that highjacked your breath, kicked your heart rate into the red zone, and made you want to peel every stitch of clothing off until you were both naked and—

"Hey," Max said, interrupting his thoughts. "Where'd you go?"

"Just deciding where to start looking for Liberty."

Max eyed him. Derek was a damn fine liar. A part of his job. He rarely got caught in a lie. But Max had always had the uncanny ability to read him. At least this time, he didn't call him out on his bullshit.

Maybe that's what had made their relationship different than all the other ones Derek had been in before or since. Max *got* him like no one else ever had.

During their time together, Max had seen Derek's unvarnished truth, and it hadn't scared him away.

Or maybe it had…

Derek's lips twisted down.

"What's wrong?"

"Nothing. Give me Liberty's address. I'm going to start there and—"

"Whoa, whoa, whoa. Who said anything about you doing this alone? She's my sister. I'm going with you."

"I work alone." Which wasn't technically true now that he'd partnered with Cesar Morales, but it was close enough to the truth that Max didn't give him any flak about the lie.

"Not this time."

"I can't have my clients—"

"If you won't take my money, I'm technically not your client then, am I? I'm just an old friend you're helping out."

"Is that what we were? *Old friends*?" Fuck. That sounded more like a recrimination. A recrimination that Derek himself had specifically said there'd be none of. "Never mind. Don't answer that."

But Max being Max, he didn't listen. He leaned in and dropped his voice to that low, intimate register that had always made goosebumps skitter across Derek's skin in the best, worst way possible. "You know it was goddamn more than that."

"We're not talking about this, remember?" It took a lot out of Derek had to say that. Mostly, he agreed. But he'd be lying—and lying so badly that *anyone* could tell that he was, not just Max—if he said that a part of him didn't want to talk about it.

Didn't want to find out where it all had gone wrong.

But none of that would help them find Liberty.

"*Jesusfuckingchrist*," Max muttered as he threw some bills on their table and stood. "Glad to see you haven't changed at all."

The way Max said it, he wasn't happy to find out that little tidbit. But what had Max expected? Derek didn't like to talk about his feelings, or his past, or god-fucking-forbid, his father. Which in some backward, roundabout way, every blowup in his life always seemed to be about the bastard who'd sired him.

How fucked up was that?

A shrink would have a field day if Derek ever stretched out on one of their couches. Not that even he had the kind of cash or the years it would take to unpack all the bullshit.

"You going to give me that address, or are you going to make me regret saying yes?"

Max gave him a tight smile that said he wouldn't budge on his position about being involved in the case. "I'd be happy to show it to you."

By the time they drove across town, picked up Derek's piece of shit car that he used for stakeouts, and got back across town to Liberty's apartment, they'd only have a few hours to kill before it got dark. Plenty of time to sit on Liberty's apartment and see who came and went.

"Fine. Follow me." He made it sound more like a challenge than a statement. They headed for the door. Once in the parking lot, Max didn't waste any time starting his bike. Through the traffic, quick turns, and short traffic lights, somehow Max managed to stick with him.

Derek drove them to his new office, a converted house in a section of town where small businesses had taken over some of the older neighborhoods. He'd hated to give up his old business location, a tiny freestanding building on a busy corner. It had been perfect over the years as he'd built his business, but not long after Cesar had joined him in his old space, they knew the one-room office with the leather couch that had frequently doubled as a bed over the years wouldn't work for a two-person PI agency.

But old sentiments aside, the new place had its advantages.

With three bedrooms, he and Cesar could each have their own office. They'd planned on stashing a bed in the smallest of the three rooms because he often worked late into the night, and the bed would be a hell of a lot more comfortable than a couch, especially for a man of his size.

Plus, he could store his stake-out jar in the one-car garage at the back of the property and not have to worry about the neighbors complaining about having to look at it.

The driveway curved around to the back, and Max parked his bike where it wouldn't be seen from the street. He caught up to Derek as he unlocked the back door and pushed his way inside.

The back door opened into a tiny kitchen. Derek had to order an apartment-sized refrigerator to fit the space. Since no one lived here, they didn't need anything more than something to keep beer, coffee creamer, or the occasional take-out leftovers cold.

Two medium-sized boxes took up all the available counter space, hiding the scratched and worn laminate. He and Cesar had some renovations lined up, but the kitchen was functional for now.

He led Max into what would have been a den and dining room area, but now it held a bunch of boxes and two desks still in pieces. The empty file cabinets sat against a wall, the drawers askew. A new mattress and box springs in their protective plastic leaned against one wall.

Max disappeared down the hall toward the bathroom while Derek took out his pocketknife and opened up boxes until he found his camera bag and his telephoto lens.

Returning to the kitchen, Derek dug out the coffee maker, coffee, and a couple of thermoses. As the coffee brewed, he glanced over his shoulder and found Max propped against the wall behind him, his gaze assessing and...

Derek couldn't quite read the expression on Max's face, the softness at odds with the crossed arms over Max's chest.

Turning, Derek said, "I don't suppose I can talk you out of coming with me."

3

Max had folded his arms across his chest when all he wanted to do was pin Derek against the counter, wrap his arms around Derek's waist, and kiss the spot on Derek's neck. The spot that had always made Derek make *that* sound. Just thinking about it sent lightning strikes straight to Max's dick.

Instead of answering Derek's question, the one where Derek wanted Max to stay behind, Max said, "I like my coffee with cream and sugar."

Derek turned away. The way he grumbled, "Yeah, I remember," told Max that Derek wasn't too happy that he had.

Though on some level, it satisfied Max to learn that Derek hadn't forgotten everything about him over the past ten years.

They stood on opposite sides of the kitchen, a few paces away from each other. Max watched as Derek carefully washed, rinsed, and dried the thermoses and set them beside the coffee maker. He'd made a large pot, and it took an excruciatingly long time for the pot to fill.

"I guess I caught your partner just in time," Max said, "I didn't know you were moving offices."

"You couldn't have known."

Of course not. When Max had disappeared, he hadn't looked back, too afraid that if he did, he'd go running to Derek and beg him to take him back. It was better this way. They'd both had their own shit they'd needed to deal with. That Max had shown up on Derek's doorstep at all, he blamed on Liberty.

Max didn't have very many good memories of the valley. All of the positive ones revolved around his sister and Derek. Considering how things had ended between the two of them, he slotted some of those memories back into the 'not so good' memory column.

The pot thankfully, mercifully, finished filling, and Derek divided the coffee between the two thermoses, leaving room at the top for Max's creamer and sugar.

Derek handed him the thermos. "There should be creamer in the fridge and sugar packets in one of these boxes. I'm going to hit the head, and I'll be ready to go."

Max doctored his and Derek's coffee and screwed on the lids. By the time he'd finished, Derek had returned, the straps of his camera bag in one hand and an old-school set of car keys in the other.

Derek locked up behind them, and Max followed him out to the single-car garage at the back of the house. What might have been a yard at one time was paved for parking. With the bike and Roadster behind the house, they didn't have to jockey vehicles. Not that it would have hurt Max's feelings if he'd had to move the Roadster for Derek.

Pulling up the garage door, Max got his first look at the shit-can-on-wheels sitting inside. Even in the shadowed garage, Max saw the patches of rust, the sun-scalded tan paint, the muffler that hung from the frame with nothing more than a coat hanger.

"You've got to be fucking kidding me. I need to get my shots updated before I climb into that."

Derek only laughed. "Wait until you see the inside." It didn't sound like an endorsement.

But this wasn't about comfort. It was about finding Liberty, and Max would do whatever it took, be around whoever he needed to, to make that happen.

Derek climbed in, and the engine spun and spun before it caught. Puffs of black smoke spilled out of the holes in the muffler before dissipating. Engine chugging, Derek backed out. Max closed the garage before yanking the passenger door open and climbing inside.

His knees hit the dashboard, and he reached down to shift the seat back, but not only was there not an electric adjustment, but the manual bar under the seat didn't work.

Derek stifled a chuckle. "Sorry. The seat doesn't adjust anymore."

Max stashed his thermos between his hip and the door since there also weren't any cup holders. He fidgeted in his seat, but no matter how he positioned himself, he couldn't avoid the spring poking into his ass.

"Good news is there aren't any airbags you have to worry about exploding into your legs."

Fuck. "Yeah. Silver lining."

Derek eased down the driveway and stopped before backing into the street. "Which way?"

Max pointed to their left. "That way. It's at Childress and Montgomery."

Derek gave him a look. "That's a crap part of town. Even the drug dealers and sex workers aren't stupid enough to stand on those corners."

"Tell me about it."

As they approached Liberty's apartment complex, they made a couple of passes around the block, scoping out the best place to watch Liberty's door while drawing the least amount of suspicion.

Derek found an alley with a decent view of Liberty's apartment, which turned out to be a much less conspicuous location to lay low and watch for Liberty than the spot in front of the other apartment complex that Max had chosen. Which he guessed was the reason Derek was the professional and not Max.

Though they couldn't see the entire front of the apartment, they could see enough.

The engine coughed, sputtered, and died before Derek could cut the engine. They cracked the manual windows. Max's only went down a couple of inches before the crank stopped turning, but on a mild March evening in Southern California, the heat wasn't unbearable.

Derek moved his seat back, attached the telephoto lens to his camera, and took a couple of snapshots. Though when darkness fell, Max wasn't convinced the photos would turn out. From his previous visits, he knew that few of the streetlights functioned, making the lighting situation less than ideal.

Even though Max knew it was his imagination getting the better of him, the area seemed to give off this evil vibe that made his worry and concern for Liberty ratchet up a few notches from its already elevated state. He shifted in his seat, trying to get more comfortable, but gave up and gave in to being miserable for the rest of the night. He took a swig of his coffee and nestled the open thermos between his thighs.

"There should be a pair of binoculars in the glove box if you can get it open."

Max practically turned himself into a pretzel, but he couldn't get his knees far enough away to get the binoculars out. He finally had to open the car door and climb out to get them. He groaned. His back and legs had already stiffened.

If he'd had something else to look at in the car besides Derek's profile, he would have said to hell with it and left the binoculars where they were.

But he couldn't sit there and stare at Derek all night, especially if he didn't want Derek asking any questions.

An hour went by. Then two. Then three before darkness fell.

Max lowered the binoculars, his knees screaming, his back aching, his heart... fuck if sitting next to Derek hadn't brought back the flood of memories. Not of stakeouts—because he'd never done that before.

But the two of them had certainly spent their fair share of time in a car together... mostly in the back seat. Just thinking about those hot, sticky nights, the kissing, the groping, the fucking, made Max hard, and sitting in that seat with his knees around his ears didn't leave much room to get an unwelcomed erection.

He shifted again, and Derek glanced over and sighed. "I know toddlers who can sit still longer than you."

"Oh yeah? What toddlers do you know?"

"I don't. Really. But if I did..."

"I gotta piss," Max said, because the alternative, telling Derek he'd given himself a boner remembering what it felt like to be buried balls deep in Derek's ass, didn't seem like a good idea.

Derek glanced around and double-checked his mirrors. No one was in sight. In fact, they hadn't seen hardly anyone all afternoon. Not the sex worker Max had seen that first night when he'd approached his sister's apartment. Not the woman who'd walked out of a back room of Liberty's apartment in nothing more than a tank top and panties, not the man with the backpack.

And certainly not Liberty.

"You can piss behind the car. No one from the apartments will be able to see you back there. Just don't slam the car door."

Max gave Derek a quelling look. "I'm not an idiot."

The return look Derek gave him called his statement into question.

He cracked his car door, the hinges creaking and groaning like the sound effects from a horror movie. He could almost hear the dark, anxiety-inducing music playing in the background.

He unfolded himself, his joints creaking and groaning louder than the damn door. Leaving the door ajar, he eased his way to the back of the car. He stood in the shadows as he unbuttoned his jeans and pulled out his hard cock.

Max didn't have to pee all that much. He'd hardly touched his coffee. But he couldn't pretend to go now and then *really* have to go in an hour or so. He braced one hand against the wall, the pointy bumps of the stucco digging into his palm.

He pushed harder, concentrating on the pain in his hand instead of the heaviness in his balls and the overwhelming desire to stroke himself to completion. At least if he jacked off, he wouldn't have to be uncomfortable sitting next to Derek all night.

And with the state he was in, it wouldn't take more than a few strokes.

Not wanting to be *that* guy, he closed his eyes and concentrated on urinating.

The hairs stood up on the back of his neck a second too late as feet scuffled behind him. A hand clamped down on his shoulder.

"Hands where I can see them," the woman said as she used her forearm to shove Max into the wall and pin him there.

Max thought about fighting or calling out, but he'd been around law enforcement enough through Derek that he knew he wasn't dealing with someone wanting his wallet or his motorcycle boots.

The woman did a quick pat-down, though with his pants unzipped and his dick hanging out, it was obvious Max didn't have a weapon around his waist. The good news? He didn't have a boner anymore.

Pulling Max back by the collar, she started walking him toward Derek's door. Derek caught the movement in his side mirror and said, "What's going on?"

She shoved Max another step forward, and Max said, "I think we've got trouble."

ALL DEREK SAW IN HIS SIDE MIRROR WAS MAX'S HANDS BY HIS head, his pants loose around his hips, and his soft dick dangling out. He would have laughed if he didn't think Max would deck him for it later.

Then another person moved from behind Max, a good head shorter and sixty pounds lighter.

"Tasha?" Derek said. "Is that you?"

Tasha stepped out from behind Max, her hands on her slim hips. "Watts. I should have known this piece of shit car belonged to you." She scanned the vehicle front to back, then leaned her hands on the door sill. "Even the department doesn't use cars this rough for undercover."

In the cracked side mirror, Derek watched as Max shoved his cock back into his pants and zipped up. Shame. Though what Derek wanted to do with that cock, he'd rather not do in front of his former FTO.

Derek twisted in his seat and put the boner-inducing thoughts of Max out of his mind where they belonged. "Max, this is my old field training officer, LaTasha Barnes.

Tasha..." He didn't quite know what to call Max, or what Max was to him at this point, so he just said, "This is Maximillian Huff."

"Hey," Max said. If he were embarrassed to have been caught with his pants down, it didn't show in his voice.

"Hey." She bobbed her chin at him but quickly turned her attention back to Derek.

Derek's stomach sank as Tasha leaned her forearms on the sill of the car. Tasha wouldn't be in a dark alley at night if she weren't working an undercover operation.

"What's going on?"

"You're stepping on our toes, Watts. I don't want you stumbling into the middle of our investigation."

"What do you have?"

She chuckled, her disarming grin belying her toughness. "You know I can't tell you that."

Despite their shared history and mutual respect, Tasha had always been a stickler for the rules, and she wasn't about to break them for him. At least not without a damn good reason. And if they were going to get anywhere, Derek would have to be the one who gave a little first. "We're sitting on an apartment down the street. Number 204. Max's sister is in the wind. We're trying to locate her."

Tasha straightened to address Max. "You file a missing person's report?"

Max nodded. "I don't think the department considers it a priority."

Though from what Max had told Derek, he hadn't spilled that bit about Liberty being a money mule to the officer taking the report, not wanting to get his sister into any more trouble than she might already be in.

She jerked her head toward Derek. "So you called this guy in?"

Max leaned a hip against the car. "What would you do if it were your kid sister?"

She glanced at the apartment complex, then back at Derek. "Stay in the car. Don't fuck this up for us, yeah?"

"We're just here to observe," Derek said. He caught the *WTF* look Max shot him in his side mirror but hoped Max would keep his trap shut. He held up his fingers. "Scout's honor."

"Spare me. Just stay in the fucking car." She started backing away.

"Hey, Tash." She stopped, and Derek said, "Good seeing you again."

She offered a flash of her generous smile. "Same."

LaTasha merged with the cover of darkness, disappearing as quietly and as quickly as she'd arrived. Derek watched his side and rearview mirrors, but he couldn't detect her hideout from the car. Was she on one of the nearby rooftops? Or peeking through a hole in one of the many boarded-up windows of the warehouse on their left?

But then again, did it matter? He'd told her they'd stay in the car. And they would. He didn't want the reputation of the PI who couldn't play nice with the undercover cops. It would be bad for business.

They sat there for an hour more, he guessed. He couldn't check the digital clock on the dash for the time because the car didn't have one. Maybe his choice of surveillance vehicles did need a bit of an upgrade.

"How long do you want to sit here?" Derek asked after the second man of the night walked past Liberty's apartment to the unit on the end of the row. "The only action this apartment complex is seeing is that woman at the far end, and I think her night is just getting started."

"I'll stay here all night if that's what it takes. It may cripple me, but—" Max must have caught movement because he raised the binoculars and thumped Derek on the shoulder with the back of his hand.

"Where?" On immediate alert, Derek raised his camera and pointed his lens in the apartments' general direction.

"That cut through, behind the stairs," Max whispered, though there was no danger anyone would over-hear.

Derek stuck his lens out his open window, made the slight adjustment in location, and started snapping pictures as a woman snuck around the stairs and scurried up, her head on a swivel until she'd disappeared inside apartment 204.

"Holy fuck," Max said. "That was the girl I was telling you about. Mina. The one that came out of the back bedroom."

They both scanned the apartment complex but didn't see any more movement. Max set his binoculars down. "Why didn't she turn on any lights? Isn't that weird? That's weird, right? What do you think she's up to?"

"Maybe she's not up to anything. It's late, and maybe she's tired and went straight to bed."

Max made a noise in the back of his throat that Derek couldn't identify as an affirmative or a scoff. "And the way she snuck in there? Who does that?"

"It's odd. But not *that* odd. You knew she lived there."

"I haven't seen her since that night, though. I've talked to a different woman each time I went there looking for Liberty, but this is the first time I've seen her since then." He cracked his door. "Maybe we should—"

Derek reached across the center console and grabbed Max's arm before Max could throw the door open and dash across the street. He didn't want to break their cover... or break his promise to Tasha. "Hold up. We're just watching tonight. Remember."

"That's what *you* said. That's not what *I* said."

"*Maxie.*" Derek almost winced at how easy Max's nickname rolled off his tongue as if it had only been ten hours since he'd last seen Max, not ten years. Being this close to Max might be infinitely more dangerous than whatever they might get into while finding Liberty.

"We need to have some patience," Derek said, feeling very little of his own. "We need to watch. We need to wait. We need to evaluate our options. We won't do Liberty any good if we go off half-cocked and scare away the very people we need to talk to."

Max sank back into his seat, the defeat clear on his face even in the low light. "Fuck. All I want is to get my sister back. If she wants me to fuck off for the rest of her life after that, so be it, but I've got to know that she's okay. She's all I've got left."

It took everything Derek had not to say that Max had him as well when he knew that wasn't true. Max hadn't looked Derek up for old times' sake. He'd looked Derek up because he'd needed help. If Liberty hadn't disappeared, he probably would have never seen Max again. It would be best that Derek didn't forget that.

"We'll get her back." Derek found it difficult to sound reassuring when he wasn't convinced himself.

"Promise?" Max had to know as well as Derek did that that may not be a promise Derek could keep. But Max needed something to hang on to, even if it were only empty words.

"Yeah. Promise."

4

MAX SWALLOWED DEREK'S LIE, AS BITTER AS IT WAS. BUT EVEN HE could admit he wasn't in the right frame of mind to contemplate the fact that they might never find Liberty. The life of a money mule wasn't necessarily known for its longevity.

Add in the fact that Liberty was a young, beautiful woman crossing into a foreign country and dealing with the criminal element. Plus, Max's concern that Liberty's penchant for speaking her mind might get her trafficked or killed.

They waited, his bladder starting to complain for real this time. The apartment remained dark, and Max let the binoculars hang around his neck. "I gotta take a leak."

"Didn't you already do that?"

"Your FTO interrupted me."

Derek fought back the chuckle but was helpless at holding back his smile. "Christ, when you started your perp-walk back to the car with your dick hanging out—"

"I wouldn't finish that sentence if I were you." Max shot Derek a look, but Derek's amused smile just widened, his dazzling brown eyes dancing.

Max started easing his door open, but there was no way he could get out of the car without making a sound, not with the rusty hinges. He considered finding a container to pee in, but the only thing in the car was his coffee thermos, and he was *not* peeing in that.

Not because of a general aversion to urinating into a container but because he didn't trust what his dick would do if it were let out into the wild with Derek only inches away. Not when it would betray his true feelings.

Max squeezed out of the car, returned to the stucco wall, and did what he needed to do. He was just zipping up when Derek made a low *pssst* that caught his attention. Turning, he saw movement on the stairs. A man with a backpack heading straight for Liberty's apartment. Max brought up his binoculars but couldn't catch the man's face before he disappeared inside.

He crept along the side of the car to Derek's window, keeping a low profile to make him less noticeable. "You get any good shots?"

Derek handed the camera out the window, and Max thumbed through the series of photos. He stopped on the photo of the man looking over his shoulder. "That's him. That's the guy I saw when I was there with Liberty."

That photo was all the confirmation Max needed. He tossed the binoculars through the window and took off for the apartment at a half-jog, half-run, not caring about Tasha, the cops, or whatever he might be inadvertently screwing up by going over there.

What he *did* know was that he wasn't going to stand there with his thumb up his ass while the person he suspected knew more than anyone else about his sister's location came and went without Max doing something about it. Derek could take photos all he wanted, but photos weren't going to get his sister back.

He thought he heard a hissed curse from Derek and the creak of the car's decrepit hinges, but Max didn't slow or glance back.

If Derek caught his eye, Max might think twice about what he was doing.

Derek's heavy footfalls hit the bottom of the rickety stars as Max reached the top. He stopped at the door jamb of his sister's apartment, not wanting to stand directly in front of the peephole in case someone heard a noise and decided to look through it.

Derek flattened himself against the wall beside Max, his grip firm on Max's bicep. A hissed, "What the fuck," landed in Max's ear.

Max turned. A dim porch light four doors down highlighted the concern, and yes, frustration, marring Derek's handsome face.

"You don't have to be here. I understand if this is going to get you in trouble with Tasha or the department."

Derek made a face—one Max hadn't seen in way too long, but one he remembered well—that stubborn face that said Derek wasn't swayed. "I'm not letting you do this alone, asshole."

Max grinned, then pounded his fist on the door, not understanding why that simple declaration made his chest tight and fill with warmth.

Maybe because it seemed like no one has had your back for what felt like two eternities?

Max put that thought out of his head. He had other things to worry about right then. The apartment door flung open, and the asshole who'd given Liberty the backpack and her marching orders stood in front of him.

No surprise came to the man's face. But considering the man's line of work, Max figured he wasn't the type of guy surprised by a knock on his door in the middle of the night.

Max shoved his way through the door with Derek on his heels. Max spun in the middle of the room. If it were possible, there was even more trash on the floor and the counters. The smell of rotting food turned his stomach. When Max finally found Liberty, they would have to do something about her living arrangement. There was no way he could let her stay there any longer.

"Where is she?"

The man shoved his hands into the front pockets of his worn jeans and rocked back on his heels, an arrogant smile on his face. "You're going to have to be a little more specific than that. I got girls all over the city. You need your dick sucked, you can find them on a corner, you don't gotta come looking here."

Before Derek could make a move to stop him, Max fisted the front of the man's shirt and shoved him up against the wall. The reverberation shook the ceiling fan, and one of the bulbs blinked out. "I'm looking for Liberty. I was here the day you sent her off on a job, remember?"

The man narrowed his eyes as if trying to match Max's face with his memory. "She ain't here. Word on the street is Marco took care of her."

By the way he said it, *care of* was a euphemism for *gotten rid of*. Max sure as hell hoped those rumors were wrong.

Derek closed in, apparently not content to stand back and let Max do all the talking. "Who's Marco?"

The smile that crossed the man's face exposed dark, meth-rotted teeth, wasn't evil or calculating. It was more of a *you have no idea what shit you're stirring*. And it looked like the guy couldn't wait to order his popcorn, sit back, and watch what happened next. "He's the guy you don't fuck around with."

Fuck.

Max released the man and took a step back. "How do I find her?"

The man straightened, the rotten, crooked smile on his face, not faltering. He leaned in and, in a stage whisper, said, "You don't."

He pushed by Max, retrieved a backpack from the floor, and grabbed a set of keys from the counter. Max stepped in front of him, blocking his path to the door. "Then where do I find this Marco guy?"

"How stupid do I look?"

Max figured he wouldn't get very far if he answered that question honestly. Instead, he decided to play up to the man's sense of honor, if the man had any left. "Come on, man, give a guy a break. She's my sister, yeah? What can you tell me?"

"Nothing more than I already have."

"What's your name, buddy?" How could Derek sound like he wanted to make a new friend when all Max could think about was rearranging that guy's face to look like a Picasso?

The man's eyes slid to Derek. "Eat shit."

The man stepped on one of the dirty mattresses, going around Max. When Max went to stop him, Derek put a staying hand on Max's arm, and he watched the man walk out the door.

He turned his anger and frustration on Derek. "Now, what did you go and do that for?"

"Because you were never going to convince a guy like that to tell you anything he doesn't want to. He's more scared of Marco than anything you could do to him."

"Fuck," Max muttered, knowing Derek was right. But how in the hell were they supposed to find Marco, much less Liberty? She could be anywhere.

From the back room came the hollow metal clang of what sounded like a hammer hitting metal. *Mina.* Max had been so focused on the guy that he'd forgotten Mina was in the apartment.

Derek beat Max to the hall and shouldered through the door

without bothering to knock, Max only a half-step behind. A shadeless lamp with a dim bulb cast the room in yellow light. A twin mattress with a pile of wrinkled, smelly clothes occupied the middle of the tiny room.

It looked as if whoever had been sleeping there had used the clothes as makeshift sheets. Either that or the person couldn't be bothered to shove them out of the way.

On the floor, next to an open cardboard box with a dried-up slice of pepperoni pizza, sat Mina. She had a hammer in her hand, and one of those locking metal cash boxes you could get at an office supply store wedged between her knees. Max recognized it. He'd bought it for Liberty for the lemonade stand she'd had when she was eight.

Max pushed past Derek and swiped the cash box from Mina's hands. "What the fuck are you doing?"

***

MINA ROSE ON HER KNEES, FALLING FORWARD AND CATCHING herself with her hand, almost hitting her head on the hammer claw. Derek snatched the hammer away from her before she hurt herself or decided to use it as a weapon.

She glanced up slowly, her eyes red and rolling around in her head. Mina tried to focus on them as they stood above her. "Hey, that's mine. Give it back."

At least that's what Derek thought she'd said. Though the way she slurred her words, he couldn't be certain. He had no clue what she'd taken, snorted, shot up, or smoked, but she was mere seconds from passing out. They didn't have much time to get the answers they needed.

Max turned the front of the cash box around, Liberty's name emblazoned on the front with pink bubble-letter stickers. It had a dented top, a sprung hinge, the locked clasp hanging from the front by a thread. "This is Liberty's. What are you doing with this?"

Mina rolled to her back and shrugged, not bothering to right herself.

Max held out a hand, and Derek handed him the hammer. Wedging the claw into the seam by the lock, he pried the top off. Cash and coins fell out, along with a passport.

Derek picked up the passport. It was Liberty, all grown up. But the name didn't match. And though Derek had seen worse forgeries, this one would never make it past the border agents. "It's fake. Why does your sister need a forged passport?"

Instead of answering his question, Max said, "What the hell has she gotten herself into?"

Mina finally rolled over, bracing her weight on one shaky arm. "She wanted out. This was her last trip. Then she was disappearing."

Derek caught the flash of hurt in Max's eyes, and Derek knew he was thinking the same thing Max was. If Max hadn't shown up at the apartment when he had, he might have never seen his sister again.

Max squatted down and picked up the cash and counted it. "There's almost four thousand dollars here."

"That's not a lot to live on," Derek said.

"No. But it might be enough to get herself started in a new life in a new town. She told me she was saving to go back to college."

"That could still be true." Derek had his doubts, but he didn't need to voice them. The look on Max's face said he already knew what his sister had told him had probably been a lie.

Mina collapsed again, her eyes drifting closed.

Max squeezed her shoulder, displaying a level of gentleness Derek hadn't expected of him considering the circumstances. But that really shouldn't have come as a surprise. As big as Max was, he had a wide tender streak he'd always had a difficult time hiding.

"Mina," Max said, his voice soft but firm. "Why were you breaking into Liberty's cash box?"

Max had to shake her again before her eyes reopened.

"She's not going to need it."

Derek squatted down as well. "What do you mean?"

She shrugged, and her eyes closed. Max shook her again. Her eyes didn't reopen, but she mumbled, "When girls are gone this long, they don't come back."

"What do you mean they don't come back?"

Derek heard the change in Max's inflection, the frustration marrying with a sense of urgency and low-key panic. Derek took the bills from Max and stuffed them in Mina's hand. "Tell us what you know, and the money is yours."

That opened one of her eyes. Max and Mina both looked at him as if he'd lost his mind. But that wasn't even close to the truth. Money talked.

"Liberty is going to need that if—" Max caught himself. "*When* she comes back."

"And I'll be happy to cover it when she does."

Max looked like he wanted to argue, but they both knew it wasn't the time or the place. Derek turned his attention back to Mina and asked his question again. "What do you mean, the girls don't come back?"

"They either get out, or they disappear. You can't cross Marco. Not and live to tell about it."

Mina's eyes rolled back. Derek felt her pulse. Strong and steady, her breathing deep and regular.

Max patted her cheek. "Where's Marco?"

"Las Rocas," Mina said before her eyes rolled up, the whites of her eyes still visible.

"We can try to pour some coffee into her, but I don't think it's going to matter much," Max said.

"I doubt she knows much more." Derek stood. "A guy like Marco wouldn't let people like Mina know where they are. These women are pawns, not players."

Max rolled up the cash and stuffed it into the pocket of Mina's shorts. If someone else came into the apartment in the middle of the night, Mina might not have the money come morning, but they had promised her the cash, and as much as Derek knew that Max was reluctant to leave his sister's money behind, a promise was a promise.

And Max didn't break promises.

Except for that one ten years ago. The one where Max had promised to stay.

Derek blew out a hot breath and pushed those personal thoughts to the back of his mind. This investigation had no room for their history. Even if Derek still had too many questions that he needed answered.

They left Mina in her room. Max cracked the front door, glancing both ways as if expecting an ambush. But none came. Derek pressed the pushbutton lock on the door. He didn't like the idea of leaving Mina alone in an unlocked apartment. She was vulnerable enough as it were.

They jogged back across the street to their car and climbed inside. Derek hadn't bothered locking it. It wasn't the kind of car even the opportunistic car thieves bothered to jack.

"Where to?" Max asked as Derek backed down the alley, did a three-point turn on the street behind them, flicked on the headlights, and headed toward their side of town.

"To get some sleep."

Max grunted, which Derek took as disgruntled agreement.

"And then?"

"Then we'll stop by the station in the morning to show Tasha those photos and see if she has any information she can tell us about Marco and his operation. That is if she's still willing to talk to me after that stunt you pulled.

5

Max took Derek's verbal slap on the chin. He'd deserved that. He hadn't gotten the information he'd wanted, but it was still worth the risk of Tasha freezing them out if it meant he had a lead to follow.

And they *did* have something. A city. Las Rocas. With what Max assumed were way too many places for a criminal to hide. But it was better than having the whole world as a possibility.

Lost in thought, Max hadn't realized they were back at Derek's office until Derek turned into his driveway too sharply. Their shoulders bumped. Though brief, Derek's body heat warmed his skin. The urge to reach across the console and link his fingers with Derek's slammed into him.

Max held back, not anywhere near ready for the kind of conversation doing something like that would generate.

Questions about the past.

Questions about the future.

Perhaps personal questions about wants, needs, and desires.

So yeah, taking Derek's hand was a definite *no go*.

Max followed Derek into the office to grab his keys and

helmet and set his dirty thermos into the sink. Derek headed for the refrigerator and offered up a bottle of water. "Want one?"

Max nodded, and Derek tossed him one of the bottles. Max drained it in five long swallows, crushing the empty plastic bottle in his fist. He would have preferred to have done that to the man's neck back at the apartment, but Derek had stopped him. Probably for the best. He'd never find Liberty if he were doing life in prison.

"Using force wouldn't have done you any good," Derek said as if reading Max's mind.

"Maybe. Then again, we might have gotten some solid info."

"You don't rough people up. It's not in your nature."

Max glanced at Derek, his words hitting a nerve. "How do you know what's in my nature? You haven't seen me in years."

"Whose fault is that?" Derek stared him down. Derek had never been afraid of eye contact. Or the difficult questions. Did Derek feed off other people's discomfort? He'd never been the one to look away first. Not back then.

Not now.

Max tossed his bottle into an empty moving box that had other trash in it. Since they'd been gone, Derek's partner must have unpacked. The coffee pot sat angled in the corner on the counter, and a toaster was plugged into the socket next to the refrigerator. The rest of the kitchen boxes had been emptied.

Max pocketed his keys and grabbed his helmet off the top of the refrigerator where he'd left it.

"Where do you think you're going?" Derek asked as if he had the right to.

"Home." It came out sounding more like a question than a statement. After all, it had been Derek who'd insisted they go home and get some sleep.

"I don't think so."

Max raised a brow. If Derek had other bright ideas of what they could do to help find Liberty, Max would do it even if it meant working through the night. The sooner they found his sister, the better. "Fine. What are we doing?"

"Oh, we're going to bed," Derek said as he dug Max's keys out of his pocket and dropped them into his. "But you're staying here."

Despite Derek's words, Max didn't even get his hopes up. Not that he should have any hopes. Derek's words weren't a seductive invitation into his bed. They were an order.

"Why the hell would I do that?"

"Because I don't trust you not to go off on your own. Liberty's got herself mixed up in some bad shit, and we can't let our emotions get the best of us."

"Heaven forbid we should have, much less show, our emotions." It was a subtle dig, but the way Derek's eyes narrowed, he hadn't missed it. "I'm not going anywhere."

"Yeah," Derek said. "I've heard that before."

Max couldn't help the ironic smile that twisted his lips. Derek always gave as good as he got. Derek walked out of the kitchen, and with no other option, unless he wanted to walk home or wrestle Derek for his keys, Max followed Derek down the hall, past what Derek said would be the two offices, to the last bedroom.

The full-sized bed had been set up on a basic frame under the window. Nothing more than a bare mattress on a set of box springs. From a box in the corner of the room, Derek pulled out two new pillows, a set of sheets, and two light-weight blankets. Max proceeded to help him make the bed, a disorienting sense of *déjà vu* rolling through his system. How many times had he and Derek done just that? A simple domestic chore that now carried so much weight.

Did Derek expect them to share a bed?

Could Max keep his hands to himself?

His natural inclination to roll over in the middle of the night and pull Derek to his chest would be hard to control. But yeah, he'd just lay on the edge of the bed and keep his arms and legs and hands and dick to himself.

When they'd finished making the bed, Derek tossed Max the extra pillow and blanket. "What am I supposed to do with these?"

"Make your bed?" Derek looked at him as if the answer was clear when it was anything but. Then it dawned on Max. He shouldn't have been surprised. "You're seriously going to make me sleep on your floor?"

"You can give the couch in the living room a try, but I've slept on it too many times. It's a man-eater. Trust me. You're better off on the floor."

Max pulled the blanket out of the plastic packaging, a knowing grin tugging on his lips as he met Derek's eyes. Derek may not talk about his feelings, but when he was tired, his guard could slip, and Max could see everything Derek felt. "Afraid you can't keep your hands off me?"

Max hoped Derek would take the bait and the challenge because Max sure as fuck didn't want to sleep on the hard floor like some kid at a sleepover.

"You wish." Derek disappeared into the bathroom.

Max laid the blanket on the floor at the foot of the bed and propped his pillow against the wall. He shucked his boots, sat down, and did the only thing he could do—scroll through his phone and wait for his turn in the shower.

The time passed quickly. The water in the shower cut off, and a few minutes later, Derek came out of the bathroom carrying his clothes and wearing nothing but a pair of boxer-briefs. Before, Derek had always slept in the nude, but the underwear must be Derek's concession to the tight sleeping arrangements.

Derek hit the light switch as he came into the room, plunging them into darkness, and flopped face-first on top of the covers, drawing the pillow to his chest. Max stood. The light from the bathroom cast a warm glow over Derek's body. Max took in the sight, remembering what it felt like to have his hands on that ass, to drive his hard dick between those cheeks, to—

"Max?" came Derek's muttered word.

Had Derek changed his mind? Did he want Max in his bed as much as Max wanted to be there? "Yeah?" He mostly managed to keep the hope out of his voice.

Derek pushed up on his elbows and glanced over his shoulder. "Stop staring at my ass and get some sleep."

Busted.

A rough chuckle rumbled through Max as he made his way to the bathroom. He found new toothbrushes under the sink and used the toothpaste Derek had left on the counter. He showered, pulled on his underwear, and carried his balled-up clothes into the bedroom. They hit the floor with a soft thump, and Max settled on top of the blanket.

He listened to the creaks and cracks of the house as he willed sleep to take him. But he couldn't get the day out of his head. And Derek had been right to take his keys. As worried as he was about Liberty, there was no telling what he would have done if left to his own devices. Probably done something that would have screwed up his chances of finding her.

"Hey, D..." Max didn't speak too loudly. If Derek were asleep, he didn't want to wake him, but if he were still awake...

Derek shifted, and he must have turned toward Max because his voice was soft but clear when he said, "Yeah?"

"Thanks." Max wasn't sure exactly what he was thanking Derek for. For helping him find Liberty. For keeping him from doing something monumentally stupid. Or for not punching him in the face when he'd showed up at the hangar out of the blue.

"You can thank me when we find her."

Max liked the sound of that. *When*, not *if*.

Even if he couldn't kick that raw, nauseous feeling roiling in the pit of his stomach that Liberty's time was running short.

DESPITE HIS EXHAUSTION, DEREK HAD STAYED AWAKE MOST OF THE night, listening to Max's every rustle, sleepy sigh, and muttered mumbling Max always used to do when he had a lot on his mind.

Instead of taking Max to the office, he should have brought Max home where Max would have been way down the hall in Derek's guest room and not fitfully sleeping a few short feet away.

But the office had been the best option. Even though Max wasn't likely to get far without the keys to his only mode of transportation, Max was crafty, and Derek wouldn't put it past him to sneak out of Derek's house and find another way to potentially screw up the search for his sister before it got started.

Or, you know, get himself killed.

Which, with the type of criminal element they seemed to be dealing with, wasn't beyond the realm of possibility.

It had been for the best that Derek had kept Max close. Except now, having Max nearby had robbed Derek of any real sleep he might have managed and left him with the worst case of morning wood Derek had had in a very long time.

Any other time, Derek wouldn't have hesitated to take

himself in hand and take care of the problem, but he didn't want Max to catch him. Or worse, have Max think Derek was thinking about Max when he did.

A fair guess, but Max didn't need to know that.

At least camping out at the office had kept sleeping under the same roof from feeling too personal. And the part about Max sleeping on the floor? That vindictive asshole in Derek had no qualms about Max losing any sleep.

Lord knew Derek had lost plenty of sleep himself in the days and weeks and months after Max had disappeared from his life.

Max softly snored as the sun rose. Derek heard Cesar's key in the back door long before standard office hours.

But Cesar wasn't the kind of guy who could work in the chaos that was the state of their current office. When they found Liberty, Derek would owe Cesar for doing all the heavy lifting while they moved offices.

A few minutes later, the scent of fresh-brewed coffee wafted down the hall, and Cesar knocked on Derek's open bedroom door. "Coffee's ready if you want some."

Derek rolled over and swung his legs over the side of the bed, scrubbing a lazy hand through his hair. "Thanks."

Cesar bobbed his chin toward a still sleeping Max who could hibernate through anything short of a 7.0 earthquake.

"Long story," Derek said. He wasn't trying to put Cesar off, but he didn't quite know how he felt about having Max back in his life, and his ability to express that ambivalence to Cesar—on little sleep and without his first cup of coffee in him—was limited.

He threw on the same clothes from the night before and padded his way into the kitchen. Cesar pushed a cup of fresh coffee into his waiting hands.

"Sooo..." Cesar drew the word out before blowing on his coffee and taking a sip. "*That* was unexpected."

When Derek's silence dragged on, Cesar raised a brow and waited for Derek to respond.

"I had an ulterior motive."

Cesar settled back against the counter, a sly, totally corrupt smile on his face. "Tell me all about it."

That too perceptive brow went higher, but before Derek could say anything else, Max pushed through the door with a nasty case of bedhead, wearing nothing but his boxer briefs and that fucking sexy shy smile that, even after all this time, still made Derek's heart jump.

"Morning," Max said. "I didn't know we had company, or I would have..." He glanced down at his bare chest and arms covered in tattoos and the bulge in his underwear. "... dressed more appropriately."

Cesar responded to Max's easy grin with one of his own after checking out Max's goods.

"Sleep well?" Cesar asked as he handed Max a clean mug.

Max poured himself some coffee and turned around. Being bright, alert, and in a cheery mood first thing in the morning had always been Max's norm. What sane person woke up like that? Looking back, that alone should have been a clear sign that the two of them weren't fundamentally compatible and had no business trying to plan a future together.

"Probably much better than Derek had hoped," Max said. He doctored his coffee and took a sip, eyeing Derek over the top of his mug, a bemused look daring him to disagree.

"Asshole." Derek didn't throw any heat behind it. He'd deserved Max calling him out on his bullshit.

Max laughed. "I'm not the one who made me sleep on the floor when there was plenty of room on that mattress for two."

"I'm out," Cesar said, "You two lovebirds can continue this argument alone."

"We're not—"

"He's not—"

Max and Derek started at the same time, but Cesar had already pushed through the swinging kitchen door.

"He's hot," Max said, his voice low but not *that* low. "You two ever—"

"No," Derek said. "Our relationship is strictly platonic. You know that two gay guys can be friends without fucking, right?"

"Yeah, but where's the fun in that?"

Instead of answering, Derek said, "These walls are pretty thin. He probably heard that."

From the other room, Cesar called out. "I did."

Max leaned in and lowered his voice, decreasing but not eliminating the chance that Cesar would overhear. "No hard feelings about the floor, yeah? I get it. I probably would have done the same under the circumstances."

Not only was Max too cheery in the morning, Derek was starting to think Max was too good for him. "Are we finished here, or do you want to talk—"

Max held up a hand, not letting Derek finish his thought. Maybe Max didn't want to talk about their past any more than Derek did. "I need a change of clothes. Unless you want to follow me all over town, I'm going to need my keys."

Derek considered his options. They had a lot to do that day, and they didn't need to waste half of the morning running to Max's place and back again.

With a half-smile and a pointed glance down at the front pocket of Derek's jeans where Derek had stashed the keys the night before, Max said, "I could get them myself if you prefer."

Derek reached into his pocket and pulled out the keys. He had little doubt Max would have grabbed something else while he had his hand in Derek's pocket. A not-too-small part of Derek would have liked that. And with *that* thought, he started getting hard.

Fuck. Having Max help with the investigation was never going to work.

Max wrapped his hand around the keys dangling in Derek's hands, but Derek held on. "Don't make me regret letting you out of my sight."

6

Max stood under the hot water in his shower, letting the warmth seep into his muscles and relieve the crick in his neck from sleeping on the floor all night.

He didn't hold the sleeping arrangements against Derek. It would have been hard for Max to keep his hands to himself if he'd woken up in the morning with his cock nestled in the crack of Derek's muscular ass.

A heaviness settled into his groin as blood ran south at the thought of snugging Derek's tight ass against him. And with what would have only been two thin layers of material between them, it wouldn't have taken much to push the material aside and take Derek from behind.

With his consent, of course.

Which Derek would never have given. Max didn't deserve Derek's forgiveness because leaving the way he had had been unforgivable. He'd like to chalk his actions up to being young and dumb, but fuck... even he didn't believe that excuse anymore.

No, he'd been scared—*terrified*—of what Derek quitting the

police department for Max meant. For them. Their relationship. Their future.

Max hadn't wanted Derek resenting him when Derek found out what a colossal mistake quitting had been.

But by running, he'd given Derek an even greater reason to resent him. That Derek was even talking to him, much less shoving all of his active cases onto Cesar's lap to help him find Liberty, spoke to the kind of man Derek was.

A man Max didn't deserve.

But a man Max still wanted.

As he glanced down at his hard dick, it was obvious that he wanted Derek more than as just a friend.

Knowing he couldn't walk around the whole day with a semi, he stroked himself. His mind wandered back to that place it always did when he jacked off to thoughts of Derek.

But now, he had more mental material in his spank bank. Derek had grown into his body over the years. The hair on his chest, the definition in his pecs, his biceps, his thighs...

And fuck, the way Derek's boxer briefs had hugged his bulge made heat flood Max's groin all over again.

It had taken everything Max had to stay on that bedroom floor and not reach for Derek, not take Derek in his hand and show them both what they'd been missing.

But Max knew not to cross that boundary, knew Derek wouldn't have appreciated the advance. Max hadn't earned back that type of trust or intimacy.

Derek didn't exactly push you away when you pulled him into that kiss back at the airstrip.

And he'd kissed you back.

Until Derek's brain had kicked back in, and good sense had overtaken his body's instinctive draw.

Over the years, Max had plenty of time to wonder if they

ever met again if their explosive chemistry would still be there, and as he stroked himself to completion, he knew that it was.

He came with a grunt, his cum swirling and mixing with the suds and the water as they circled the drain and disappeared.

Quickly, he finished his shower. He had more important things to think about than how he'd made the biggest fucking mistake of his life when he'd walked away.

Max put on deodorant and brushed his teeth, his hair a damp mess. Water dripped down his chest and into the towel tucked low around his waist as Derek's unmistakable knock sounded at his door.

"Coming," Max hollered out as he worked his way through his cramped studio apartment, tossing the covers over his bed and stuffing the dirty cereal bowl and coffee mug into the other-wise empty sink.

He wasn't the neatest guy, but he wasn't a complete slob. Usually.

Unlocking the door, he stepped back as Derek pushed inside, his energy up, that *go get 'em* vibe rolling off him and filling the tiny apartment.

"How long of a shower did you take?" Derek asked by way of greeting.

Max shrugged, trying to hide his smile. He didn't think Derek would appreciate knowing that he'd been jacking off to thoughts of Derek no more than a few minutes before. "As long as necessary," Max said, holding Derek's steady gaze.

Before Max could say something that he shouldn't, like *want to join me in another one?* he glanced away and pulled clean clothes from the dresser. Turning his back to Derek, he dropped his towel.

"Oh, hey, whoa," Derek said. "What the fuck? You couldn't have gone to the bathroom to get dressed?"

Max pulled up his underwear and turned around with his

jeans in his hands. He put one leg through and then the other. "It's not like you haven't seen me naked before."

"Yeah, but..." The gruff words died in Derek's throat, and Max couldn't help but notice how Derek's eyes drifted to Max's crotch as Max stuffed his junk away and zipped up.

"If you keep looking at me like that," Max said. "I'm going to start thinking you're interested."

"I'm not."

For the first time in memory, Derek broke eye contact first. *Hmmm. Interesting.*

When Derek glanced back, whatever he'd been thinking or feeling had been buried, and *PI* Derek replaced *maybe interested* Derek. "We sitting around here all day, or are we going to find your sister?"

Max shook his head to get his mind out of the gutter and back into the game. The truth was, Derek wasn't interested. If Liberty weren't in danger, Max truly believed Derek would have sent him packing that first day.

"What do you have planned?" If Max had had any great ideas of his own about how to find Liberty, he wouldn't have had to look Derek up. As it stood, Derek *had* been Max's bright idea.

"I downloaded those pictures I took last night onto my phone. I thought we could take them down to the station and talk with Tasha and see if she has any information she's willing to share."

Max laced up his shoes. "Do you think she'll talk to us after last night?"

"Doubtful, but only one way to find out."

"What about this Marco character Mina told us about?"

"I've got Cesar digging into Marco and his operation in Las Rocas. Cesar knows his way around the darknet. I'm hoping he'll be able to track some information down for us. Even if he doesn't, I think a trip across the border to Las Rocas is in order.

Nothing like boots on the ground to help dig up information. We'll check off the towns where Liberty could have gotten off the bus, and then head to Las Rocas."

Pocketing his wallet and grabbing his keys, Max said, "Sounds like it could be hazardous to our health."

Derek considered Max for a brief moment, his gaze assessing, and Max felt like an unknown specimen under glass. "It could be dangerous. I'm not going to lie. You don't have to go. It might be easier for me to slip across the border by myself and—"

Max pulled himself up straight. "If it's dangerous for us, it's got to be infinitely more dangerous for Liberty. I'm not staying here and hiding behind your skirts."

That reluctant twitch of Derek's lips was all the approval Max needed. He stepped past Derek out onto his second-floor landing, waited for Derek to head down the stairs, and locked up behind him. He slid into the passenger seat of Derek's Roadster and smoothed his hand across the leather. Christ, you didn't know what luxury was until you felt the interior.

"The PI business seems to agree with you." It wasn't a judgment as much as an observation, but some of his... not jealousy, because Derek deserved everything he'd obviously worked so hard for, but even Max heard the awe in his voice.

"I can't complain. And Cesar and I joining forces will allow us both a better work-life balance. It's taken a lot of long hours, late nights, and a few close calls to get to where we're at."

"Close calls?"

Derek winced as if he'd said more than he'd meant to and pulled out onto Travis Street and headed toward the station. "Do you have the name of the detective who took your missing person's report? Maybe we can stop by and see him while we're at the station and ask if he has any updates."

"I do, but I'm not holding my breath. And don't think you

can say something like 'a few close calls' and gloss right over that without me putting you on the spot. With this traffic, you have time to talk and fill in the details before we get to the station."

DEREK STIFLED A GROAN. IF HE HAD BEEN PAYING MORE ATTENTION to what he was saying instead of picturing Max's naked ass as he'd bent over to pull on his underwear, maybe then Derek wouldn't have made that stupid slip of the tongue.

"The close calls weren't even *that* close." Derek didn't want to talk about the few times he hadn't been sure he would come out of an investigation alive. He'd lived. That was the important part. He didn't like dwelling on the past.

Don't like dwelling on the past? Then why can't you get Max out of your head? He's definitely from your past, and you should have let him stay there where he belonged.

"Come on, D," Max cajoled, with that *you know you wanna* half-smile on his face. "You don't have to tell me all of them. Just tell me one."

A horn honked behind him, and Derek hit the gas and skated under the green light as it turned to yellow, leaving all the cars behind him to miss the light. He focused his sights on the road ahead. "It was a stalker case with a celebrity."

"Oooh, was it that country singer, Janis Malcolm? She had that ex that—"

"Still reading those celebrity rags, are you?"

"Hey, I don't do drugs, don't drink excessively, I don't sleep around... *too much*. It's my only vice, and I refuse to give it up."

Derek laughed. "Fine, I'll give you your celebrity rags. But I'm drawing the line there."

What's the matter, don't want to think about Max's sexploits?

Freud might have something to say about your inability to think about him with another man without getting that sick, queasy feeling in the pit of your stomach. Do you think he's been pining away for you all these years and hasn't been with anyone? A sweet, charming, handsome man like Max wouldn't have to look far and wide to find someone who wants to have sex with him.

"Are you going to tell me, or am I supposed to keep guessing?"

Derek cruised under the next traffic light as it turned from yellow to red. The three cars behind him followed him through the light.

"Christian Fogerty," Derek said. "He—"

"Topped the Country music charts for the past three years. Everyone's heard about that case. Mainstream media had a field day with that. Hell of a way to be outed is all I can say. Poor bastard. I don't get why people even care where other people put their dicks or their twats. It's literally no one's business but their own."

"Yeah, well, this fan of Fogerty's took exception to it when the rumors came out."

"Didn't that dumbass jump the fence, break into Fogerty's house, and find him in bed with his lov—"

Max's hand flew to his mouth as the realization hit. "Oh, my fucking gay god. It was you that the crazy-ass stalker shot, wasn't it?"

What had given it away? The tight grip Derek had on the steering wheel? The muscle twitching by his right eye? The way he couldn't seem to catch his breath? Fuck. Why had he even brought it up?

"How many of your clients have you slept with?"

Derek barked out a laugh. "That's the question you want to know? Not how big is Christian's dick, or if he's a bottom or a top, or—"

"*Biiig*," Max said with a sincere confidence. "I saw the leaked dick pics online. And if I had to guess, I'd say bottom, but only because not many guys can take a dick that big," Max swept his eyes up and down Derek, his gaze assessing as a smile came to his lips. "Unless you—"

"You finished?"

"I'll shut up now. Continue. You were in bed with your client when—"

"He wasn't *exactly* my client at the time."

"Got it. You were in bed having crazy kinky sex with your... *boyfriend*?"

"Friend."

Max grinned. "You don't seem like the fuck buddy type, but more power to you and, fuck, I'd fuck Christian Fogerty any day of the week, and if he wanted to top then—"

"Stop," Derek said, but he was laughing. Derek hadn't expected this conversation to go that way. He pulled into the station's parking lot—the station he used to work out of no less —and parked in a visitor spot. Near the back of the lot, he spotted Tasha's SUV. "Looks like we're in luck. LaTasha's here."

"Wait, she doesn't know we're coming?"

"Under the circumstances, I thought it was better she didn't know that ahead of time."

"Smart." Before Derek could open his car door, Max added, "And I'm glad you have someone like Christian in your life. From what all the tabloids say, he seems like a really decent guy."

"He was. Or *is*. I mean, I haven't exactly seen him since I was shot. I think the whole stalking thing is something he'd like to forget, and I guess having me around reminded him of that."

"How did I not know? How did anyone not know it was you?"

"I have a friend with the press. He managed to squash all

mention of me, and the police reports conveniently left my name out. I probably have my father to thank for that, but I've hardly spoken to my old man since I quit the force, so I'd only be guessing."

Derek worked to keep the strain out of his voice. As if his fucked up history didn't matter. But, fuck, it wasn't easy.

"A reporter friend or reporter *friend?*" Max waggled a brow, and Derek recognized Max was doing what he could to lighten the mood.

"Christ, get your head out of the gutter for one second, Huff."

Max glanced away, and when he looked back and met Derek's eyes, his smile was gone. "I'm glad you're putting yourself out there. All I've ever wanted is what's best for you."

Derek kept the *then why did you fucking leave?* to himself. He didn't want to seem needy. Or pathetic. But Max must have seen the unasked question in his eyes. Max's mouth opened and closed, but no words came. When Max finally did speak, it wasn't what Derek had expected to hear.

"So... you got shot?"

"My side. Through the muscle. It was a small-caliber bullet. Full-metal jacket instead of a hollow point. I got lucky. If the guy had been a better shot or had used hollow-points, it could have been a lot worse."

Max made a lifting motion with his hand. "Let me see."

Derek popped his door and stuck his leg out. "I'm not showing you my scar."

"Show me." If Max's words had come out as a demand, Derek would have likely refused, but spoken softly like that, more of an ask... as if Max seeing would make it better, even if the damaged tissue had healed long ago.

Derek settled back into his seat, not quite understanding why he was lifting his shirt even as he did so. He rarely thought about the scar anymore. Random hookups never asked, and in the few not-so-serious relationships he'd been in since Max, he'd told the guys he didn't want to talk about it. No one had ever pushed him the way Max had. Derek couldn't decide if that was a good thing or a bad thing.

Max ghosted a finger over the scar marring Derek's right side. Goosebumps flashed across Derek's flesh, and he only just managed to suppress a mild shiver. "How did I not notice it last night?"

"It's not that noticeable." It had been long enough ago that the angry red scar had faded to silver.

"It's pretty fucking noticeable. And badass."

Derek laughed the way he knew Max wanted him to. He dropped the hem of his shirt and went to step out of his car.

"Hey, D?"

Derek stood and ducked his head into the car. "Yeah?"

Max leaned across the center console, his voice somehow thick and soft at the same time. "I'm really glad that asshole was a bad shot and didn't use hollow-point bullets."

7

MAX HELD OPEN THE STATION'S DOOR FOR DEREK, UNABLE TO quell the nausea rolling in his belly. If that bullet had gone an inch to the right, Derek might not have been walking through the door at that very moment. Derek stopped just inside, and Max nearly bumped into him.

Derek turned. "Stop babying me. I'm fine."

"Yeah, but—"

"That bullet happened a long time ago. I'm here. I'm healthy. Let's talk to Tasha and see what she has to say, okay?"

Max nodded and followed Derek down the hall. Being shot might have happened a long time ago, but it was as if it had happened a minute ago to Max. Not what? Three years now, if Max remembered the articles correctly? It wasn't as easy to push it out of his mind as Derek had.

The station wasn't a standalone building like a lot of police stations. This one was more of an annex set at the end of a strip center in the middle of the San Fernando Valley. Derek had told him one time it was to better serve its citizens with community policing.

The desk sergeant recognized Derek, and he let them through after signing in and picking up their visitor badges. They walked through a maze of halls and desks and past the bullpen where they held their briefings. Most of the officers barely glanced up from their desks. A few waved at Derek. A couple of the old-timers raised a curious brow when they saw Max trailing behind.

Max didn't know what they thought of him, which was probably for the best. Derek had been a fast-tracked up-and-coming officer who'd received accolades at a young age. Did they blame Max for robbing the department of a good officer?

The low-level hum and buzz of activity at the station held a hectic vibrancy that made Max's heart rate kick up a notch even as a civilian. Derek didn't have to ask for directions. He turned right and stopped in the open doorway of the first door on the left.

Tasha came around her desk, dressed in street clothes, not the black tactical pants and black T-shirt that she'd worn the night before.

She frowned at the sight of them. "Should have called, Watts. I'm just heading out."

Derek caught her arm, and she stared at his hand for a moment before Derek must have thought better of it and let his hand drop. "If I had called first, would you have talked to me?"

"Not sure why I should go out of my way to help you when the two of you went out of your way to ruin our night."

Derek made a face. "To be fair, that hadn't been our plan." He gave Max the pointed look he deserved. "Did we fuck it all up?"

Tasha sighed and stepped back into her office, allowing Max and Derek to follow her inside. Derek closed the door behind him, and Tasha retook her seat behind her desk.

She slid a pen back and forth between her fingers. "Luckily for the two of you, no. My sergeant was pissed, though, when he heard. I wouldn't stick my head in his office on the way out to say hello if I were you."

"That's my fault," Max said, not wanting Derek to take the heat for what he'd done. Derek was already going out of his way to help him. He didn't need the department coming down on Derek for something Max had dragged him into. "I didn't think—"

"Clearly," Tasha said. Her dark brown eyes held his, and although she was almost half of Max's size, he swallowed hard. She turned her attention back to Derek. "Why are you letting this guy drag you into trouble?"

Instead of answering the question, Derek pulled out his phone and showed Tasha the photos he'd taken of the man at the apartment. "You know this guy? He brought the backpack that Max's sister left with. He's one of the last people we know who saw her before she disappeared."

Tasha leaned back in her chair. "You didn't get anything out of him, did you?"

"Nothing helpful," Max admitted.

"We couldn't even get his name. But one of Liberty's friends at the apartment gave us the name of one of the bigger fish down in Las Rocas, Mexico. Marco. All we have is a first name. I was hoping you might be able to connect some of the dots."

Tasha chewed on the end of her pen as if contemplating what she was and wasn't willing to tell Derek. "This is a dangerous game you're playing."

"We don't have much of a choice. None of your guys are going south of the border to find her. You know that. We know that. All we need is a little information."

"You know that's not how this works, right? The flow of

information is from PI to law enforcement, not the other way around."

Derek leaned forward, his forearms on his knees. "I can find out who this guy is on my own. But it could take a couple of days. A couple of days that Liberty might not have. I'm asking for a little give here."

It was a testament to Derek as a former officer, as a PI, as a decent man, that Tasha even contemplated helping.

She glanced at Max. "Who's the detective assigned your sister's case?"

"Detective Corbel."

Tasha punched a couple of numbers into the phone on her desk, spoke to Corbel, and within a minute or two, he walked into her office. He had a babyface and hadn't yet learned the fine art of schooling his expression. When Tasha had Derek show him the photo and asked if he had any information, he looked at Tasha as if she'd lost her mind.

"Go ahead," she said. "If the captain has a problem with you speaking to them, he can take it up with me."

Corbel shrugged, the *it's your ass* expression clear on his face. Leaning against the wall, he pulled a notepad out of his uniform's breast pocket and told Max and Derek what he knew.

"On the streets, that guy goes by the name of Pelón, he—"

"Bald?" Derek said. "The guy had hair."

"Yeah, well..." Corbel must not have known what to say about that, so he continued. "He's a low to mid-level guy mixed up with a group known for stealing and stripping cars. Some drugs and prostitution are thrown in there for a little bit of variety, but car parts are this group's bread and butter. Parts are sold here, and the money is moved back across the border. They have a whole stable of young, white women running the money across."

"How many of those girls make it back to the States?" Derek

asked, not afraid to ask the question that had lodged in Max's throat.

"Hard to tell," Corbel said.

"Guys like Pelón," Tasha said, "prey on the runaways, the homeless, the desperate. Those aren't the type of people who usually have a strong support system of family and friends looking out for them and reporting them missing."

"So if a bunch of these women never make it back across the border, you might not ever hear about it." Max had read about things like this happening, but it was still disheartening to hear it directly from law enforcement.

"Exactly," Tasha confirmed.

"Didn't you say that Liberty told you that this was her last trip, and then she was getting out of it?" Derek asked.

"Wait." Corbel couldn't hide his irritation. "Your sister is involved with these guys?"

Fuck. Max hadn't wanted to get his sister in trouble with law enforcement, but he would face that possibility over the chance of never finding her again.

Derek watched as the beads of sweat formed on Max's upper lip. He knew Max wanted to protect his sister, but they needed all the information they could get if they were going to do that. "Tell him."

Max scrubbed both hands through his hair, leaving a couple of tufts sticking straight up, making him look a little maniacal. "Yes. The morning I was there, this Pelón guy came to the apartment with a black backpack for her to take. She told me she was getting out, that she needed this one last trip to help her pay for college. So, yeah. It sounds like she'd made the trip before, and that would mean she made it back safely."

"Makes sense," Tasha said. "If you find a good mule, you'd want to make sure nothing bad happened to them."

"Unless they knew she was getting out," Corbel said, which did nothing to stem the cold sweat problem Max was having. "Who knew she was getting out?"

Max raised his hands. "It's not like I have her friends list. But one of her roommates, Mina, and of course Pelón, was there when she said it. We caught Mina breaking into Liberty's cash box. Maybe she knows more than she's willing to admit."

"You should have told me that from the start," Corbel said.

"Yeah." The defeat in Max's voice tightened Derek's chest. He hated that Max was going through this. If Derek had a sibling in trouble, he would be out of his mind with worry. That Max had been able to hold himself together this long was admirable. "I get that."

"Mina told us that Marco was in Las Rocas, so we assumed she headed there, but she could have gotten off the bus before then and disappeared. And we don't have any idea where to find him in the town. If she did go there, did she give money directly to him or a middleman? Las Rocas looks big enough to have a lot of places for a guy like that to hide."

"Marco?" Corbel glanced at Tasha, his eyes wide. She gave an almost imperceptible shake of her head.

"Tasha," Derek said. "Don't hold out on us. Who is this guy?"

She glanced over Derek's shoulder through her window into the station's bullpen as if concerned who might be around to overhear. "He's Costa's right-hand man. Marco does all of his dirty work."

"Who's that?" Max asked.

Tasha tossed her pen onto her desk. "He's a somewhat new player. Moved in to fill the void when the Mexican government took down a rival cartel. It created a vacuum. Costa's savvy, opportunistic, and—" she glanced from Corbel to Derek to

Max, her face softened, almost sympathetic. "He's *trouble*. And on the run. He escaped from a Mexican prison, killing a couple of the guards on the way out. This guy doesn't have anything to lose, and he proved he'll do anything not to go back to jail."

"Great," Max said, his color now gone.

"If Costa or Marco has her, you won't be able to get close to either one of them. I'm warning you two, stay away from these guys."

Derek stood. There wasn't much more Tasha was going to tell them. Even if the department had an idea where they were hiding out, there was no way she would tell him that kind of information, despite their history together. He nodded to Tasha and Corbel. "Thanks for your time."

Max stood as well, and they all shook hands. They had more information, but it wasn't as helpful as Derek had hoped. He opened the door. His mind turned inward, and his eyes locked ahead as he ran through different ways they might be able to find Liberty without getting her or themselves killed.

They walked past the bullpen, turned a couple of corners, the exit door in sight, when Derek heard a voice that made dread lodge in his throat with spiked claws. He picked up his pace and heard Max's footfalls do the same.

"Still running, boy?" Derek's father's voice cut through all the buzz, all the chatter, all the ringing phones and clacking keyboard keys. In the absence of sound, Derek's ears buzzed, and his feet grew roots on the scuffed industrial linoleum, refusing to budge.

Max caught Derek's bicep, his grip firm but somehow still gentle when he leaned in and grumbled in Derek's ear. "Just keep walking."

But of course, Derek couldn't do that. He knew it. Max, with a sigh, knew it. His father knew it as well, or he wouldn't have said a word. The station wasn't the time or the place for family drama, but it wasn't Derek who'd started it.

Derek turned as his father strode toward them. His father's shirt was tighter across his belly, his temples grayer, his scowl lines deeper.

"Been caught in another celebrity's bed?" His father had a hell of a way of greeting people. For a guy who'd made sure Derek's name had never shown up on any of the police reports, he didn't seem to have an issue airing their dirty laundry at the station.

But that was just like a bully—couldn't pass up a chance to be a dick.

With as level of a voice as Derek could muster, he said, "Haven't been forced into retirement yet?"

His father grunted and bobbed his chin at Max. "What's he doing here?"

Derek elbowed Max in the gut to keep him from saying whatever he'd opened his mouth to say. The same rules that applied to encounters with bears applied when dealing with his father. You certainly didn't want to poke them, but you also couldn't show fear.

"We're here on a case."

People started returning to their conversations and typing on their keyboards once they realized no fists would be flying. His father's scoff could easily be heard over the background noise. "What's wrong? Did a celebrity break a nail?"

Derek had to give his father points for consistency in assholery. He'd been bad enough during Derek's early years on the force, but he'd reached a whole new level when Derek had the audacity to leave the department. And in the years since, his father's contempt of Derek hadn't flagged. Derek didn't know which had hit his father harder, that his son liked dick, or the fact that he wasn't man enough to follow in his father's footsteps.

Max tugged on Derek's arm, but Derek wasn't finished. "It's a missing person's case out of Mexico."

Leaning in, his father said, "Leave the investigating to the professionals before you go and get yourself killed."

"Awh, gee whiz, *Dad*, I didn't know you cared."

His father stared at him. Derek stared back, prepared to maintain eye contact all day. News flash, he was a grown man, and that condescending scowl and blotchy red face didn't intimidate him anymore.

As a kid, his father had seemed larger than life, a man no one wanted to mess with. Now... now he looked and sounded exactly like what he was—a pathetic, aging bully who clung to what was left of his career by his torn and bloody fingernails.

The department probably only kept him on out of the captain's twisted sense of loyalty.

His father wasn't relevant. He was a dinosaur on the brink of extinction.

"Yeah, well," his father said, "I don't."

Those words didn't land the way they used to, like an atomic bomb to the chest. You hear that shit enough over the years, it loses its power. Once Derek had accepted that his father had the problem, not Derek, then his old man had lost his ability to wound him.

Mostly.

Derek turned and walked away. Something he should have done when he'd first heard his father's voice.

Max followed Derek out the door. "That's seriously fucked up."

Derek laughed, but it came out sounding bitter. No surprise there. "Tell me about it." Back at the Roadster, he leaned against the front fender. "Maybe you had the right idea all along."

"Wait, I was right about something?" Max rocked back on his

heels, his smile only half-cocked, so it wasn't completely devastating. "Do tell."

"You getting out of this place." Derek stared off at nothing over Max's right shoulder. "Sometimes, I wonder how things would have been different if I had gone with you when you'd walked away."

8

Of all the things Max might have predicted would have come out of Derek's mouth, that would never have made the list in the history of *ever*.

"What did you say?" Max couldn't have heard him right. Derek's run-in with his father must have hit him harder than he let on.

Derek focused on Max again. "Nothing. Forget I said anything."

"Nuh-uh." Max stepped closer, effectively blocking Derek's escape unless he wanted to go over the hood of his car with its pristine paint job or go through Max. And if he tried to do the latter, Derek would have one hell of a fight on his hands because Max wasn't letting that comment go without exploring it further. "Tell me what you meant."

Closing his eyes, Derek sucked in a breath and let it out, his pupils large, his eyes clear, his voice low and gruff when he said, "I mean, maybe I shouldn't have let you walk away."

Max stepped closer, one foot between Derek's legs, a finger

snagging one of Derek's belt loops. "Maybe I should have stayed."

"You mean that?"

Max ran the back of his knuckle down Derek's cheek, the day or so worth of stubble prickly against his skin. "Yeah. Sometimes."

Derek's small smile trembled at the corners. "But not always?"

Max shrugged, not as if he didn't care, but as if he didn't know. "We both had a lot of growing up to do if we were ever going to work."

Max leaned in. Instead of shoving him away, Derek looped his fingers in Max's belt loops, closing the gap between them.

Their lips touched, and Derek's breath escaped him. "Awh, fuck," Derek muttered as he deepened the kiss. Max had planned on taking the kiss slowly, wanting to give Derek a chance to pull away or tell Max to fuck the fuck off, but the way Derek took control of the kiss, the way he breathed Max in, the way he pulled him closer until Max's hard cock pressed against Derek's hip, *slow* was no longer an option.

Max wanted to grind up against him. He wanted to strip Derek naked in the parking lot, but the sounds of the traffic on the street reminded him that not only were they not alone, but they were also in front of a police station. The last thing either of them needed was to catch a public indecency charge when they still had so much they needed to accomplish.

Max broke the kiss, and Derek sagged. Pressing a kiss to Derek's forehead, Max's mind was a jumble of thoughts, his chest tight. Could Derek still have feelings for him? Or had he caught Derek at a vulnerable time after that confrontation with his father?

Fuck. Was Max the dick here?

"No," Derek said. "You're not a dick. I know the way you

think. If you think you somehow took advantage of me when my guard was down, then fuck you for thinking I don't have any agency of my own."

Whoa. "I didn't mean to say that out loud." Max chuckled. "But, okay, then."

Max took a step back and held out his hand.

Derek glanced at it. "What?"

"Give me your keys."

"Why would I do that?"

"Your hands are shaking." Had Max done that to him? Was it his kiss, his touch that had made a grown man tremble? Or was that the adrenaline-induced after-effects from running into his father? Either way, Derek was in no condition to drive.

"You just want to get your hands on my car."

"There are lots of things I want to get my hands on," Max dropped his voice to that low octave he knew Derek had always loved. "Your car is just one of them."

Max strapped into the car, the throaty purr of the engine settling deep into his bones as he pulled out of the parking spot and into mid-day traffic—which was a lot like morning traffic, only the sun was higher and the middle fingers not as prevalent.

"When are we crossing the border?" Max asked, his left knee bouncing with his impatience. They only had minimal information to go on, but it was more than he had even twenty-four hours ago.

Derek cut him a look that showed his impatience with Max's impatience. Somehow at the same time, that look said to leave the work to the professionals.

"Don't make me regret agreeing to let you come along. You haven't exactly shown yourself to be calm, dispassionate, and an asset to the investigation."

"She's my fucking sister." The light turned green, and he

zipped around a work truck belching exhaust and weaving in its lane. "Dispassionate isn't an option."

"I'd settle for just not screwing anything up," Derek said, his look both cutting and pointed. He didn't break eye contact until Max did.

"Okay fine, I'll do my best not to fuck up. It's just..."

Max didn't know how to explain how much his baby sister meant to him. How much the guilt of his absence in her life weighed on him. If—*when* he got the chance to make it up to her, he didn't know how he would make things better. He only knew that he would.

If she let him.

DEREK WAS SURPRISED TO FIND CESAR STILL AT THE OFFICE WHEN they'd pulled into the parking area at the back of the house. He didn't wait for Max. His frustration was still in the red zone, knowing full well that Max was a loose cannon in the investigation, and it would take an enormous amount of concentration and energy to keep him contained, no matter what Max had promised.

Yeah, and the more energy and brainpower you expend trying to keep him between the ditches, the less energy and brainpower you have to keep your mind from going places it shouldn't. Like fantasizing about having Max in your bed again, all that raw power and passion and—

"Hey, I didn't expect you two back today," Cesar said as he came down the hall from his office and met them in what was shaping up to be the reception area.

Derek shoved his tormented thoughts about Max into a deep, dark box in the back of his mind where they should be and should stay. He glanced around the room. The new furniture had arrived while they'd been gone. Cesar had arranged the new club chairs across from the couch and coffee table he'd brought from his old office. He'd also set up the lamps and side tables and the refreshment station with the single-cup coffee maker and mini-fridge for their clients.

Hell, he'd even hung up some of the artwork on the walls.

"Damn," Max said as he came into the room. "This is starting to look like a real office."

Derek turned to Cesar. With Max's case, the brunt of the responsibility had landed in his lap. "I appreciate all your hard work. I—"

Cesar cut him off with a casual wave of his hand. "It's fine. I would have waited for you to help, but the mess was driving me insane. Plus, I'm saving up the goodwill for when I need a favor in return.

Derek nodded. "Noted."

Cesar bumped his chin toward the hall. "Follow me. I've got something I want to show you guys."

Cesar headed for his office, and Max waggled his brows at Derek. No, Cesar didn't mean he had *that* kind of thing to show them. Derek shook his head and muttered, "Get your head out of the gutter, Huff."

Max chuckled but followed Derek down the hall. Yes, Cesar was attractive, but Derek seriously doubted his partner wanted a three-way. Besides, as much as Derek could appreciate Cesar's sex appeal, Derek just didn't see him that way.

All protests to the contrary, could that have something to do with having never gotten over Max?

Derek turned into Cesar's office. Cesar had taken the backroom, giving him a view of the yard and the trees. Derek would have preferred that room for his office versus having a view overlooking the traffic on the street in front of the house, but Cesar was doing all the work, and he couldn't fault the guy for picking the nicer office. He would have done the same.

"Whatcha got?" Max scooted around Derek and stood behind Cesar to get a better view of the computer screens.

Yes, *screens*. Cesar was a bit of a computer geek. Not one of those savant hacker types, but he knew his way around the computer and the darknet. One of the many reasons Derek knew Cesar would be an asset to the agency.

Derek pulled one of the chairs around while Max leaned against the lateral filing cabinet beneath the window. Cesar had information up on all three of his screens.

"I searched Liberty's credit history, trying to find any credit cards she might have that we could trace, but no luck. At least not under her given name." Cesar glanced over his shoulder at Max. "Does she have any aliases?"

Derek caught the slight sag in Max's shoulders. When Max spoke, his words came out soft. "No. Not that I know of, but that doesn't mean anything."

"Considering where she lives and the company she keeps, I would expect her to live on cash mostly," Derek said, "which only makes her that much harder to track."

"I did get this, though," Cesar pointed to another screen, with a clear picture of Liberty. "This was her crossing the border twelve days ago."

Wait. How had Cesar gotten into the Border Patrol's database?

Cesar must have known what Derek's next question would be because he glanced over at him with a cocky smile and said, "Don't ask."

"At least we know for certain that she made it across the border." Max leaned in to get a better look at the photo, his hand on the back of Derek's chair. That close, Derek smelled the rugged scent of Max's cologne, or aftershave or whatever the fuck it was. It was probably just the way Max naturally smelled.

All testosterone and brimstone.

If Derek didn't know better, he would say that Max had bewitched him, but he knew that wasn't possible. Though it was as good an explanation of the power Max had over him as anything else Derek had come up with over the years.

"That picture there," Max said. "She still has her backpack. The one that Pelón gave her back at the apartment. How does she get through without getting caught with all that money?"

"She probably has the cash strapped tight to her body so they wouldn't find it in her backpack when her stuff goes through security," Cesar said. "Plus, it's much easier to get your backpack stolen than for someone to find the cash on your body. Border Patrol won't find the cash unless she gives them a reason to do a body search."

Glancing through the set of still frames Cesar had found, then showed a border patrol dog passing Liberty and then Liberty walking away from security towards the buses. They clearly hadn't had a reason for anything more invasive than a walk through a metal detector.

"Where was that bus headed?"

"Tres Colinas, Ensenada, and Camalu," Cesar said. "I haven't been able to get the security footage from the bus company. Not sure I'll be able to either. Without that, I have no idea where she got off."

"Now we're getting somewhere." Max tapped Derek's shoulder with the back of his hand. Even before the contact, he'd felt Max's excitement building. In the time they'd been gone, Cesar had come up with way more useful information than they'd been able to at the station.

"That's not all. I did some searches for that Marco guy you were telling me about." Cesar made a face. After six months of working together, Derek had gotten better at reading his partner's expressions. This one worried him. "Marco is into some serious shit. It may be chop shops and low-level drugs and prostitution in the US, but he's started gaining a foothold in Mexico and other parts of Central and South America. As this Costa dude's right-hand man, he's got a brutal reputation."

Derek frowned. Max grimaced, and the leather on Derek's chair creaked under Max's tight grip.

Cesar continued. The bad news kept coming. "I searched for news articles in California, New Mexico, Arizona, and Texas. There have been a smattering of reports of missing women—suspected drug and money mules that have disappeared after crossing the border. The problem is more pervasive and ongoing than we first thought. In total, there are twenty-three women unaccounted for between all four states over the past few years. But those are just the ones that were reported. I suspect the number is way higher than that."

"*Jesusfuckingchrist*," the word rolled out of Max on a sharp exhale of breath. It wasn't unexpected news, but to have Cesar find proof of what they believed to be true only made the situation worse and more urgent.

Max's haunted gaze met Derek's. "We've got to get down there. Now."

Derek stood and clamped a hand on Max's shoulder, unsure if the touch was more to offer Max comfort or to keep him from running out of the office and heading to Mexico on his own.

If he put off going down to Mexico any longer, he risked having to chase Max across the border. Derek adjusted his mental plan.

Cesar must have sensed the urgency as well. He turned to Derek. "You two head down in the morning. I can feed you information as I find it. I put some feelers out and set an alert on some of the darknet sites that Marco tends to use to get the word out on what he has to offer. If anything comes up about Liberty, I hope to find it."

Derek straightened. "I guess we'll get out of your hair. We've got some prep to do if we're heading out first thing tomorrow."

Cesar reached into the top drawer of his desk and handed Derek his car keys.

"What's this for?"

"You can't take the Roadster down to Mexico and not get noticed, and your beater will break down before you hit the border."

A sensible guy, Cesar had a sensible four-door sedan. Derek took the keys and pocketed them. "Thanks, man. You're chalking up the brownie points."

"We're partners. That's what a partner is for."

Derek clapped him on the back and headed out of the room, catching Max's quick thanks as he followed Derek out to the cars.

"Where to?" Max said as he folded himself into Cesar's Chevy.

"We'll drop by your place to get your passport and pack a bag, grab some Chinese takeout, and head to my place."

The grin Max shot Derek would have had him reaching over the center console and kissing those lips if, you know, they weren't *not* doing that. "Still don't trust me not to head out on my own, do you?"

"Not the least little bit."

9

Max shoveled the last of the lo mein noodles into his mouth and washed it down with the dregs at the bottom of his bottle of beer. He sat back on the couch, Derek's eyes on him as Max rubbed his full belly.

Despite the worry about Liberty and having had lunch, he'd been starving and had made up for it by demolishing more than his fair share of the food Derek had bought.

"What?" Max asked when Derek didn't look away.

"Where did you put all that food? And how the hell do you not weigh four-hundred pounds by now?"

Derek had been looking at his body, had he? Max grinned. "Good metabolism."

"Fucker," Derek said without any heat. "I'd have to run for the next five days straight if I'd eaten all that. I thought we'd have enough left over to heat up for breakfast."

Max glanced at the numerous empty cartons on the coffee table. They'd been so hungry they hadn't even bothered with plates. Or a real table. He picked up the nub end of a spring roll Derek hadn't finished and popped it into his mouth. "Sorry."

Derek shook his head. "No, you're not."

Max chuckled. "Nope."

Since Derek had paid for dinner, Max gathered up the trash and dumped it into the kitchen garbage can. He went through the back door and got his small duffel out of the back of Cesar's car. They didn't have a clue how long they'd be gone, so Max had thrown in a few changes of clothes, his toiletries, and had called it good.

When he returned to the den with his bag hooked over his shoulder, he asked, "Where do you want me?"

Derek paused whatever he'd been doing on his phone, his gaze hot. For a moment there, Max thought Derek would say something like *in my mouth* or *sitting on my face*. But then Derek's phone pinged, and the raw desire cleared from his face.

"Sleep wherever," Derek said at last before diving back into his phone, his tone dismissive with a heaping helping of ambivalence tossed in.

What had Max done now? He'd cleared the coffee table, left to get his bag, and now Derek had turned on *full asshole* mode. Was Derek mad at Max for something he'd done or was Derek pissed at himself for wanting him?

Max backed away and headed down the hall by himself, opening closed doors, searching for the guest room. He found Derek's sleek, sterile office and the guest bathroom before finding the room he was looking for.

For a brief second, he thought about setting himself up in Derek's bedroom and seeing what would happen if Derek found him naked in his bed, but he thought better of it. He didn't need to push any more of Derek's buttons or take advantage of his goodwill. After all, it wasn't every day that a PI of Derek's caliber took up a case pro bono, and it would be stupid of Max to push his luck.

He dumped his bag on the queen-sized bed. The room— smaller than the office—had little furnishings besides the bed and a set of bedside tables on either side of the black leather headboard. A dresser sat against the opposite wall next to the closet. Though the furnishings were upscale, like Derek's neighborhood and car, nothing else was in the room. No decorations on the walls, no knickknacks on the tables or dresser.

Just a room. Cold. Sterile. Much like his office had been. It was as if Derek didn't live a life here and had just filled the rooms because they needed filling. Then again, a workaholic like Derek probably spent most of his time at the office or on the road.

Max quickly showered, giving his dick the most basic of cleanings because every little touch or brush of his hand seemed to set him off. For a brief second, Max had allowed himself to think about that searing look Derek had given him in the den. Even after rinsing in cold water and climbing out of the shower, he couldn't get rid of his hard-on.

Max stomped into his room with his towel knotted at his waist. Fuck if he couldn't even think straight when he was walking with a stiffy. But then Derek had always done that to him. It hadn't taken much back then, or now it seemed.

But just because he was still attracted to Derek didn't mean they had anything else between them besides physical chemistry and years of old memories and regret.

Regret on Max's part. Maybe not so much on Derek's.

Would Max do it all differently if he had a chance to do it all over again? He didn't know. Those years he'd spent away had given him the chance to grow the fuck up, to learn about himself and his place in the world. He wasn't sure he would have survived if he'd stayed.

But fuck, where would he be, *where would he and Derek be*, if he had?

Max dropped his towel on the hardwood floor, pulled on a pair of clean boxer briefs, and propped himself against the headboard. He shot a quick text to his apprentice, Jordan, asking how his clients had taken his canceling appointments and if they'd rescheduled for another time. He couldn't afford to lose the business, but he refused to not be involved with Liberty's search.

Even though he hadn't been in her life for years now, that didn't mean he wasn't protective of her and didn't feel responsible for her wellbeing. He couldn't get the thoughts out of his head of where she might be if he'd stuck around. Would she be in school? Would they be sharing a place? Would they even be friends?

But for all the reasons he'd had to stay back then, he knew now that leaving and getting away from his toxic parents had probably saved his life.

But at what cost to Liberty?

To Derek?

A shadow fell across his doorway, and Max glanced up. Derek muttered a curse and snatched Max's damp towel off the floor. "What the fuck, Max. You raised in a barn?"

Max rolled to his feet. A barn would have been an upgrade, and Derek fucking well knew it. Max pushed Derek back, his hand in the middle of Derek's chest, holding him against the wall. "I was going to get that in a minute. What the fuck is wrong with you?"

Derek's chin came up, his eyes blazing, the towel in question wrapped up in Derek's clenched fists. "Nothing."

"So you're just being an asshole to be an asshole then?"

"Forget it," Derek said, as he tried to brush Max's hand away.

Max wasn't having any of it. He pressed his palm more firmly in the center of Derek's chest, Derek's heart thundering beneath his hand.

Max leaned in closer, their shared air mixing in the space

between them, the wasabi and beer thick on Derek's breath. "What the fuck is eating you?"

"You really want to get into this now?"

Max dropped his hand. "There's never going to be a good time. Now's as good a time as any."

"You fucking *left*. Practically up and disappeared. If you hadn't have left that..." Derek's voice cracked, and he cleared his throat. "If you hadn't left that fucking note, I would have filed a missing person's report. One minute you're in my life, and the next, you'd vanished."

"I had my own shit to work out. And let's face it, Derek, as much as you told yourself you wanted to be a detective, you hated it. But you shouldn't have used me as your excuse to quit. You couldn't lay all that at my feet. I didn't want my past screwing up your career."

Derek shoved Max out of his space, his hands on his hips, the harsh light from above highlighting the exasperation on Derek's face. "I chose you."

"No. You were running from your father's infamous legacy. Don't you *dare* spin that as some martyred declaration of love."

Max broke eye contact first, but it was Derek who walked away.

***

"*Hey*," Max called out as Derek left. It was either walk away or put a fist through something Derek shouldn't... like the wall... or Max's face. "Don't walk away from me."

Derek kept walking down the hall toward his bedroom. Too afraid that if he stopped, he'd blurt out something he hadn't even admitted to himself in the past ten years.

That he was still in love with Max.

What the fuck was Derek supposed to do with that?

He'd deluded himself into thinking that he was over Max, that his spat of failed short-term relationships and hookups was because his work hours didn't afford him much time for a personal life.

But the fact remained, he could easily see himself watching Max grill on the back porch, or them doing the mundane things like running errands or waking up together in a puddle of arms and legs and sated bodies.

Jesus Christ, he needed to find Liberty and find her fast.

The scary truth was if Max asked Derek to take him back, even after all Max had put him through... Derek would.

And he kind of despised himself for his weakness.

His saving grace? He figured Max was smart enough not to ask.

You never could tell him no. For your sake, let's hope you're right.

The floorboards shook as Max stomped down the hall after him. Derek half expected Max to grab his arm and spin him around in the hall. Instead, Max followed Derek into his bedroom.

"I wasn't finished talking." Max slapped the light switch as he came through the door. Derek squinted against the harsh brightness.

Max had had the last word when he'd walked away. It seemed fitting that Derek should get a turn. But it didn't seem as if Max was willing to let the subject drop, even with their early morning the next day.

Derek rounded on him. "What the fuck is wrong with you? *Now* you want to talk?"

If Max wanted to talk about it, then they'd fucking talk about it. After all, this talk was ten years in the making.

A vein ticked at Max's temple, and his breath came hard and fast. Derek gave him a sharp shove that did nothing to spur the man into talking. "Where was Mister Talkative ten years ago?

Where was *this guy* when you walked away? Why didn't he stay and talk ab—"

Derek cut himself off. With each sentence, his voice rose octave by octave. This wasn't the calm, adult conversation he'd wanted. Unfortunately, it was his scared, hurt, newly-out young self who'd come to *this* conversation. He took a few calming breaths, his voice nearly abandoning him when he said, "Why didn't *he* want me."

The air whooshed out of Max, the flush of anger subsided, and his strong shoulders sagged. He swallowed audibly. "You thought I didn't want you?"

Derek let out a sharp, incredulous laugh. "What the hell else was I supposed to think?"

"That I loved you. That I thought I was doing what was best for you. That—" Max's voice cracked, and he shook his head, glancing at the ceiling as if he thought he'd get the answers from above. "*Fuck...*"

Derek's breath caught. That one word, spoken with exasperation, frustration, and realization, made the knot in Derek's gut loosen a fraction.

Max stepped forward, closing the distance between them. "It was never that I didn't want you." He stepped closer still, their bodies nearly touching. Max's hand came up, his thumb rubbing across the short stubble on Derek's jaw.

Derek didn't fight the touch like he knew he should. He leaned into it, blowing out the heat, the animosity, the *hurt,* letting himself focus on Max and the here and now, on the sincerity on Max's face, on the tremor in his tone, on the soft look in his eyes.

Was it possible to fall even harder for a man who had tipped his world upside down? Derek closed the infinitesimal gap between them—their bodies touching from thigh to hip to chest —and waited for Max to finish his thought.

Instead of talking, Max dipped his head. Derek saw the kiss coming, knew it would devastate him, but he did nothing to stop it.

Max's lips brushed against Derek's. Derek grunted at the soft blow to his heart. Fuck if he could resist Max. And fuck if he even wanted to try.

Max broke the kiss all too soon, his voice thick and his eyes awash with unshed tears. "I'm not sorry that I left. I wouldn't have survived staying. But I am sorry that I left *you*."

Derek didn't completely understand. He'd known that Max had been in a bad spot before he'd left the valley. That the toxicity of his parents and extended family had made it nearly impossible for him to stay and have it not affect his mental health.

Despite Derek's love and support, Max had been in a dark place.

"I would have gone with you."

"That's what I was afraid of. And I—" The words fell away, and whatever Max wanted to say vanished. Max cupped Derek's face. "I had to make a clean break, but I missed you so fucking much. Every goddamn day."

Derek pulled him in for another kiss. A kiss that didn't stay soft for long. It tasted, teased, tormented.

Over the months and years after Max had left, Derek had kept loose tabs on him through various online searches that weren't necessarily on the up and up, half afraid he'd stumble onto Max's obituary.

But when none came, the time between checks gradually lengthened until he could push the urge to check on Max to the back of his mind and keep his hands off the keyboard and dodgy search engines.

Which explained why Derek hadn't had a clue that Max had rolled back into town.

Even if Derek could have forced words past the cloying lump in his throat, he didn't want to admit the truth—that maybe, just maybe, Max had been right to leave.

Not that that realization had made what Max had done hurt any less.

Max deepened the kiss, stepping into Derek until the back of Derek's knees hit the side of the mattress. Derek knew he should stop, knew that if he let his knees buckle the way they wanted to, that if Max followed him down onto the bed, there would be no stopping what happened next.

And damn it, Derek so didn't want to stop. Max still smelled the same as he did, that potent mix of virile male and healthy musk.

Wrapping a hand around the back of Max's neck, Derek pulled him down onto the bed. Max followed willingly and eagerly, the soft grunts and sighs arrowing straight to Derek's dick.

By the time they'd settled in the middle of the bed, with one of Max's legs wedged between Derek's, Max's hard cock pressed against Derek's hip, Derek was ready to accept anything Max was willing to give.

Max explored Derek's mouth and licked and nipped at his lips and chin and that tender part of Derek's neck that always sent an army of goosebumps marching across his hot flesh. Max reached for the hem of Derek's shirt.

Derek broke the kiss long enough for them to strip off their clothes and dispose of those as well.

The low hum of approval from Max made Derek's dick even harder. It stood straight out from his body, a drop of precum catching the light.

Max rubbed it off with the pad of his thumb, bringing it to his mouth and sucking his thumb clean. His eyes closed for a fraction, and when they opened, his pupils had blown. "I've always fucking loved the way you taste."

Derek pulled Max on top of him, going for another kiss, loving the way he tasted in Max's mouth. The mattress sunk beneath their combined weight, their dicks aligning for the first time in a very, *very* long time.

Derek ground against him, the sensations intimately familiar and brand new all at the same time. They weren't the same men they were back then, but not everything had changed either.

Max had bigger muscles than before and more tattoos that Derek would have to explore later. The mat of chest hair had grown thicker, but there was still the bump on his collarbone where he'd broken it as a kid. There was the same birthmark—the splatter of darker skin near his throat that always drove Max mad when Derek put his lips and tongue to it.

Max skimmed a hand down Derek's torso, supporting himself on one elbow and straddling one of Derek's legs. His fingers followed the column of Derek's neck on down to his overly sensitive nipple. Then Max moved on to Derek's ticklish ribs. He paused at the puckered scar on Derek's side and kissed it before blazing a trail through the hair beneath his belly button. And finally, to where Derek wanted Max the most.

Running his hands through Derek's short-cropped pubes, Max circled Derek's base with a single finger. Derek strained upward, needing the touch, the pressure of Max's hand on him.

Max chuckled, the low throaty sound energizing Derek's dick. "You want me to touch you?"

"Bastard," Derek managed, raising on his elbows to stare down at him. "You know damn well I do."

"Do you want my hand?" Max licked and kissed his way up Derek's neck and nibbled on his earlobe. "Or do you want my mouth?"

Even after all this time, they both knew the answer to that

question, but fuck if Derek didn't dig the way Max was going to make him say it.

"I want your mouth, and you fucking well know it," Derek all but growled.

Max reached farther down between Derek's spread legs, cupping Derek's heavy balls. "That's my guy." They both stilled, and Max blanched. "Not that you're my guy, I mean, I know this is a one-off and—"

Derek caught Max's chin in his hand. "I know you didn't mean that the way it came out. Don't worry. I'm not planning a trip to the jeweler and an elaborate proposal."

"Just so that we're on the same page."

"Yeah, sure." Derek's head agreed, but his heart, that was another matter that he'd rather not delve into right then. He didn't want to kill the mood or think about what that meant for now or for the condition of his battered heart in the long term.

Not that he expected a long term.

They'd find Liberty, and then they'd go their separate ways. He couldn't expect any more than that and be able to watch Max walk away again and not have his heart splinter.

Max shifted and started kissing his way down Derek's torso. Derek put a staying hand on Max's chest.

Max glanced up, the heat and unleashed desire back in his eyes. "You change your mind?"

"I should wash up before you go any further. I'm not exactly out-of-the-shower fresh."

Max pushed Derek down and braced his weight on his hands, his hard cock sliding down the seam of Derek's leg. "I won't stop you if that's what you want to do, but I've always loved your smell. It fucking turns me on."

Derek relaxed. Fuck it. If it didn't bother Max, it sure as hell didn't bother him. "Go for it."

Go for it.

Max couldn't hold back his grin. His devious chuckle brought a smile to Derek's lips as well.

He didn't stop to think about the consequences of what they were doing. All he knew was that he wanted Derek, and he wasn't going to stop unless Derek wanted him to.

But Derek didn't.

Derek's hands went to Max's head as Max started kissing his way down Derek's body, Max's hair just long enough for Derek to fist his fingers in.

Fire sparked and rolled in his belly, his cock straining as he licked and sucked on Derek's flat nipple. Derek hissed in a breath. His nipples had always been super sensitive. Looks like *that* hadn't changed.

"God, I fucking love that talented tongue of yours. I could come from just your tongue." Derek's arms wrapped around Max's head, holding him tight as Max teased Derek's nipples into hard peaks.

Then Derek's hands went to Max's shoulders, pushing him

downward. "But I need you on my dick. I want your hot breath and your warm, wet mouth."

Max groaned, his precum slicking Derek's thigh as he moved farther south. He loved Derek's dirty talk. For a guy who could use silence as a weapon in an interrogation, how free he was with words in the bedroom was even more devastating.

The muscles in Derek's belly fluttered beneath Max's lips, his hips flexing, precum freely spilling from Derek's slit. Max wanted to reach out and smear it over the head of Derek's dick with his finger, but he wanted to do it with his tongue more.

Max shifted between Derek's legs. Holding his weight on one arm, Derek's big, beautiful cock jutting up in front of Max's face. He glanced up at Derek, checking in one last time. Derek's gaze locked on his, a laser beam in full-lock mode.

Catching Derek's base with his hand, Max angled his tip toward his mouth and watched Derek as Derek unabashedly watched him take him into his mouth. Derek's eyes fluttered closed for a fraction of a second, but when they opened, they held a banked fire that threatened to flame and consume them both.

"That feels so fucking good," Derek said as Max licked the salty moisture from his slit and ever so slowly took him to the back of his throat. Max groaned. Derek grunted and gently thrust into Max's mouth. Max relaxed the back of his throat, taking more of him until his nose settled in Derek's pubes and Derek's dick cut off his air.

Max's lungs heaved, begging for oxygen. Pulling back, Max sucked in some much-needed air and started with a steady rhythm, taking Derek deep and shallow, his tongue working the thick vein on the underside of Derek's girthy cock.

Derek clasped his hands behind his head, staring down at Max as his dick disappeared. "I could watch you suck me off all fucking day. That mouth, those lips, the—"

Max took him impossibly deep again, loving the way he stole the words from Derek's lips, the thoughts from his head. Max loved the power he had to silence a man who prided himself on his self-control.

Max wanted more of that. Wanted more of Derek giving into the pleasure and relinquishing some of that precious control. He spat into his hand and ran his fingers down Derek's taint, slipping into Derek's crack and toying with the tight bundle of muscles.

Derek's head fell back as he pushed against Max's probing finger. Derek had always loved getting fucked. Max would have been content sucking Derek off, but Max was willing to give Derek more.

"Fuck, yeah," Derek said on a soft exhale as the tip of Max's finger breached the tight ring of muscle.

Derek twisted and grabbed a bottle of lube out of the bedside table and tossed it to Max along with a short ribbon of condoms. Max sat on his haunches between Derek's splayed legs. Derek's hand went to his own dick, and Max lost himself watching Derek's lazy, unabashed strokes as he pleasured himself.

Max ripped off a condom packet and turned it in his fingers. "You sure about this?"

"About the condom or about me wanting you to fuck me?"

"I'm fine using a condom. I'm talking about the fucking part."

"It doesn't have to mean anything. It can just be sex. A one-off, right?"

Before it could escape, Max bit down on the audible *umpf* as Derek's words hit. Even though those had been Max's words, it hurt more than a little to hear Derek say them.

Knowing he shouldn't expect more—*didn't deserve to expect*

more—but wanting more all the same. Max forced lightness into his words. "Nothing wrong with meaningless sex."

Max tore the condom packet with his teeth and tamped down on the frisson of disappointment that made his chest tight, and his heart shrink.

A little self-respect should have had Max rolling off the bed instead of rolling on the condom. But then again, Max hadn't always done what was best for him. And as much as Max knew this might hurt later, he wasn't turning down a chance to have Derek splayed and willing beneath him once again.

He slicked up the condom and poured more lube on his fingers to slick up Derek's hole. He knocked Derek's hand off his cock and replaced it with his own hand as he worked a finger inside Derek.

"You're so fucking tight," Max said, his dick straining, wanting in on the action. Derek had always been an eager bottom, but he'd rather not rush things and hurt Derek in the process.

"I don't want your finger," Derek groused. "I want your dick."

Max didn't have to be told twice. As it was, he was already close to coming. That's what happened when you'd spent most of the day half-hard. He went down to his hands, their pelvises grinding against each other as Max hovered above him.

The 'just sex' comment still stung, but as Derek stared up at him, desire, lust, and fire in his eyes that matched Max's own, he pushed that out of his mind.

Derek was a skilled liar, which made him so good at his job, but Max didn't think it was only Max's dickful thinking that the sex meant something to them both.

Cock straining, he opened his mouth, not sure exactly what he wanted to say.

Derek's hands went to Max's hips. "Don't ask me if I'm sure or any bullshit like that. I'm not some kid you have to coddle."

"Kid?" Max huffed out a clipped laugh. "I'm not interested in the twenty-something twinks. You should know me better than that."

"Then tell me what you want." It was a request as much as a dare. And fuck if Max hadn't missed that directness in his bed.

If he hadn't missed *Derek* in his bed.

Max lined up on Derek's hole and gently rolled his hips, catching Derek's strangled gasp with a kiss as Max breached his hole. He took the kiss deep before pulling back, wanting to watch the delicious strain of ecstasy on Derek's face as he pressed in further. "I want to be buried balls deep in your ass. I want to watch you break apart, and I want to fuck you back together again."

A knowing grin teased at the corners of Derek's lips. Whatever he'd been about to say caught in his throat as Max sunk to the hilt. Before Max could start pulling out, Derek's hands on his hips held him still.

Derek blew out a breath. "Give me a sec." The tightness around Max's cock lessened as Derek willed his body to relax. Derek rolled his hips, easing Max out a bit before pulling him back in again. The low rumble of Derek's self-deprecating chuckle rolled through Max's chest. "I forgot how big you were."

Taking Derek's body cues, Max slowly pulled out, going almost to the tip before stroking back in again. Max didn't say what he wanted to say, that he hadn't forgotten one damn thing about how Derek felt, smelled, tasted. It had been imprinted on his mind, not in indelible ink, but chiseled in stone. One of those precious memories that would go with him to the grave and beyond.

THE WAY MAX GAZED DOWN AT DEREK, ALL HEAT AND WARMTH

and heart, was more than Derek could take. This wasn't the quick, easy, mindless fuck he'd expected, and it pained his heart too much to allow himself to go back to where they used to be.

He couldn't take the slow, the sensual, the lovemaking. He needed raw hunger and rough sex. Forget connecting on a deeper level because that would threaten the carefully constructed wall around his heart and blow it the fuck up.

Derek didn't think he'd survive that.

Not again.

He took Max by the ears, brought him in for a heated, hungry kiss that left them both short of breath. "Fuck me." An order, not an epitaph.

Max grunted, his pupils nearly blown. Rising to his knees, he looped his arms around Derek's thighs. He plunged in and out. Stretching and filling him. Max's breaths came fast as he slammed into Derek again and again.

Max's heavy balls slapped against Derek's taint, the scent of musk and sweat filling Derek's nostrils. Fire built in his groin, sending incendiary sparks throughout his system, setting his nerve endings alight.

Reaching down, Derek grabbed his dick—the tip and his abdomen already soaked with precum. He stroked himself to Max's deliciously brutal pace, his climax racing to catch up. He felt the first pulses of his orgasm at the base of his spine.

Max dropped Derek's legs and came down on top of him, burying his face in the crook of Derek's shoulder, his savage pace unrelenting. Max's teeth sank into the soft flesh of Derek's shoulder, not hard enough to bleed, but hard enough to push him over the edge.

Derek groaned, his head thrown back as the pleasure washed through his body. Within seconds, Max stiffened, his pants harsh in Derek's ear, his breath hot on Derek's skin as Max kissed and sucked at the tender spot beneath the teeth marks.

Strokes, now slow and languid as they both came back to themselves, Max kissed Derek again, the roughness gone, leaving only the tenderness in its devastating wake.

"How's the shoulder?" Max asked as he shifted and took his weight on his forearms.

Derek felt the faintest of pulses beating in the skin where Max's teeth had sunk. He ran a finger over the faint indents in his flesh. No man had ever marked him the way Max had and did. No one had dared. But fuck if that thought didn't have Derek's spent dick twitching again. "Never better."

Max grinned, slowly pulling out and laying on his side. His breath still unsettled from his exertion. Derek rolled to his side to face him. A part of him still unable to believe that Max was in his bed again.

In his *life* again.

Don't forget that the only reason he showed up at your door was because he needed something from you. He'd known where to find you. If he'd wanted to come back for you, he would have.

Derek buried those thoughts. Not because he didn't think they were true, but because he *knew* they were. There would be plenty of time on the drive down to Mexico for self-recrimination. He didn't have to ruin a good after-sex buzz and do it now.

And if he were honest with himself, he wanted to live in that tiny bubble where he could delude himself into thinking what just happened was more than what it was. At least until the morning.

After ten years, he'd allow himself that.

Max rolled out of bed and padded into the bathroom as the sweat dried on Derek's overheated skin. Max returned with a warm washcloth and cleaned Derek up, his hands gentle, his thoughts turned inward.

Max disposed of the washcloth and stood in the bathroom

doorway, his shoulder against the jamb, his dick soft and nestled in the trimmed hair around the base. "You hungry?"

"Not really." Derek pushed up to an elbow. It was an effort, with his body still sated and sluggish from sex. "You?"

Derek started to climb out of bed. Max held out a staying hand. "Not really. More tired than anything."

"Same." Derek rolled back onto the mattress, uncertain if Max wanted to stay with him for the night.

Max turned off the bathroom light and snagged his underwear off the floor before killing the bedroom light. "Okay, I guess I'll—"

"Do you want to stay?" The words come out sounding weird, even to Derek's ears. A collision of need and uncertainty.

Max cocked his head, the expression on his face Derek couldn't quite read. "Is that an invitation or a consolation prize?"

Derek sensed that Max wanted more, but Derek didn't know if he was in a place where he had more to give. To deflect the heavy question, Derek injected a little humor. "We both came. I don't think they give out consolation prizes to the winners."

Instead of hopping into bed the way Derek thought Max would, he took a step back.

"I don't want you thinking this is more than it is." Max's face twisted. It looked as if those words tasted bitter on Max's tongue.

"I'm a big boy, Maxie." The old endearment rolled off Derek's tongue before he could stop it. If Max heard it, he did a great job of hiding it. "I can take care of myself."

Max stared down at the balled-up underwear in one of his tight fists as he contemplated his choices. Then his fingers relaxed, and the material fell from his hands. He looked up and said, "Yeah, I'd like to stay."

Max crawled into bed and lay on his back, his fingers laced behind his head, and stared up at the ceiling, mirroring Derek. Had everything changed between them? Had nothing changed?

Were they both headed for a fall? Or could they be adults and keep the past where it belonged—behind them?

Long after Max succumbed to sleep, Derek lay awake in the darkness, scrolling through his phone while Max softly snored beside him. For reasons he'd rather not contemplate, he took a photo of Max curled up behind him. Maybe to prove that it had happened when his brain questioned his sanity. Or maybe because he was pretty damn sure it would never happen again.

Emotions swirled. Having sex with Max had been the best and worst decision he'd made in years. He almost texted Joss. He'd been there for Joss through the hardest years after Joss's partner had died, but Derek hesitated.

Because Joss would tell you what a colossal mistake you'd made. Face it. You don't want to hear the truth. Or an I-told-you-so.

But the enormity was too much to hold in.

He pulled up Cesar's number and attached the photo to his text.

Derek: *So... this happened.*

He put his phone down, not expecting a return text so late, already feeling a bit better for having put it out there.

Cesar's reply came almost immediately: *Is this a good thing or a bad thing?*

Derek thought about his reply and decided he'd go with the truth: *Seemed like a good idea at the time. Now, I don't know.*

Though he and Cesar had been partners for six months or so, their friendship was still developing. And while Cesar knew he and Max had a history, they hadn't delved much into the telling confidences phase of their friendship. But Cesar had a good head on his shoulders, and Derek was learning to trust his intuition and judgment.

Cesar: *I know these situations can be minefields to navigate. Be careful. And don't get ahead of your skis.*

Which was the PC way to say, don't let your dick do all the thinking.

Derek: *I get it... but fuuuuck.*

Cesar: *Lol. That good?*

Derek wasn't one to go into details about his personal life, but then again, he'd started this.

Derek: *You have no idea.*

Cesar: *You're just trying to make me jealous. Now get some sleep. I'm here if you need to talk.*

Derek: *Thanks.*

Setting his phone aside, Derek let the long day pull him under. No surprise to Derek, he woke to find himself hard and balancing on the edge of his king-sized bed. Max had been the only man he'd ever slept with who always managed to claim precious real estate in the middle of the night.

At least the tight hold Max had around Derek's waist kept him from tumbling off.

In the early morning dawn, Derek lay there, fully aware when Max's breathing changed as he woke. Derek had more to worry about than Max taking over his bed. He had to worry about Max taking over his thoughts, his dreams, his... *heart.*

It would be so fucking easy to roll over and fall back into Max's arms and into old habits that his body found impossible to forget.

Max pulled him in tight and pressed a kiss between Derek's shoulder blades before releasing him and rolling away. How was Derek supposed to keep from thinking there was more between them when Max did tender shit like that?

Derek climbed out of bed and padded into the bathroom, the scent of sex still lingering in the air from the night before. Max didn't follow, and Derek didn't ask him to. Taking a shower together would undoubtedly waste more time than they had. He couldn't forget the real reason Max had come back into his life—to find Liberty.

Derek just hoped he didn't let Max down. For all of their sakes.

When Derek made it to the kitchen, with his overnight bag packed with enough essentials to last him a few days, Max was already there. The coffee pot gurgled, and bagels heated in the toaster.

Even though he'd smelled the coffee as he'd walked down the hall, seeing Max in his kitchen, his hair damp, his feet bare the way he'd been a million times before, knocked Derek back a step. He recovered before Max could turn around and catch it.

"I hope you don't mind that I made myself at home."

"It's fine." Derek's ability to lie under pressure paid off in many ways. This was just one of them.

Derek went for coffee. The toaster popped, and Max spread the cream cheese on the bagels and slid one across the counter to Derek. "I didn't want to waste time cooking this morning. But if you—"

"No." Derek took his plate and coffee and leaned against the counter, a few precious feet separating them. "I'd rather get on the road. It's going to be a long day."

Max grunted around a bite of bagel. "What do you really think our chances are of finding her?"

Derek could have lied and made it believable and sound more optimistic than he was, but Derek didn't want to give Max any false hope either. Yeah, he'd promised to find Liberty, but they had both known at the time that that wasn't necessarily something that was within his control.

Derek decided not to sugarcoat it. "Slim."

The word must have landed like a sucker punch, the grunt from Max, harsh and guttural. "That's what I thought."

THEY FINISHED EATING IN SILENCE, LEFT THEIR DISHES IN THE SINK, and readied two travel mugs with coffee for the road. Within minutes, they were in Cesar's car.

They filled up on fuel and stocked up on cash, not knowing how much money they'd need or if they'd need to pay for information or buy their way out of trouble.

They headed south on the 405, fighting rush hour traffic through the valley, past Los Angeles, and down through San Diego. It wasn't until they were past the Coronado bridge that the roads started opening up, and they could manage any relative speed.

The tension knotted the muscles in Max's neck, and he had to work them to keep the low-grade tension headache from turning into a full-blown migraine.

His right knee bounced, and he didn't bother stopping it. It was the only outlet he had for his nervous energy.

He groaned as they neared the Tijuana border crossing and saw the long line of cars, trucks, buses, and semi-trucks ahead of them. "You've got to be fucking kidding me."

Derek glanced at him, having said few words on the long

drive down. "You expected something different?"

Max raised his hands and let them fall to his lap. "Hell, I don't know what I expected. At this rate, we'll be lucky if we make it across the border in an hour or so. *Fuck*."

"I don't know what else you want me to do." After hours of fighting traffic, the strain seemed to be wearing on Derek. Max heard it in his voice.

Max bit back his frustration. It wasn't Derek's fault that Southern California's traffic sucked or that it looked like half of the state's population had chosen that day to cross the border.

"I'm just anxious to find her. I feel like we've wasted a lot of time that we could have been down here searching for her."

"That time bought us some valuable information. It will probably save us more time in the long run now that we have some idea of where to start looking."

"I know you're right... in here." Max pointed to his head. "But in here," he said, pointing to his heart, "I have a harder time accepting that."

They fell into silence again, Max's knee still dancing as their car inched forward. Derek glanced over occasionally as if he had something he wanted to say but didn't know how to say it.

If it had been about Liberty, Max doubted Derek would have hesitated to speak up. It didn't take a genius to figure out where Derek's mind had drifted. A few cars from the booth and the border agents, Derek draped both hands over the wheel, his focus out the windshield when he said, "Do you regret it?"

There were many things in Max's life that he regretted, but the night before wasn't nearly one of them. "Do you?"

Derek's chuckle came out parched and dry. "I did sleep with a client."

"That's bullshit, and you know it. Besides, you refused to take my money, so technically, I'm not your client, just your ex. Try again."

Derek inched up another car length, eyes focused forward. For a man who could stare even the hardest of men down, he avoided eye contact now. "Do I think sleeping with you was the smartest thing I've ever done? No. Do I regret it?"

Max tried to breathe through the wait, but his lungs refused to function. Then Derek caught Max's gaze, the heat and desire flaring in those deep brown eyes. "Not for a minute."

The car behind them honked. Derek held his hand out across the center console. For a second, Max didn't take it, but who the hell was he kidding? He wanted that touch and that connection as much as Derek did. Max twined his fingers with Derek's as another horn blast sounded behind them.

Derek squeezed Max's hand, only letting go long enough to give their passports to the border patrol agent and fill out their forms for their visitor's permit. They were through faster than Max expected. Even though they suspected Marco was in Las Rocas, they had no idea if Liberty had made it that far south. He plugged Tres Colinas into his phone's GPS, the first town after the border crossing that Liberty could have gotten off the bus.

Tres Colinas was a small town not far from the Pacific coast. Maybe they'd get lucky, and someone had seen her. With her long legs, her hair dyed a bright red, and a face that turned heads, she was the type of woman many people wouldn't forget.

And Max counted on that.

Derek drove the main road to Tres Colinas, following the GPS, having never ventured that far south before, unlike many of his friends and fellow Californians had. It wasn't a resort town like Cancún or Cozumel that drew all the tourists, partiers, and spring breakers. It was better known for its sleepy, off-the-beaten-path kind of vibe.

They kind of place you went to get away.

But Derek wasn't naïve enough to think that bad shit couldn't go down in a sleepy town. Sometimes small towns were a hotbed of drugs and other meanness precisely because they were out of the way and often overlooked.

Derek's phone pinged with an incoming text as they arrived on the outskirts of town. Max picked up Derek's phone. "It's Cesar."

Derek rattled off his password, and Max opened up his messages. Belatedly, Derek remembered the string of texts he'd sent to Cesar the night before. The last thing he wanted was for Max to find that incriminating string of messages. He stomped down on the urge to take back his phone.

But it was too late now.

"He sent the photos of Liberty from the border crossing. At least now we have something to show people."

As Derek had feared, Max scrolled too far up, and the photo Derek had sent Cesar the night before caught Max's eye.

Derek tried to snatch the phone out of Max's hand, but Max easily switched it to his other one out of reach. "Why is there a picture of me in your bed on your message feed to Cesar?"

Making a *give it here* motion with his hand, Derek said, "Just give me the damn phone."

"Not until you answer me. It's a valid question."

Derek made another grab that Max deflected, the car veered into the other lane. A motorcycle beeped its horn, and the rider sped around them, flipping them the finger over his shoulder.

"You're going to get us fucking killed."

Derek checked the mirrors, yanked the wheel to the right, bumped up over a broken curb, braked in a vacant lot, and threw the car into park. Earning himself another round of much-deserved angry honks. But fuck, he *really* didn't want Max reading his texts.

Didn't need the man he once loved to know how vulnerable he was. "Give me the fucking phone."

Max clamped the phone to his chest. "What are you hiding?"

Derek closed his eyes, and he gathered himself. He opened them, hoping his desperation wasn't blatantly evident. "*Please.*"

All Derek got was one of Max's maddeningly calmly raised brows. The one that called Derek out for being unreasonable. But Derek didn't think it was unreasonable to want to keep his private texts private.

Fuck. Max wasn't going to quit until he knew the truth. "Fine," Derek said. "Read the fucking texts if you want to know."

"I don't want to read it. I want you to tell me why it's there."

It was humiliating enough that Derek had poured his heart out to Cesar, but it was even worse being caught having done it. Derek was the one his friends went to for his sage advice. He was the strong one, the clear-headed one. The one who always knew what to do.

But with Max, Derek's emotions were all a blur, his heart already starting to twist in the wind. He barely knew which way was up when it came to Max, and he didn't think he had the capacity to think rationally.

Because, fuck, having Max in his life again—even if he sent it careening over a cliff—Derek didn't have the will to stop it.

"*Derek,*" Max said in that tone that said he'd been trying unsuccessfully to get Derek's attention.

Derek glanced over at Max's outstretched hand with his phone in it. He took it back and pocketed it. "Thanks."

He shifted the car into gear, then slammed it back into park again. At this rate, he'd owe Cesar a new transmission by the time they got home. "I was talking to Cesar about last night. About *us.*"

Max took his words in, nodding as he digested them. "So, you do regret it then."

Max's voice had lost its usual vibrancy, and Derek's chest squeezed. He should have said yes and left it at that. Maybe then Max would keep his distance, and they could find Liberty without Derek losing his heart in the process.

But that wouldn't be fair to Max.

Them falling into bed together was as much Derek's doing as it was Max's.

"No. I don't regret it. But I honestly don't know what or how to feel about it yet."

"You could have lied to me. You could have told me that you were showing Cesar the newest notch on your bedpost, and I would have believed you."

"I don't want to lie to you, Maxie."

Max huffed out a laugh, "But you do it so well."

Derek knew Max was only trying to lighten the mood, but Derek also knew he had to set Max straight. "I lie for my job if the case warrants. But I try not to lie to the people I care about."

Max's smile sparked in the bright Mexico sun. "You care about me, huh?"

Derek could have tossed him a flippant *fuck you* and drove away, but he cursed the part of himself that couldn't leave it at that. "I never stopped caring, Maxie. Never once."

"I figured you hated me."

"Hate's a very strong word. A few years there in the beginning, when you were at the top of my shit list, I felt many things. Pissed, betrayed, abandoned, unloved. But I never hated you."

Max caught his hand behind Derek's neck and pulled him in for a brief, tender, sweet kiss that told Derek one important thing—Max still had the power to devastate him.

Max broke the kiss before either of them could take it any deeper and pressed their foreheads together. "That's good to know."

A CHICKEN LANDED ON THE HOOD OF THEIR CAR, PLUCKED A BUG off the windshield, and squawked at them. In the time that they had parked in the vacant lot, a small flock of chickens had surrounded them, picking at bugs in the scraggly, shin-high grass.

"I guess that's our cue to leave," Derek said, breaking the silence that wasn't quite awkward but wasn't quite *not* either.

Besides, they would have all the time in the world to discuss their relationship, then and now, after they found Liberty. But to hear that Derek didn't hate him the way Max had always feared lifted a weight off Max's chest that he'd grown so accustomed to, he'd forgotten it was there.

If he'd known how Derek felt, perhaps he wouldn't have stayed away as long as he had.

Did they have any kind of future? Max didn't have any clue. But it felt like they'd taken their first real step towards something new.

What about last night? What about that slamming-good sex, the ball-busting orgasm? Seems like a giant leap forward right there.

Maybe, but the physical had always come easy for them. It had been the talking, the real communicating, that they'd had a harder time with. Not that either of them was necessarily that much better at expressing themselves now, but Max liked to think that he'd learned a few things, grown a bit, and yes, matured in the years since he'd been gone.

But would it be enough?

The car bounced as Derek drove off the curb and pulled into the early afternoon traffic. For a smaller town, the streets were heavy with cars, mopeds, and pedestrians. Mostly locals, but the tourists were also easy to spot.

There were vendors on the street and a bustling market in a huge vacant lot. If nothing else, maybe they could see if some of the shop owners had seen Liberty. It was a long shot—hell, all of it was a long shot—but they had to try.

"Wanna plug the bus station into the GPS? I figured that's as good a place to start as any," Derek said.

Max searched for the nearest bus station on his phone and hit *Go.* Within minutes, they'd pulled into the station's parking lot.

Max pocketed his phone. "Want to text me those pics that Cesar sent you? I figure we can cover more ground if we split up."

The bus terminal was less of a terminal and more of a small, single-story building with six diagonal lanes out front where the buses parked. If the building held more than a ticket agent, some chairs for the waiting passengers, and perhaps a bathroom, Max would be surprised.

"I'll go in with you," Max said. "I need to hit the head. But I'll check with the vendors and bus drivers while you ask around inside."

"Sounds like a plan."

After relieving himself, Max made his way out to the four waiting buses, climbing into each one and showing the drivers the pictures of Liberty. With his terrible Spanish, it was a slow go, but the drivers' English was better than his Spanish, and they managed to communicate. If Max had known how critical learning the language would be, he would have paid better attention in school.

Unfortunately, none of the drivers had remembered seeing his sister. But these were just four of many buses that must come through the station. No way could he talk to all of them.

He stepped off the last bus and headed for a line of vendors on the sidewalk, his stomach growling in protest. He ordered a couple of bottles of water and four soft tacos. He paid and showed the woman the picture. She showed it to the man with her, but they both shook their heads.

Max tried to keep that sinking feeling from settling in his gut. He'd known from the start that finding Liberty wouldn't be easy, but a part of him had hoped for a different outcome.

Derek joined him as Max pocketed his phone and picked up the water and the bag of food.

"Any of that for me?" Derek asked.

Max handed him a bottle and the bag. "Two each. I didn't know what you'd want, so I just got tacos."

"Tacos are never a bad choice." Derek smiled. It wasn't a special smile meant only for him, but a smiling Derek still packed a powerful punch. He'd buy Derek tacos every day if it made him smile at him like that.

Without anywhere to sit and eat, they leaned against the wall of the bus station and watched people come and go. Max figured it was too much to hope that Liberty happened to walk by, but the few red-haired women he saw, he gave them an extra-long look even if they were too short or too old.

He unwrapped a taco and took his first bite. He chewed,

swallowed, and took another bite. "I take it that you struck out inside the bus station."

"I asked everyone who would stand still long enough to listen. The ticket agent just shrugged. I asked the janitors and anyone that looked like they might work there. No one recognized her."

"Yeah. No luck with the bus drivers or the vendor. There are still a couple more vendors I need to go to when we finish eating, but I'm not hopeful. She could be anywhere."

"We've just started. Don't lose hope."

"Yeah. No. I'm not. I mean, sure, I'm disappointed, but I didn't expect to walk up to the first person and have them point me in Liberty's direction either."

They quickly scarfed their meal and tossed their trash in a nearby can with the swarm of angry flies diving and buzzing.

"Let's knock these last few vendors out and try some other places."

It didn't take long for the other vendors to tell them the same thing everyone else had told them. They hadn't seen Liberty. Or if they had, they didn't remember.

They spent the rest of the afternoon asking in bars, restaurants, and shops up and down the streets near the bus station, but when they met up again, they'd both come up empty. Max's feet ached and throbbed as the sun started to set.

"I don't know if I can go another step," Derek said. "I'm fucking spent."

"Same." Max leaned against the wall of a tobacco shop across the street from the busy market in the vacant lot.

The vendors had started packing up their wares. He and Derek had been so focused on the businesses that they hadn't had time to run through the market. Derek leaned a shoulder against the wall next to Max, his focus across the street.

He batted Max with the back of his hand to get his attention and bobbed his chin at something. "See that booth, the second one on the left?"

Max located the booth. A squat older man with a balding head and what looked like a disapproving wife glanced around the market, his eyes darting. The hand at his side kept going to his front pocket. A younger man with a hoodie over his head took one quick look around before sliding into the man's booth. The wife spat at the young man's feet, but he only laughed at her.

The two men made a sloppy exchange, and the kid disappeared into the crowd. They couldn't tell what was bought and sold from where they stood, but they had a pretty damn good idea.

"You think that shop guy is selling drugs from his booth?" Max asked.

"Looks like it."

The wife scowled at her husband and hit his arm with the back of her hand. "I don't think he's getting any tonight."

"Fuck, she's pissed." Derek straightened, and Max followed him across the street. "I think he might be someone we need to talk to."

"That drug sale might have nothing to do with Marco."

"Maybe not, but I'd be surprised if he didn't have a hand in it somehow. This is supposed to be his area if what Cesar found out is correct."

"Fuck," Max grumbled as he dodged a moped and hurried across the street before an oncoming cabbie could run him down. "What the hell was Liberty thinking getting mixed up with these guys? If anyone should have known better, it should have been her."

Derek paused on the other side of the street, his gaze assessing as he stared at Max. "How so?"

Leave it to Derek to pick up on that little slip of the tongue.

Max should have kept his mouth shut. There was a reason he'd never told Derek much about his childhood. And he planned on keeping it that way. "Nothing. Forget I said anything."

Max started to walk away, but Derek caught his arm and spun him around. "Tell me. It might be important."

Lifting his chin, Max said, "I said, forget it."

It would take a much bigger man than Derek to drag his past out of him.

Max saw the moment when something clicked into place, and Derek made the connection. "Does it have anything to do with the real reason why you left?"

Max shrugged off Derek's hand and started walking again.

"Are you ever going to tell me?" Derek asked as he fell into step beside him.

"Not if I can help it."

Derek let the conversation drop, probably because he knew he wouldn't get anywhere with Max when they had a vendor to talk to.

"*Hola*," the squat man said. He had a sheen of sweat on his face that matched the rivulets running down Max's back. What Max wouldn't give for a little air conditioning and a cold beer right then.

Before Max could use his broken Spanish, Derek whipped out his phone and spilled off a long sentence in Spanish. The only word Max caught was *Liberty*.

The man didn't even look at the picture. He darted a glance at his wife, who shook her head. Derek and the man talked back and forth, Derek's voice remained calm, but the man's voice raised, his hands gesticulating in short chopping motions.

But Max wasn't really watching them. He had his eye on the wife. She stopped packing up their bins and crossed her arms over her generous belly. She swiped a sweaty lock of hair off her face, her lips going flat and her features solidifying as Derek and her husband talked.

Max caught another word. *Marco.* And wished like hell he could follow the conversation. The wife must have decided she couldn't stand back and watch any longer. She pushed her husband away from Derek, her voice a harsh whisper as she chewed her husband out.

Derek lowered his voice and said to Max, "She doesn't want him talking to me about Marco."

"That much I got."

The wife broke away from her husband. "*Vamos,*" she said as she shooed them away.

Derek held up his hands. They backed away and headed across the street.

"So what did the guy say?" Max asked as they got to the other side. His stomach gave a low growl. A bagel and two tacos hadn't been enough considering the long day they'd had.

Derek pointed to a cafe a few stores down with some tables on the sidewalk. "Let's get a beer and food, and I'll tell you all about it."

THE WAITER DELIVERED TWO BOTTLES OF COLD BEER, TOOK DEREK'S and Max's food orders, and hurried over to another table. They were smack in the middle of the dinner rush. Derek had no idea how long the food would take to get out, but he had a cold beer and a hell of a view with Max sitting across from him, so Derek couldn't complain.

"When you look at me like that, it makes me forget why we're here," Max said.

Derek took a swig of his beer, letting the cool liquid wash away the dust and dryness. "Sorry."

Max opened his mouth, but instead of pressing him, he took a sip of his beer as well. "What did the guy tell you?"

Derek was thankful for the change in subject. While he didn't know what to make of the night before, he'd been thinking about a repeat all damn day, and he'd rather Max not know about that. "That he hadn't seen Liberty. That they have too many tourists coming through the market for him to remember every red-haired woman that passes by."

"Fuck, we can't catch a break."

"I don't know about that. He sure got squirrelly when I mentioned Marco's name."

"Yeah, his wife didn't seem too thrilled about it either. She—"

Max's gaze shifted over Derek's shoulder, and before Max could tell him not to look, he glanced around and saw the vendor jog across the street. The man glanced over his shoulder at the market as if he'd snuck away. The man headed directly for them and dropped a piece of paper on their table. Without a word, he turned around and headed back to his nearly dismantled booth.

Derek read the scrap of paper and held it out for Max.

"Las Rocas? Looks like everything points to Las Rocas."

"I'm assuming it has to do with Marco. It goes along with what Mina told us."

"Do we give up here, abandon the other two stops and head straight there?"

"Seems like a better idea now than sticking with the original plan."

"We're just going to stroll into town and start asking for Marco?"

Derek shrugged. "You got a better idea? Asking around for Liberty has gotten us nowhere. Maybe we need to start with him if we want to find her. After all, if she made it to him, he could be the last one to have seen her."

The waiter came and brought their food. They didn't hesitate to dig in. Around a mouthful of cheesy enchiladas, Derek said, "I'm not going to lie, it could be pretty dangerous."

"If this is where you think you're going to tell me to stay behind and leave it all to you again, then fuck you."

There wasn't much heat behind Max's words, only determination. Derek chuckled and washed down his food with more beer. "I'm not asking you to stay behind."

"Damn right, you're not."

"I'm just saying that things might get a little dicey. We're going to have to watch our backs. These aren't the kinds of guys you want to mess around with."

"I'm not naïve. I know better than most how the world works."

There it was again, that hint of something more from Max's past that he refused to talk about. Derek knew that Max hadn't had the best start in life. He'd seen the trailer where he'd grown up the few times he'd gone with Max to take his sister home from school when she was younger. But Max had never said much about his family.

Before Derek could ask any clarifying questions, Max held his gaze over a bowl of chips and salsa and said, "Don't."

Fine. Derek got it. Max's childhood was off-limits. He could appreciate that. It wasn't like his own father was a real winner— all those commendations from the police department notwithstanding. Just because his father did his job well did not negate the fact he was the most toxic person in Derek's life.

Funny how his father could put his life on the line for total strangers and be a right bastard to his son.

"Hey, where did you go?"

"Nowhere," Derek said. He pushed his half-full plate away, his appetite gone.

"You're not going to eat that?"

"Help yourself."

Derek waved down the waiter and paid their bill while Max finished off the rest of Derek's food. Max stacked the plates when he finished, sat back in his chair, and drank the last of his beer.

Max stifled a yawn. "Fuck, I'm beat."

"How far is Las Rocas from here?"

Max pulled out his phone and mapped the distance to their destination. "A couple of hours at least. It's not all that far, but it's mostly back roads, it looks like. We can head that way if you're up for it."

Derek shook his head. The sun had already set, and he would rather not traipse across a foreign country in the middle of the night, especially when he could fall asleep where he sat without any problems. "Let's get a room and start fresh in the morning."

They left the cafe and drove around town until they found a motel. Since it wasn't a tourist town, their options were limited. The motel was a low-slung two-story job that looked like it had been imported from the States sometime in the fifties. A concrete block and stucco construction. Derek knew this because an exterior wall was crushed in, the building blocks exposed as if the end unit had been used for crash dummy testing.

Derek only paid for one room. Considering he and Max had already had sex, he didn't see a reason to waste money— even if the rooms were budget-friendly. Which was the nice way of saying even the roaches probably avoided the place.

He didn't hold out much hope that the interior would be

much nicer than the exterior, but all they needed was a bed and a roof over their head for the night.

They scored a first-floor room. Derek parked in front. Slinging their bags over their shoulders, Derek turned the key in the lock. It took a boot at the bottom edge of the door by Max to un-stick the door. Max entered first and turned on the light. The first words out of his mouth were, "I'm not sleeping on the floor."

Derek followed Max inside and dropped his bag. "I'm not making you sleep—"

Derek stepped around Max and got a good look at the bed. "Well, fuck."

He'd known when he'd gotten the room that it only had one bed. He should have thought to ask about the size. It wasn't a roomy king. It was a full-sized bed, at best.

"That's gonna get cozy," Max said.

"I can go back and see if they have another room. But I'm too tired for any monkey business if that's what you're worried about."

"I'm not the one who had regrets, remember?" Max held Derek's gaze, and Derek felt the cutting edge of Max's recrimination.

"I didn't say I had regrets."

Max held his hands up and took a step back. "Sorry. Unresolved feelings."

They were both exhausted. Max had to be stressed and worried about his sister, so Derek let the comment go without a response. It wouldn't do either one of them any good to get into an argument now.

"You want the shower first?" Derek asked.

Max sat on the edge of the bed and leaned against the headboard with a heavy sigh. "Go ahead."

Derek cleaned up as best he could in the rusty water and

came back into the room with a threadbare towel wrapped low around his waist. Max glanced up from whatever he was doing on his phone, his eyes snagging on Derek's crotch before roving higher.

"All yours," Derek said as he put his bag on the bed and rummaged for a clean pair of underwear. He caught the flash of heat in Max's eyes. "I mean the shower. The shower is all yours."

The hint of a smile fell from Max's lips. "Yeah, I know what you meant."

Derek climbed in on the right side of the bed, knowing Max preferred the left. The mattress sagged, and the bed frame creaked under his weight. He had to use both thin pillows to prop himself up in bed. The shower turned on, and he called Cesar to give him an update.

The phone rang and rang. Usually, Cesar was quick to answer his phone. Derek almost hung up when he finally answered.

"Everything okay?" Cesar's voice was barely a sleepy whisper, and Derek had to strain to hear him.

Had Cesar been asleep? Derek pulled the phone away from his ear and checked the time. A few minutes past eight. He was about to ask Cesar if he'd woke him, then he heard a muffled voice say, "Who is it, babe?"

"Hold on a sex—I mean *sec*," Cesar said. He must have put his hand over the mic because all Derek heard were muffled voices and the click of a door latch.

"I'm back," Cesar said, his voice at a normal level.

"*Babe*, huh?" Derek couldn't help but give Cesar a little shit. "Since when is someone calling you *babe*?"

Cesar released a harsh breath. "I ran into him at Sneaky Pete's."

"You never struck me as someone who'd pick up a guy at a gay bar, take him home, and fuck his brains out."

"It's my ex. It's complicated."

Derek chuckled, the humor of their similar predicaments not lost on him. "Tell me about it."

After a few moments of silence, Derek asked, "Was it good?"

Derek heard a soft thud as if Cesar had thumped the wall with the back of his head. Maybe he was trying to knock some sense into himself. Maybe that was a strategy Derek could try. "*Sooo* fucking good. But you didn't call to get an update on my sex life."

"No, but if you want to talk…"

"I don't even know what I'm feeling right now. How did you deal with sleeping with Max?"

"I haven't. Not really. Too much baggage to unpack in the middle of searching for his sister. Which *is* why I called."

"You find something?"

Derek gave Cesar the update, telling him about the note the vendor had left them about Las Rocas and their plans to head there instead of the other bus stops.

The silence dragged on before Cesar finally said, "I don't think going to Las Rocas is such a good idea. You don't drive into the middle of the bear's den and start prodding it with a pointy stick. Not if you want to survive."

"I don't see where we have a choice. Flashing pictures of Liberty all over the city isn't getting us anywhere."

"Do me a favor."

"What's that?"

"Don't do anything until I can do a little more research tonight. I've focused more on Costa and Marco than I have the location. Let me see what else I can dig up."

"You don't have time to do research. You've got a man waiting in your bed to—"

"I doubt he's staying."

"Is that what you want?" They'd had little more than surface conversations about previous relationships. But now that Derek had opened the door with that photo he'd sent of Max on his bed, he figured Cesar's relationship was fair game as well.

"Right now, I don't know what I want."

"One day at a time, right?"

"Sounds like solid advice."

"It should," Derek said. "It's yours."

13

Max woke with a raging hard-on, his back snuggled up against Derek's chest, and Derek's magnificent, stiff cock nestled into the crack of his ass. Derek shifted as he woke, pressing that dick ever harder against Max's flesh.

"You need to either put that thing away or put it to good use," Max said.

Max was in a hurry to get the hell out of town and down to Las Rocas to find his sister, but fifteen minutes one way or the other wouldn't make much of a difference.

But instead of taking Max up on his offer, Derek shifted away. "I didn't bring any supplies."

Max rolled over to face Derek. "There are plenty of things we can do that don't require condoms or lube."

Derek leaned in, his kiss brief, but it left Max even harder than he had been before. "I think we should hit the road."

"Didn't Cesar want us to wait until he got more intel for us?"

"I figured we could start heading that way. We'll wait for word from Cesar before we do anything."

"Yeah, sure." Max climbed out of bed, letting go of his disappointment. And while that kiss told Max that Derek was still into him, there had been a hesitancy that spoke to all the reservations Derek had about him as well. Not that Max could blame him. He couldn't barge back into Derek's life and expect everything to go back to the way things were.

It didn't take long to pack their bags and check out of the motel. The sun rose over some distant hills. People were on the streets going about their business. A horned lizard scurried across the ground, disappearing into scrubby plants in a nearby flowerbed.

They stopped at the first café they came to for coffee and breakfast. They sat in the car in the parking lot and ate.

Derek's phone rang as they finished up. "Hey, Cesar. You're on speaker."

"Morning, boys," Cesar said, his voice thick. Probably from lack of sleep, if Derek knew Cesar. "I've been trying all night to find something useful."

"I thought you had company," Derek said. Max raised a brow, wondering what was going on, but Derek held up a finger. "I didn't expect you to work all night on this."

Cesar chuckled, but he didn't sound the least bit amused. "I was working on our problem for a couple of hours then went in to check on him. Looks like he snuck out when I wasn't looking."

"Who does that?" Max asked, unable to hold the question back. "What an asshole move."

"I guess that's why he's my ex," Cesar said. "Do you guys want to talk about what I found out about Marco and his operation, or do you want to get into the nitty-gritty of my epically bad decisions and shitty sex life?"

"Tell us what you found," Derek said. "We're ready to hit the road."

"Turns out Marco is into more than just the car stripping and money laundering in the US. In Mexico, he's into much more. Drugs, but that's no surprise. That's almost a given with these boys. But there's a much darker side. There's chatter that he is involved in human trafficking as well. So there's possibly more to the disappearances of some of these women he's using as money mules. Maybe they aren't disappearing on their own."

Max cut in. "You think he's selling them?"

"Unfortunately, that may be the case. I found some chat groups that mention something about a southern trade route. We're talking Central and South America. Guatemala. Honduras. Columbia. I've only found bits and pieces of the chatter. But I did find a cattle auction site. But I don't think they're talking about beef. I think it could be a front for auctioning some of these women to the highest bidder."

"No need to have a site on the darknet for cattle sales." Derek snuck a glance at Max as if he wasn't sure how he was taking the news.

Truth was, human trafficking had been one of Max's biggest fears. Liberty was a striking woman. If her mouth didn't get her killed, her looks could get her trafficked.

Why hadn't she listened to him when he'd asked her not to go? Money was tight with him only recently opening up his tattoo shop, but he would have found a way to help pay for college if that's what she'd wanted.

She had no reason to trust you. You ran out on her the way you ran out on Derek. Either one of them would be a fool to put their trust and faith and their future in your hands.

When they found Liberty—not *if*, because not finding her wasn't an option—Max would spend the rest of his life earning back her trust if that's what it took to have her back in his life. He'd fucked up once. He wouldn't do it again.

What about Derek? You going to earn his trust back, too?

Derek had no reason to give him a second chance, but Max hoped like hell he could find a way to make it up to him.

But Max couldn't think about a future life with Derek with Liberty still out there somewhere.

Was she scared? Was she in pain? Beaten? Drugged up?

Dead?

Derek shifted the car into reverse, and Max shook the disturbing thoughts out of his head. Somewhere in his musings, Derek and Cesar had ended their call.

"Sorry. What did I miss?" Max asked.

To his surprise, Derek reached across and took Max's hand. Their joined hands came to rest on the center console, and Max took much more comfort in the gesture than he should have.

"You didn't miss much. Besides the human trafficking angle, all Cesar found was that Marco seems to spend a lot of his time in the central area of Baja, California, which isn't any different from what we got from that note from the market guy. All we have is Las Rocas, not his exact location. But maybe we'll get lucky."

"What if we make our own luck?"

Derek cut his eyes to Max. "I love the way your mind works sometimes."

The *other times* remained unspoken, but Max would have to live with that for now.

Max didn't know if his idea would work, half-baked and ill-thought-out as it was. But between him and Derek, maybe they could flesh out a plan before they rolled into town.

"What if instead of looking for Liberty, we look for Marco? Since he or his men were probably the last people to see her."

"Wait, isn't that what I suggested last night?" Derek asked.

"It is. But what I'm suggesting is that instead of us trying to find Marco, we let him come to *us*. Maybe we pose as buyers. For drugs. Women. I don't know."

Derek's mouth pursed in thought, his free hand dangling over the top of the steering wheel as he sped along the two-lane road. Houses, businesses, and pedestrians fell away until they were in the countryside.

Max had a hard time not staring at Derek's profile and the several days' worth of stubble that had sprung up along his jawline. What Max wouldn't do to be able to nip at that jutting, confident chin and work his way down from there.

And fuck, he was hard again.

He reached down to adjust himself, but Derek caught him. "Stop it. Wherever your mind just went, stop."

"Why's that?" Max shouldn't have pushed Derek for an answer. Undoubtedly, it would be something he wouldn't want to hear.

"Because I'm not opposed to pulling off the road and blowing that hard-on you're packing behind that zipper."

"*Jesus Christ*," Max groaned. "Now you've made it worse."

Derek chuckled. "Sorry, not sorry."

Max made a *get on with it* motion with his hand, desperate to steer the conversation in another direction before he took the wheel and drove them off the road himself. "If you are not going to pull over, let's figure out a plan. I need something to soften my dick, and you aren't helping."

"Okay..." Derek thought for a moment.

"What's the one thing that someone who wants to remain hidden hates worse than anything?"

"Being exposed?"

"Exactly. We could go into Las Rocas like loudmouth Americans and bumble our way through town, looking for Marco. We do that in enough places. I'm sure he'll come looking for us. If only to shut us up."

"And here we thought just *looking* for Marco would be dangerous."

"You want to sit on the porch while the big dogs go play?"

Max laughed. He knew Derek was only egging him on. They

both knew *that* wasn't going to happen. "Just try and keep me leashed."

The GPS binged, and Derek turned off on a side road that looked like it led farther and farther away from civilization.

"Mmmm," Derek said, clicking back into their conversation. "I always wanted to tie you up."

"Fuck." Max glanced down at his lap. "Now you've got me going again."

DEREK STRETCHED HIS BACK AS HE DROVE DOWN LAS ROCAS'S main drag, a mid-sized coastal town with tourist shops and restaurants across the street from a small harbor.

Not the kind of harbor with the big motor yachts and luxury sailboats with their own crew. This was the type of harbor with two-man shrimp boats that had been around since before the cold war. Little wooden dinghies sat anchored to the shore with a tatty piece of knotted-together rope tied around marginally sufficient-sized rocks on the shore.

They drove past the sandy beach dotted with sunbathers and a few brave souls in the frigid Pacific surf. Past the food vendors, merchant stalls, and other respectable businesses, until they got to the outskirts of town and pulled into a bar with a naked lady on the sun-faded sign.

Derek pulled into the parking lot and shifted into park. "What do you think?"

"That if you wanted to shrivel my dick, you've done a damn fine job of it."

"This place may not have anything to do with Marco, but this looks like a good place to start."

"Oh, goody." Max turned up the sarcasm as he read the sign. "Look, they serve food."

"No, joke. I could eat."

"Here? Are you fucking kidding me? I don't think I'm up to date on all my shots."

Derek unfastened his seatbelt and slapped Max's arm with the back of his hand. "It can't be that bad."

"If you catch something here and die, I'm having 'It can't be that bad' engraved on your headstone."

Derek laughed, "And if you catch something and die?"

"Have it say *I told you so.*"

Derek barked out a laugh. He'd missed Max's biting humor. As much as he wasn't sure where this thing with Max was headed, Derek could honestly say that having Max walk out of that hangar had been the most surprising and intriguing thing that had happened to him in a very long time.

"Come on," he said as he cracked his door. "Let's see what kind of trouble we can drum up."

They walked into the titty bar, Derek's eyes skimming across the naked woman dancing for a few men tossing pesos on the stage.

"*Hola,*" Derek said to the bartender as they strode up to the bar, and each pulled up a stool. He didn't have to elbow his way to the bar. That early in the day, there wasn't anyone else in the place. "*Dos cervesas, por favor.*"

"What kind?" The bartender's English was probably better than Derek's Spanish. He sounded more Californian than the Californians did.

"Cervesa Sol?" Derek said, looking at Max.

"Modelo," Max said, as he settled on the seat.

"One Sol and one Modelo coming up." The bartender pulled the iced-down bottles out of a couple of beat-up Igloo coolers and popped the tops.

He set the beers on cocktail napkins in front of them. "Anything else? We have food. Menu's limited, but it hasn't killed anyone yet."

"That you know of," Max added.

The bartender shrugged. "You want food or not?"

They looked at each other. No one dying wasn't a ringing endorsement, but Derek's stomach was about to start digesting itself, so they might as well take their chances. Max nodded when Derek raised a questioning brow at him. "Sure, we'll eat."

They ordered off the menu, which was nothing more than a handful of items printed on a half-sheet of paper. They waited an inordinate amount of time for their food to arrive, considering how deserted the place was.

But that gave them time to watch and observe. Women came on stage and left in a continuous parade, song after song. Derek counted five or six before it looked like the round of women started over again. No one complained about the repeat performances.

Their food came. The enchiladas came out cold, the guacamole warm, and the grease so thick it congealed on the plate. After powering through a few bites, Derek pushed his plate away. Either Max's tamales weren't as bad, or he had a stronger stomach than Derek.

Or maybe Derek needed to go ahead and order that headstone for Max.

"Something wrong with the food?" the bartender asked as he came out of the swinging doors that led to the kitchen. He had the audacity to sound offended.

"Naw. I have an appetite. Just not for food," Derek lied as he tipped his bottle back and polished off the last of his beer.

He kept their tab open, and he and Max wandered toward the stage.

14

THE WOMAN PERFORMING CAUGHT MAX'S EYE, AND HER DULL EYES brightened. Whether it was from attraction or the fact that she had new blood watching her dance, Max couldn't tell. He assumed the latter.

She shifted her focus from the men in front of her and danced her way toward them. She had pert natural breasts and a G-string highlighting a killer ass that even a gay man could appreciate.

A sourness rolled through Max's belly as she turned and shook her ass in his face. He'd been in titty bars before, and, let's face it, more than his fair share of gay bars that showed off all the goods to be embarrassed about the nudity aspect, but the sheer desperation of *this* place made his skin crawl.

He'd known enough men and women working in the sex industry in the States to recognize someone who was in the business because they *wanted* to be that it made it easy for him to spot people who were there because they *had* to be.

With the half-dead eyes and fake flirtatious smile, the woman in front of him seemed more desperate than willing.

The woman hitched her thumbs in her G-string and slowly worked it over her hips and down her legs.

Derek played the loud, obnoxious American and whooped beside him. "Work it, baby. That's right. Oh, man. Look at that ass."

The woman half turned, taking Derek's hand and putting it on one of her ample ass cheeks. Was that allowed?

Derek caught Max's eye with a wide grin. If Max hadn't been deep inside Derek's ass the day before, he'd have believed Derek was bi or straight.

The woman kicked her G-string away and turned around, her trimmed bush now at eye level as Derek's hand fell away. She looped a hand around Derek's neck and pulled him closer for a kiss. For a moment, Max thought she'd pull Derek in and suck his dick out through his throat. Derek must have caught it too because he pulled a ten-dollar bill from his front pocket and handed it to her as the song she'd been working ended.

She took the bill, a spark in her eyes. This time when she smiled, it almost looked real. She picked up the money on the stage. From a casual count, she'd probably made about twelve dollars US, and that included what Derek had given her.

Max and Derek took seats at an empty two-top table near the stage, ordered more beer, but let them warm in their hands. Max put the bottle to his lips, faking a sip. At the rate the day was going, with other bars they needed to visit, if they didn't go easy on the alcohol, they'd be plastered by the end of the day.

And neither they nor Liberty could afford that.

Derek scooted his chair around to Max's side of the table, their arms brushing as they waited for the next performer to come on stage. The handful of men near the center of the stage laughed and drank and generally ignored the two gringos who had invaded their space.

Stage lights flashed, and new music came through the

speakers—some pop song from the US that Max had heard before but couldn't remember the artist. The speakers popped and hissed as the beat wormed its way through Max's system.

Derek elbowed him in the ribs as the next woman appeared from backstage, but it wasn't the new performer Derek had his eyes on. It was the woman Derek had given the money to. She came in through a side door dressed in only her G-string as she bypassed the other men and headed in their direction.

"*Hola,* sexy," Derek said, sounding more like a Texan on his first foray into Mexico than a man who spoke the language fluently. Max wasn't sure what game Derek was playing, but he was up for it.

"Americans?" she asked, her accent thick, but Max had no doubt she knew the language well enough. At least he hoped so. He wouldn't be very helpful if he had to keep asking Derek to translate. She glanced at Max, a predatory gleam in her shrewd eyes as she lasered in on him. "Lap dance?"

"*Cuanto?*" Max asked. He'd remembered enough Spanish that he at least knew how to ask *how much.*

She looked him up and down, her confidence high when she said, "Twenty."

Derek laughed. "That's steep."

She slapped a hand on her ample ass and gave it a sultry rub. "Not for this." Her chin went up, and Derek took out two twenties from the fold of bills in his front pocket and handed it over. The smile slipped from Max's face when Derek bobbed his chin toward him and said, "For him, *por favor.*"

Max cut him a look, but the amusement in Derek's eyes told Max he was laughing on the inside. *Motherfucker.* Max wanted to get his hands on something, and right then, it was around Derek's neck.

The men hooted and hollered as the woman pulled the small table out of the way and started dancing for Max. All in all, it was the longest four minutes of Max's life. The woman put his hands on her breasts, and he had to pretend to love the contact. She turned away, putting her ass in his face before straddling his lap and grinding against his crotch.

For the first time since he'd kissed Derek back at the hangar, his dick was soft. It wasn't just that he wasn't attracted to her. It was everything. The seediness and desperation inside the bar. The fact that he suspected the woman didn't want to be there any more than Max did. Plus, he couldn't get his mind off the idea that maybe Liberty was out there somewhere being forced to do the same thing that this woman was to another man in another bar in another town.

Except *that guy* might not have Liberty's best interests at heart.

When the song ended, the woman locked her wrists behind Max's neck. "You like?"

"Yeah, sure, terrific." Max had difficulty keeping his voice from raising and having his words come out sounding more like a question.

The woman reached a hand down and grabbed his crotch. The corners of her lips turned down. She said something in Spanish that he didn't catch, but Derek threw his head back and laughed.

Max cut him a glare, but it didn't stop the laughter. Derek had to wipe the tears from his eyes and catch his breath. He handed the woman another twenty, and she stuffed it in her G-string and went to work the new guys that had walked into the bar.

"What the hell did she say that was so goddamn funny?" Max asked as he pulled the table closer again.

"She said that in her country, they have pills for men who have problems getting it up."

Max scrubbed a hand over his face. "Fuck me."

Derek shrugged. "She did say that *that* was an option as well. She said she would give you a special price."

"For fuck's sake. Can we get out of here already?"

"Not yet. That whole show wasn't so that I could get a good laugh at your expense. I had my reasons."

MAX CROSSED HIS ARMS OVER HIS CHEST AS IF HE DIDN'T BELIEVE A word of what Derek said. "Why didn't you clue me in on it before you sicced that woman on me?"

"There wasn't time."

"Well, there's time now. So spill."

Derek took a cautious sip of his beer. The warm liquid didn't quench his thirst. It only made him grimace. "I wanted it to be more believable that we were in the market for women when we went back and talked to the bartender. I think I have an idea for a cover."

"I'm all ears." Max almost took a swig of his beer but must have thought better of it.

"We pose as guys looking for women and drugs for a client's party boat he'll be docking in Cabo."

Max's brows rose as he contemplated Derek's plan. "Could work. We ask around enough places, maybe Marco or one of his lackeys will find us."

"Exactly."

They waited until the new group of men got their drinks and took a table by the stage before leaving their nearly full beers behind and made their way over to the bartender to pay their tab and ask some questions.

Max hadn't said anything, but the tension rolled off him, and Derek knew that he only had a certain amount of time before Max's patience ran thin at their slow progress.

Derek feared if Max's patience broke, *that* Max would be difficult to control.

"Anything else?" the bartender asked as they walked up.

Derek and Max glanced at each other as Derek leaned in. The bartender stepped back and crossed his arms over his chest, his gaze wary and scanning between Derek and Max.

"Can I ask you a question?" Derek said.

"Is this the part where you tell me you're a cop?"

Derek smiled the most disarming smile he could muster. "We don't look like cops."

The man raked his eyes up and down Max. "Not him. *You.*"

Derek glanced over at Max, who kind of gave him one of those *busted!* half-smiles.

"You kinda do," Max said, entirely unhelpful.

Fuck. Well, one of the things that made Derek such a good liar was that he tried to keep a grain of truth in those lies so he could sound convincing. He could deny his history all he wanted, or he could fess up.

"In a former life," Derek admitted.

"And what do you do in *this* life?"

"I find things." Derek didn't elaborate. It was the truth. Not that he was going to tell the bartender the *whole* truth. Not if he expected Marco or his men to come looking for them.

Even though it would be hard for anyone to overhear them talking between the men chatting and the music pumping from the speakers, Derek lowered his voice. "Right now, I need to find a few women. And some drugs. Maybe some E. Or some heroin. Coke. A little something for everyone, if you know what I mean. I've got a guy with a boat docking in Cabo in a few days, and he and his buddies are looking for a good time while they're in port."

"Can't help you," the bartender said as he started to turn away.

"Yeah, sure," Max said. "I get it. Can I borrow a pen before we go?"

The bartender looked skeptical, but he reached into his back pocket and handed Max a pen. Max scribbled Derek's number in the center of a damp ring of condensation on a cocktail napkin. "Call us if that changes."

"It won't."

Derek pulled some bills out of his pocket—more than enough to cover their tab and then some—and laid it on the napkin and slid it across the bar. "This guy's got stupid money. And he likes spending it. He would make it worth anyone's time."

"Good for him." The bartender took a step back, but not before palming the money and putting it in the till.

Derek caught motion out of the corner of his eye. A woman stepped out of view of the window in the kitchen's swinging door. Was that the woman from the lap dance?

He tapped Max's arm with the back of his hand and jerked his head toward the exit. Max followed him outside.

"Fuck me, that's bright," Max said as they squinted into the now mid-day sun. His eyes teared up at the glare, and he wished he'd brought his sunglasses from the car.

"Where next?"

"Find another bar. Put our number out there. We're bound to hit someone who at least knows someone who can pass the word along that we're in the market for some fun."

"Jesus Christ," Max said. "I feel like I need a shower, and it has nothing to do with the sweat rolling down my back. How do you deal with people who think people are just another good to be sold?"

"To be fair, most of my clients are wives who think their husbands are cheating or celebrities with stalkers that haven't crossed the line enough for the police to do anything about it."

They started walking down the street and into the busier part of town. The scent of the ocean lay thick in the air, and if he listened hard enough, he could imagine he heard the crash of the surf on the shore in the lull between passing cars. "Luckily, I don't have to deal with that element as much."

"Hey," a woman's voice said as they passed the alley behind the bar.

Max stopped and backed up. "It's the woman from the bar."

Derek reversed direction, and they entered the alley. A battered milk crate propped open the bar's rear door. The woman glanced over her shoulder before walking their way.

She'd put on a pair of short shorts and a tight t-shirt. The makeup was still on her face, but she had her hair down and a cigarette between two fingers. She looked like a woman at the end of her shift.

"I have friends who might be interested," the woman said. "You'd have to find someone else for the drugs. But for the girls, we could make a deal."

So she *had* overheard his conversation in the bar. Derek could appreciate her entrepreneurial spirit. She saw a good thing and wasn't afraid to go after it. Why not cut out the middleman? Derek almost felt bad that he didn't really have any work for her.

He and Max exchanged a glance, and he could tell Max didn't want to keep up the ruse. He knew what Max was going to do before he did it, but he let it play out. Derek didn't think a woman who chanced making a deal behind her boss's back would tell the man information that might hurt him and Max.

At least he hoped she wouldn't. But this was about Max's sister, and Derek would let him call some of the shots.

Max pulled up the photos of Liberty on his phone. "We're mainly looking for one girl." He handed her the phone. "Have you seen her?"

She glanced at the photo. She hid her emotions well, but a muscle ticking next to her left eye gave her away. She glanced over her shoulder at the bar's back door. Still empty. "Why you come down here looking for women if what you want is white? You can't get enough of that where you come from?"

"There's a reason we came down here looking for a white woman. You're a smart lady. I'm sure you know the reason why."

She sucked on her cigarette and stared back at them through a cloud of exhaled smoke. Derek had a feeling she had a really good idea of what he was talking about.

"Please," Max said.

"Why her?"

Max didn't even look at Derek before he spoke. Probably because he didn't want to see Derek shake his head. Derek had known it could be a problem bringing Max down to Mexico with him, but he understood where Max was coming from and did nothing to stop him from answering with the truth.

"She's my sister."

The woman took one long, last drag and dropped the cigarette on the ground, crushing it with a thin rubber flip-flop with puppy teeth marks on the toe. "You don't know what or who you're messing with. You think you do..." Something dark passed behind her eyes. A not-so-distant memory? A trauma? A nightmare? "But you don't. Go back where you came from. You'll thank me later."

15

THE REST OF THE DAY PASSED BY IN A DIZZYING HAZE. MAX HAD long since lost count of the number of drinks they'd bought and never drank. He hated to see all the alcohol go to waste, especially since he needed a drink now more than ever, but he never lost sight of the real reason they were in Mexico.

Bar after bar, they decided to fuck discretion and handed out their number to anyone who would take it, telling them of the party boat they needed to fill with women and drugs. Would word ever get back to Marco and his men? Max had no clue. If nothing else, maybe they'd get a call from Marco telling them to knock it the fuck off.

But Max was determined to stay down in Mexico as long as it took. Derek might have to get back to his real life soon. After all, Cesar couldn't hold down the fort forever, and Max couldn't expect Derek to work for free until the end of time.

If Max had to sell the tattoo shop to fund his stay, he would. But he hoped like hell it wouldn't come to that.

Between the tension and exhaustion and the constant drip of adrenaline every time he caught a quick movement out of the corner of his eye as he remained on high alert, his body ached in ways it hadn't since before he'd left home as a teen. He'd forgotten how exhausting and unsettling it was to have to continually look over your shoulder every minute of every day, waiting for the next thing to blindside you.

"You look done in," Derek said as he let them into the room they'd rented for the next few nights.

Max stepped into the room. Derek hung back and glanced down the shadowed row of rooms.

"What's the matter?" Max asked as he turned back to the door. Derek held his hand up, and Max halted.

A few long, drawn-out seconds passed before Derek lowered his hand and came into the room. He locked the deadbolt and stuck a chair under the rickety doorknob, but the jamb was so rotted a toddler could have kicked it down.

They didn't delude themselves that they were safe for the night.

"Are you going to tell me what that was all about?"

Derek flopped down into one of the chairs next to the table under the window. He parted the curtains and stared into the darkness, though with the lights on inside, he wouldn't be able to see anything. Finally, he pulled the blinds closed, making sure they overlapped at the center so no one could see in.

He glanced over at Max. "I thought I saw someone by the office watching. But can't be sure."

Though this motel was cleaner than the one the previous night, the walls were thin, and they heard competing radios in the other rooms, the upbeat Mexican music at odds with the dread gnawing in Max's belly.

Max glanced at the door. If anyone wanted to come after them, there would be little he or Derek could do to stop them.

He dropped onto the corner of the bed, relieved to have the weight taken off his tired feet. "I can't decide if I want them to find us here or not. A part of me wishes they would so we could maybe get on with this and find Liberty."

"If they don't find us and kill us, that is. I'm sure it wouldn't be too difficult for a guy with Marco's reputation to make a couple of stupid gringos disappear."

"I'm hoping it won't come to that."

"You and me both."

"You still think we're going about this the right way?"

Derek scrubbed a hand down his face. Faint dark circles ran under each eye, and the worry lines between his brows had formed deep trenches. Max didn't know anyone else who would have dropped their lives and helped him with the impossible.

But Derek had.

"I think it's foolhardy. I think it's reckless. I think it's danger-ous... and I think it's the best move we have. If Liberty's in danger, we don't have the luxury of time on our side. We have to find her as quickly as possible. If that means painting a target on our backs, then I say hand me the brush and stand back."

The sudden tightness in Max's throat made it hard to talk without his voice cracking. Then he thought, to hell with it if it does. "I—" *Fuck.* "I still can't believe that you're here. Helping me. I can't tell you how much this means to me."

"Stop it." Derek's eyes swam with excess moisture. "You're going to make me fucking cry, and I *won't* forgive you for that."

Maybe it was the exhaustion that took over Max's brain or lowered his defenses, or maybe it was just fucking time to ask the hard question.

Max didn't know if he had the stomach to hear the answer, but he asked anyway. "Does that mean that you forgive me for leaving?"

Derek huffed out a humorless laugh. "I'm not going to lie and say I understand why you left. I know you had your reasons that you thought were valid at the time. It was a long time ago. We were both different people…"

Max couldn't breathe, couldn't think. In the silence, while Derek contemplated what he'd say next, all Max heard was the erratic beat of his heart. He hadn't realized how much Derek's forgiveness meant to him until the possibility of having it arose.

Derek stood and sat on the bed next to Max. Max smelled the smoke on Derek's clothes and the hops on his breath. "But I don't think you intentionally set out to hurt me."

The roaring in Max's ears went silent as if someone had turned off a fire hose. If Max didn't know better, he would have thought his heart had stopped beating, but he felt it hammering against his sternum, so he knew that hadn't happened. "What are you saying?"

Derek held out his hand, and Max threaded his fingers through Derek's, the warmth of his skin seeping into Max and warming parts of him that had grown so cold over the years. "I'm saying I forgive you."

"*Christ.*" Max ducked his head and pinched the bridge of his nose until the backs of his eyes no longer stung. The blotchiness that burned on his face, he could do nothing about. "I can't tell you how long I've waited to hear that. Honestly, I never thought I would."

Derek's sad, crooked smile nearly broke Max's heart. "Until this moment, I'm not sure I thought I would have said it either."

That time, the tear fell before Max could do a damn thing about it. Derek made a sound in the back of his throat, wrapped an arm around Max's neck, and pulled Max into his side. "Sorry. I didn't—"

"No. It's not that. It's the relief." Max sat up to see Derek's face even though he'd rather be snuggling up against him. "I didn't know how heavy the guilt weighed on me until you said that."

"I think I might know how you feel. It's like this mass that had made its home in the middle of my chest has vanished. My lungs don't know how to breathe now that that heaviness is gone."

"I really am sorry, D. I never wanted to hurt you, and it guts me that I did."

Derek cupped Max's cheek. He had about three days' worth of whiskers on his face, as did Derek, but he kind of liked the scruffy version of Derek. It gave Derek that hot, Indiana Jones ruggedness. Max didn't wait for Derek to go in for the kiss. He leaned in and claimed Derek's dry, chapped lips.

But Max didn't care how they felt. He deepened the kiss, wanting Derek to feel his relief and his sincerity. All of Max's bottled-up emotions that had built up over the years, the guilt, the blame, the self-recrimination poured out into the kiss.

Derek fisted a hand in Max's T-shirt as if expecting Max to disappear on him again. But the joke was on Derek. Max had no intention of going anywhere. And if Derek thought he would be rid of Max as soon as they found Liberty, then he didn't know Max very well.

He'd had already made the mistake of leaving Derek once. He wouldn't be that quantumly stupid again.

Where did that leave them now? Who knew. He wasn't in a hurry to define anything or put their newfound relationship into some sort of box to be put up on the mantle and appreciated from afar.

As they came up for some much-needed air, Max would gladly take whatever Derek would give him. He wasn't inherently greedy. But the fact that Max still wanted it *all*—and wanted it all with Derek—couldn't be denied.

But any sort of healthy relationship needed more than two bodies thrown together in extenuating circumstances.

"You hungry?" Derek asked.

"I'm exhausted. I'm relieved. I'm emotionally spent. Food is the furthest thing from my mind."

Derek stood. "You've got to eat. We can't survive on beer nuts, pretzels, and street tacos. I'll go get us something to eat."

Max stood as well. "I'll go with you."

Derek pushed him back down on the bed, and Max didn't have the energy to stand again. "Stay here. Take a shower. I'll be back in no time."

"You shouldn't go alone. If there's someone out there—"

"You never could sit back and let me take care of you, could you?"

Max cracked a smile. "Is that what this is?"

"I'm trying."

Giving in, because he couldn't see a way past Derek without a fight, Max said, "Okay. But, Derek?"

"Yeah?"

"Watch your back out there."

As it turned out, you *could* live off of street tacos. Four of them each, to be exact. And queso. And refried beans. And the best handmade tortillas Derek had ever put in his mouth.

"I'm not upset that the only open thing you could find was a taco truck," Max said as he stuffed the last bite of his fourth taco into his mouth. He swallowed and wiped his hands and mouth. "I'm selling up in the valley and moving my shop across the street from that guy. I *need* that man in my life."

"Nope," Derek said before he could stop himself. "I just got you back in my life. You're not disappearing on me again."

There was no bite to Derek's words. No hostility. No recrimination, only a glint of humor in Derek's words.

"I don't have a whole lot of illusions that my leaving will be something that we look back on in years to come and laugh about, but thank you for your grace and understanding. And if you have to spend the next ten years giving me a little grief about it, I'll gladly take it."

"I'm not trying to give you grief. I just don't want the subject to be so taboo that we're afraid to bring it up. It happened. We're moving past it."

Max started stuffing their empty containers into a plastic bag, cleaning up the mess they'd made at the table. "I always knew you were special. Back then, I just hadn't realized *how* special. I don't des—"

"Stop. Don't you dare finish that sentence." Derek had to come to terms with some things and dig deep to find forgiveness, but a part of him always knew forgiveness was in him. Knew that if Max asked for it, Derek would be hard put to deny him.

But he also wouldn't allow Max to denigrate himself. There was so much that Max didn't deserve. A shitty childhood, for one. That didn't make him undeserving of forgiveness.

Of love.

Whoa there, buddy. Hold your horses. Cool your jets. Take a dozen breaths, and take a step back. Don't let all this go to your head. Forgiveness is one thing. Falling for him is another.

The fucked-up thing was, there was no falling for Max *again*. Because he'd never stopped loving him. Pathetic, maybe. But it was the truth.

Didn't mean that they had a future together.

But they didn't have to worry about the future or whatever the attraction between them meant. All they had to do was take it one day at a time. That's all anyone could do.

"You deserve all the things, Max. I don't want to hear any different."

Derek didn't wait for a response. Max sat back, his mouth open as if he had something to say but didn't know what.

"I'm taking a shower. We should head to bed early. We've got a lot of ground to cover tomorrow," Derek said.

"I'm just tossing the trash out. Don't want the roaches finding us."

Derek killed time in the bathroom, brushing his teeth and finding a change of clothes until Max came back into the room and put the chair back under the door. But Derek's stalling wasn't lost on Max.

"You could have hopped in the shower. I can take care of myself. You may be the tough PI, but I've held my own in plenty of fights. A guy comes after me, he's going to wish he hadn't."

"I know." In Derek's head, he did. The rest of him had a hard time not worrying. Yeah, Max was a big dude, and someone would have to be stupid to mess with him, but Derek doubted that Marco and his men were like any of the run-of-the-mill gay-bashing assholes they might run into at the local bar back home.

By the time Derek got out of the shower, only the television's glow illuminated the room. Max lay on the bed with one leg thrown over the sheet. It wasn't exactly the North Pole in their room. But at least the air conditioning worked well enough that they weren't covered in sweat.

Max had the volume turned down as he mindlessly scrolled through the channels.

"You can turn it up if you want. I don't mind."

"It's not that," Max said. "I'd have to blast it to hear it over the music next door. Besides, there are only five channels, and they're all in Spanish."

"I'm going to call Cesar and give him an update."

"I'm betting he won't be a fan of our little change in strategy."

As it turned out, Max hit it on the head.

"You two are doing what?" Cesar screeched into the phone,

his voice going so high that it cracked. "You've got to be fucking kidding me. You two are going to get yourselves killed. You know that, right?"

"You have a better idea that won't take the better part of six months to find all the important players?"

The silence from the other end of the phone told Derek that while Cesar didn't like their plan, the immediacy gave them little opportunity to sit around on their hands.

"Speaking of which," Derek said. "Have you found out any more information that could help us?"

"I've worked my ass off all day. Put some people I trust on it as well. And no, nothing. Costa and Marco may not be running one of the big cartels, but they're careful. Either there isn't much more information out there about them, or they have everyone too scared to talk. The latter would be my guess. You can't have the reach of even a smaller organization like Costa's and Marco's and not leave tracks. Even on the darknet."

"What do you think their move is going to be?"

"If Marco was smart—and Marco wouldn't be in the position he's in if he was stupid—then he'd leave you two the fuck alone until you wore yourselves out and came home. He doesn't need to attract the attention of the authorities."

"For Liberty's sake, I hope not."

"I do have one thing, though. I dropped by Liberty's apartment, and that friend of hers, Mina, was there. I managed to convince her to give me Liberty's cell phone number."

"You're fucking kidding me." The relief came immediately and so strong that Max picked up on it and hopped out of bed. Derek pressed the speaker button on his phone. "I put you on speaker."

"Hey, Max. I was just telling Derek that Mina finally gave up Liberty's cell number. I think even she was starting to worry."

"If she's a mule like Liberty, she's in potential danger as well if she crosses the border," Derek said.

Derek's comment had barely left his mouth before Max asked, "Did you find anything else?"

"I have a resource at her cell phone provider. I have the list of numbers she called and texted. All that stopped the day she crossed the border."

"I was afraid of that," Derek said.

"Yeah. Like I said, no calls or texts that day, but I did get one last ping in Tres Colinas before it all went silent."

Max started pacing the room. "Did you try to call?"

If Cesar was annoyed by Max's obvious question, it didn't show in his voice. He was the same, unflappable Cesar. "I'll send you the number. But, yes, I texted. And calls immediately go to a voicemail that isn't set up."

"It's off. Or out of battery." Derek sat on the edge of the bed, but there was no way he'd be able to cage Max's restless energy.

"Or someone took it from her," Max grumbled, color rising along the back of his neck. A vessel at his temple throbbed. "We were just fucking there yesterday. We should go back. We should—"

"Hold up," Cesar said, the voice of reason to a couple of guys going on too little sleep and too much adrenaline the past few days to be thinking as clearly as they should. "As much as I'm not a fan of your plan to have Marco or his men come to you, I think it's a better option than stumbling around Baja hoping to find the one person who may have seen her. Because even *if* that person had seen her, that was days ago. She could be anywhere now."

"Agreed," Derek said. Glad to have someone else he could trust to bounce ideas and plans off of. "Max?"

Max stopped his pacing and rubbed his hands down his

face. The long deep breath he held and released seemed to drop his frenetic energy a fraction. "Yes. Agreed."

"I'll continue to monitor for calls, texts, pings in case the phone turns back on."

Derek clicked the phone off speaker and held it to his ear. "Thanks, Cesar. Go to bed. You've earned it."

"I can't sleep anyway, so at least this gives me something else to focus on. I'll call you tomorrow and—"

"Wait. Why can't you sleep?"

"It's nothing. Forget I said anything."

"*Cesar.*"

Cesar sighed, and Derek heard the springs on Cesar's desk chair groan the way it always did when he leaned back in his chair. The two muffled *thunks* he heard must have been Cesar putting his feet up on the corner of his desk. "I got a text from a guy named Saxon Grey. Apparently, my ex has a boyfriend. That boyfriend wants to meet."

"What the hell for?"

"He wouldn't say. Fuck, Derek, if I had known my ex wasn't single, I never would have slept with him."

"I take it they weren't in an open relationship."

"Only in my ex's head. He's such a fucking prick. I should have known something was up when he insisted that we hook up at my place."

Derek glanced at Max. He'd had the same feeling when Max turned up at the hangar looking for his help. But at least in their situation, Max wasn't a cheating piece of shit.

Max finally stopped pacing long enough for the exhaustion to kick back in. He sat on the bed, leaned against the headboard, and started scrolling through his phone.

"You know you don't have to give this guy the time of day, right? You had no idea your ex wasn't single. That wasn't on you. That was on your ex."

"I know. But I'm... intrigued, I guess you could say. Though I can't imagine what this guy has to say that he thinks I need to hear."

"Just... be careful."

Cesar laughed. "You think he wants to beat me up?"

"I don't know what to think. If you wait until I come home, I can go with you and watch your back."

That time, Cesar's laugh felt more genuine. "Forget it. I'm not taking you with me. You've been in the PI business too long if you think there is a boogieman under every rock."

"No, just long enough to know they're under there. Now get some rest. We'll catch up tomorrow."

He hung up the phone, unable to disconnect Cesar's concern as easily as he could the call.

He crawled into bed next to Max. "Mind if I turn off the TV?"

Max put his phone on his bedside table and plugged in his charger. "Go ahead."

They lay in the darkness for a while, lost in their thoughts.

"I can hear your mind whirling from over here," Derek said, his own mind uneasy.

"You volunteering to take my mind offline?"

You volunteering to take my mind offline?

Max wanted to slap himself in the forehead. Strangled light filtered beneath the curtains allowing the security lights to seep in, turning the room a dark, hazy gray.

Instead of Derek laughing him off or telling him to get his mind out of the gutter where it had been his entire adolescent and adult life, Derek said, "It's not the worst idea I've heard tonight."

Max stilled, the blood redirecting south as Derek's words hit his brain. "Don't even joke."

Derek rolled to his side and scooted closer, wrapping an arm around Max's waist and dropping a leg over Max's thigh. "What makes you think I'm joking?"

Derek leaned up on one arm, covering Max's lips with his. The second his tongue raked across Max's bottom lip, Max opened for him, allowing Derek to deepen the kiss.

Their tongues touched and tangled, and there were so many more things Max wanted him to do with that talented tongue. So many more places for him to explore that would bring them both pleasure.

But Max took what Derek gave, not wanting to pressure him into anything more than he willingly gave. Derek stopped and looked down at him. In the near darkness, it was hard to read his expression, but something was off.

"What's wrong?" Max asked.

"I was going to ask you the same thing."

"I'm laying here, and you kissed me. What could be wrong?"

One of Derek's hands trailed down Max's chest. Goosebumps broke out all over his skin, and his dick strained against his boxer briefs.

"You're never this passive. You don't lay back and take it. You go for what you want. Like that kiss you laid on me back at Joss's hangar."

"I don't want to scare you away. I figured I would follow your cue."

Derek straddled Max's hips, their cocks aligning as Derek braced his hands on either side of Max's head. "Then tell me what you want."

To forget.

To let his mind go numb even if it were only for a few brief moments, and to feel something other than the constant, nagging dread that had been gnawing at Max ever since Liberty disappeared.

If Derek wanted him to tell him what to do, he wouldn't put up a fight.

He put his hand at the top of Derek's head and pressed downward. The thought of having that tongue and that warm mouth on his cock made him instantly hard.

"That's more like it." Derek's devilish grin as he started moving down Max's body only made him harder. He groaned as Derek licked and nipped at his sensitive nipples, sending electric shocks straight to his groin.

Derek breathed in deep as if he wanted to suck Max down

deep into his lungs where he'd never escape. Which was perfectly fine with Max. The one thing these last ten years had taught Max was that he didn't want to live the *next* ten years without Derek.

The first ten had been excruciating enough.

But then Derek hooked his fingers in the waistband of Max's underwear, and the past fell away. All that remained were the two of them.

As soon as Derek exposed the tip of Max's cock, he licked the drop of precum from his slit. He gently held Derek's head, keeping him there. Derek's chuckle reverberated down Max's shaft, and Max bucked up against him. The teasing licks had him ditching his underwear.

He lay beneath Derek, fully exposed, and watched as Derek took him in his hand. "Fuck, I love your grip."

The long, slow stroke ripped another groan from the back of Max's throat. Derek cupped his balls, taking the heavy weight in his hands, then he took Max to the back of his throat.

Max fisted his hands in Derek's hair when he bottomed out. He strained for the release that wasn't far away. Derek pulled off, and Max was about to complain, but Derek spat into his hand and reached down and slicked up Max's hole. It wasn't lube, but it would do in a pinch.

"I want that hole," Derek said. "It's so fucking sexy."

With a little more spit, Derek breached his hole. The extra tug and friction had Max pressing back against Derek's finger. With a hand on Derek's head, Max guided Derek back to his dick.

"Fuck me," Max said. "With your mouth, with your finger."

Sensations rolled through Max, a constant cascade of currents electrifying his body. Derek flattened his tongue, trailing it up the underside of Max's cock before taking him into his mouth again.

And that finger... that finger worked its way inside. It would be too much to take Derek's dick without lube, but his finger Max could fucking take.

With his mouth and hands, Derek worked Max into a near frenzy. Max stared down his torso, watching his dick disappear again and again and again. All that suction and wet warmth. Then Derek's finger went deeper, brushing against his prostate. Those shocks and shudders exploded, a warehouse full of fireworks lit with the flick of a single match.

"Coming," Max managed to warn. Derek didn't pull off. He only increased the cock-throbbing suction. Colors splintered behind Max's eyelids, catapulting him into another realm—another world where being with Derek for now, for always, was more than a fantasy. It was real life.

Derek gently removed his finger and released Max's spent cock to grab his own. Even in his languid post-orgasmic haze, Max would never forget the sight of Derek on his knees between Max's thighs as he pumped his engorged cock. A roar ripped from Derek's throat, the cords tightening, the veins distended on either side of his neck.

Derek fell to one hand as he came, the hot spurts landing on Max's abdomen.

Falling to the side, Derek slowly caught his breath. He finally got out of bed with a groan. Max would have opened his eyes to watch that magnificent ass walk across the room if he had the strength. But between his mounting exhaustion and the massive dump of post-orgasmic prolactin into his system, all Max could do was lay there.

As Max sunk into oblivion, he vaguely became aware of Derek cleaning him with a warm damp cloth, and a strong arm holding him tight against a warm body.

The words he longed to say but knew he shouldn't poised on the tip of his tongue... *Love you.*

Not only did Max sleep all night, but he hadn't budged since Derek had snugged him up against him the night before.

But Derek didn't get a wink of sleep, not after those two little, monumental words dropped from Max's lips as he'd sunk into sleep—*Love you.*

Could those words be real? Did Derek want them to be? Or had they just been a reflexive muttering as Max's sated mind had shut down?

Three little questions. Derek still didn't have the answers for them when he climbed out of bed early the next morning and stumbled his way into the shower.

He had his hands on the shower wall, his head ducked between his shoulders, the hot water pelting his neck and back when the shower curtain fluttered. Max stepped in behind him.

Derek turned and reached for the soap.

Max leaned in for a kiss, pulling back before either of them could take it any deeper. "Thanks for last night. I haven't slept that well in a long time."

The half-smile on Max's lips fell when he got a good look at Derek's face. "What's the matter? Is it Lib—"

"No." Derek cut Max off, not wanting him to think the worst. "And nothing's wrong. I just couldn't sleep last night, is all."

He would have liked to have been able to tell Max that he'd spent the night devising a clever plan to find Liberty that didn't involve making themselves a target for a lethal man.

Or at least have mapped out a list of places they needed to hit that day.

But nope. Derek had accomplished nothing as his mind had whorled and twisted. And by Max's tone and expression, Max had no memory of the bombshell he'd dropped the night before.

Max moved Derek out of the water spray and rinsed his body. The hot steam dissipated as the water ran cold. Max hissed in a breath, and goosebumps erupted over his body. "Fuck. You used up all the hot water."

"Sorry."

Max narrowed his eyes and moved out from beneath the spray, allowing Derek to rinse off. "There's still something wrong that has nothing to do with you not getting any sleep last night. So spill."

Derek should have climbed out of the shower and let Max soap up by himself, but he stayed there and tried to decide if he would tell Max the truth.

Not communicating well is part of what destroyed your relationship to begin with. If you want a chance at something beyond a quick fuck or a blowjob in a seedy Mexican motel, then maybe it's time to say what's on your mind.

"Last night, before you dropped off to sleep, you said, 'Love you.'"

Max's hands stilled in the suds on his chest, his expression giving nothing away. "Did I?"

"Yeah. You did." Derek said it with enough force to let Max know that he had no questions about what he'd heard.

Instead of immediately answering, Max rinsed the soap and shampoo from his body and hair and turned off the water. Derek pulled the curtain back and handed Max a dry towel, taking one for himself as well.

When Derek thought Max would dry off and get dressed without answering, Max glanced over at him. "I didn't leave because I didn't love you anymore. You get that, right?"

Not an outright declaration of love, but Derek had to give Max bonus points for his willingness to be vulnerable and put his feelings out there.

"What are you saying?" Derek asked, not wanting to assume anything.

"I'm saying that if I could take it all back, that if I could have made better decisions that day, I would do it like *that*."

Max snapped his fingers, but they were damp, and no sound came. His expression turned sheepish. "Well, you know what I mean."

"So, you want a reset button, is that what you're saying?"

Max stepped into Derek, pushing him back against the wall. Max bore his weight on the hand by Derek's head, boxing him in with his body. Derek could have shoved him away if he'd wanted to, but every cell in his body would have rebelled if his brain had given it that order.

"Yes." Max couldn't say it any clearer than that. "But pressing that button isn't up to me. That's up to you. Let me know if you want to press it too. Yeah?"

A part of Derek wanted to slap his hand down on that reset that Max offered and right a ship that had been listing for years. But Derek knew it wasn't as easy as it sounded, and a part of him knew that he'd be setting himself up for more heartache if he didn't proceed with an abundance of caution.

Derek nodded. "You'll be the first to know."

Max leaned in, claiming Derek's mouth the way only Max ever could. It left Derek hard and questioning why he was hesitant to move the beginnings of this new relationship forward. But Derek didn't want to make a rash decision. Life had taught him to think things through. *This time,* if he took that leap of faith, he wanted to make damn sure what waited for him at the bottom before he did.

Max backed away, and they both turned their focus to the reason they were in Mexico in the first place. Derek dressed and stepped into his shoes, his feet already complaining about the long day ahead.

"I need some coffee," Derek said as he glanced out the window from behind the curtain. No one waited outside their room. "I think the office has some."

"You're not worried about getting sick?"

"I'm desperate. I'm willing to take my chances that those stomach bugs can't survive a good scalding in a coffee pot."

The attendant at the front desk let them fill their travel mugs with coffee before they hit the town again.

They climbed into the car, and Max said, "I've been thinking about that ping from Liberty's phone that Cesar found in Tres Colinas. Maybe we should go back there. It was her last known location, and we were only there a day. Maybe if we give it a little more time, something will surface."

Derek shifted into drive. "I think we have a solid plan, but if we don't turn up anything today, then we can head back in the morning. Sound good to you?"

Max nodded. "Then let's make today count."

17

Derek was relentless.

One of the qualities Max was growing to love about him. And undoubtedly, one of Derek's many fine qualities that made him such a good PI. He flat out didn't give up.

From bar to store to market, they gave out their number and told their story about looking for women and drugs for an upcoming boat party. But they'd only been met with suspicion—which was valid—and nobody called. Or texted. Nothing. Not even a nibble.

At some point in the middle of the day, they thought they were being followed. They approached the guy, only to have him run. Turned out it was a hell of a lot harder to find what they wanted than what they'd originally thought.

Which was why they walked down the street that evening, still five or six blocks from their car, and discussed their plan for the next day.

"We should stop back into these two bars on the way to the car before we head back to the motel, and if we get up early," Derek said, "we can be in Tres Colinas before it's light and start searching again. Maybe go back to the bus station. There may be a bus driver, or ticket agent, or janitor that had seen her but wasn't working the day we stopped by, and then—"

Max shoved him into an alley as they passed one. Easy to do when Derek's guard was down, and he was more asleep than awake. Even Derek's back hitting the yellow stucco wall behind him barely raised his eyes above half-mast.

"What did you do that for?"

"Stop for a second. Take a breath and listen to me."

Derek lost the battle to keep his eyes open. "I'm listening."

"We've been everywhere in this town. No one has confessed to having seen Liberty, and no one seems to give a flying fuck what we're looking for. No one has called, texted, or approached us, except that one kid, and I think he was after our wallets."

Derek made a noise in the back of his throat. It could have meant anything. At least it was enough to know Derek hadn't fallen asleep on his feet.

Though it was dark, the streets had a lot of traffic, and Mexican music mixed with some hip-hop from a club at the end of the block. If people noticed them in the alley, they didn't pay them any attention.

At the other end of the alley, two cats fought, their screams drowning out the sound of an occasional honking horn. One of Derek's eyes opened a fraction before slamming closed again. If Max didn't get Derek back to the room ASAP, chances were he'd have to carry him there.

Max continued, even though he wasn't positive Derek had registered anything he said. "This town is a bust. That idea was a bust. Marco's not dumb enough to take the bait. Let's call it a night, get some sleep, and get up early like you said."

The muscles in Derek's face went slack, and his head lolled to the side as his knees buckled. If Max hadn't been there to prop him up, Derek would have fallen to the ground.

He took Derek by the shoulders and gave him a shake. "Hey. You hear anything I said?"

Derek's eyes fluttered open. If Max hadn't known better, he would have suspected someone had slipped something into Derek's drink. But since all the drinks they'd bought had been for show, being drugged would have been impossible. It was just the fatigue and lack of sleep pulling Derek under.

"I'm going to drive you back to the motel, and we're going to get that sleep."

Derek made a sound that seemed disappointed. "So, no back-alley blowjob then?"

"You thought I pushed you in here to blow you?"

The back of Derek's head hit the stucco, making a hollow thunk as he tried to maintain eye contact. He shrugged.

Max reached a hand down to cup Derek's junk, only to find Derek as hard as he'd been the night before. "Fuuck. I don't mind returning the favor," Max dipped his head and grumbled in Derek's ear, "but you're going to have to wait. What I want to do to you, I don't want to do in public."

That hand to Derek's groin did more to wake him up than a bucket full of water to the face probably would have. Derek wrapped an arm around Max's neck and brought him in for a kiss.

The hairs on the back of Max's neck rose a second too late. He caught movement out of the corner of his eye. A hand fisted in his shirt and shoved Max to the ground.

His head hit the asphalt with a *thunk*, sending an array of stars across Max's field of vision. Nearby, he heard the unmistakable sound of a fist hitting flesh. Derek grunted.

Max scrambled to get to his feet, but he slipped in something wet. The next thing he knew, three guys were on him. He didn't know if this was a good old-fashioned gay-bashing or if Marco's men had caught up with them.

The men didn't give him any time to contemplate that question. The fists came first, and then the feet as his attackers landed blow after blow, kick after kick. Max tried to fight or roll away to a defensive position. In the end, all he could do was curl up into a ball and try to protect his face and head.

But he had to help Derek. He wasn't in any kind of shape to fight for himself.

As quickly as the attack came, it ended. Max coughed and spat out blood from a split lip. He called out to Derek. A groan was the only reply.

Then a cargo van pulled up, and the same hands that had punched him now lifted him and threw him through the open side doors. He struggled, but the men overpowered him with ease. As soon as he landed on the bare metal floor of the van, he scrambled back toward the door. *Derek.*

No more had that thought flashed through his mind than Derek landed in the van next to him. The doors slammed closed, and the van took off.

Streetlights shined through the two back windows of the box van. The light coming and going as they passed under streetlights. Between them and the driver was a solid metal partition.

"You okay?" Derek asked, feeling Max's face in the near pitch black.

Max coughed again and wrapped an arm around his aching ribs. "Never better. You?"

"I'm awake if that's what you're asking."

Max sputtered out a laugh even though it fucking hurt to do so. The van turned, and soon the streetlights and sounds of the town faded. They bumped down a road, making them grunt and groan with each hard hit in the potholes.

With a solid partition between them and the drivers and the door latch stripped from the inside, they had no way out. Max couldn't tell how long they'd been riding in the back when the van finally came to a halt. The driver and passenger side doors opened as another vehicle pulled up. There were some raised voices. An argument.

"Hey Maxie," Derek said, his voice weak but wide awake.

"Yeah?"

"Our plan worked."

Max stifled his laugh. "High five."

In the dark, their hands collided as someone threw open the side doors of the van.

———

ONE OF DEREK'S EYES HAD NEARLY SWOLLEN SHUT, BUT THERE wasn't much to see in the dark except for what looked like an abandoned warehouse. He might have smelled fresh-cut weed, but with the blood caking in his nose, it was hard to smell much.

Four men half-dragged, half-carried him and Max into the building. From somewhere, he heard raised voices too far off to hear what they were saying. A small part of him was glad their plan had worked, but a much larger part of him wondered what the hell they'd gotten themselves into.

When he'd pictured making contact with Marco or his men, it had been by phone, text, or maybe someone approaching them in the bar. He hadn't counted on them making contact with their fists and steel-toed boots.

Which made Cesar's warnings all the more dire.

The men dumped him and Max into a small room and slammed the door. He patted his pockets, but his phone was gone. He didn't remember someone taking it off of him, but the whole beating was a blur. At least in the room, the moonlight shone bright enough that they weren't in total darkness.

The door opened up again almost as soon as it had closed. A man tossed a bucket into the room. "*Por neccecitos,*" the man said before the door closed again with the distinct sound of a padlock locking.

Derek kicked the bucket away. "I'll be damned if I'm going to piss and shit in a fucking bucket."

"Pretty sure we're going to be here awhile. I'm sure we'll be fucking thrilled to have it."

Beside him, Max pushed himself to his feet. Derek didn't like the way Max cradled his ribs. If one of them were cracked and punctured his lung, their little escapade could turn deadly.

"How are the ribs?" Derek stood and leaned against one of the walls.

"Bruised. But not broken. I know what the hell broken feels like."

When had Max had broken ribs? Derek raised a brow, but Max shook his head, that same frightened, feral look in his eyes that he got whenever the subject of Max's childhood came up. Derek let it drop. If Max didn't want to talk about it right then, he wouldn't push the issue. Turns out, there was a lot about Max he didn't know.

The high windowsill was over Max's head. He reached up and grabbed the edge, muttering a curse as he winced in pain.

"Here." Derek linked his fingers together to give Max a leg up.

Max stepped into his hand and looked out the window. From the exertion, Derek's nose and eye developed a pulse of their own. Above, Max tapped on the glass and the frame before stepping back down. "The frame is sturdy. And that's some industrial-grade glass or something. We couldn't punch through that. And honestly, even if we did, I don't think the opening is wide enough to get our shoulders through."

"Fuck." Derek slid down the wall and sat again, his swollen eye pulsating. With a little bit of grousing, Max managed to sit beside him.

They sat in silence for a while. The only sounds they heard were the sounds of an old building settling. Occasionally, Derek thought he might have heard voices, but he could have been imagining it.

"Do you think they're going to kill us?" Max asked, sounding more defeated than scared.

"Eventually, yeah, maybe. But I think if that had been the plan all along, they'd be dumping our bodies in a back alley somewhere and wouldn't have brought us here first."

"Probably waiting on instructions from Marco would be my guess."

"Same."

Derek didn't know how long they sat there. Long enough for his body to get stiff and the adrenaline to drop off, allowing the pain to creep in. There was a silver lining, though—his nose was so swollen that he couldn't smell how bad the room stank.

Max picked at the dried blood on his puffy lip. His head fell back against the wall. "I'm sorry I—"

"Don't," Derek said. He rolled his head to the side so Max could see the sincerity in his eyes—well, his *eye* at least. "This isn't your fault. We're going to get out of this and find Liberty and—"

Max's derisive laugh cut him off. "You don't have to blow sunshine up my ass, D. I know what's up. I know we'll be lucky to get out of here in something other than a body bag."

"It's not over. Not by a long shot." Derek didn't know if he was telling himself that as much as he was telling Max. Because the truth of it was, Max was probably more right than Derek was.

Derek held out his hand, and after a moment's hesitation, Max linked his fingers with Derek's.

"I would have thought you would want to deck me, not hold my hand."

"Despite all this," Derek waved his hand in the general direction of their ten-by-ten prison. "I'm really glad you stormed back into my life. And if this is where it ends, then I'm glad we got to spend these past few days together."

Max squeezed Derek's hand, then wrapped his arm around Derek's shoulder and pulled him into his chest. Derek settled against him, trying not to put too much pressure on his ribs.

"It's okay," Max said. "You're not going to break me. I promise. Now get some rest. I'm sure we're going to have an interesting day tomorrow."

Despite the throbbing in his face and the dread swirling in his stomach, the sheer exhaustion pulled Derek under.

When Derek woke the next morning, Max lay behind him, his front to Derek's back, Max's strong, protective arm tight around Derek's waist. For a minute, he let himself concentrate on that and not the hard concrete beneath him or how his eye had swollen completely shut during the night.

Derek shifted, and Max stirred behind him, nuzzling the back of his neck and placing a soft kiss on his shoulder.

Max snugged him in tighter. "I missed this."

Derek snorted. "You missed getting beat up and thrown in a storage room in a rundown warehouse somewhere in the middle of Mexico?"

"That part, I could have done without. No, I missed having you in my life. Of waking up to you in my arms. We're going to get out of here so that we can have many more mornings like this, preferably with a bed under us."

For the first time, Derek didn't have that niggling thought in the back of his mind, reminding him he needed to protect his heart when it came to Max. The voice was silent for once.

He didn't know what that meant for a future that involved Max, but the constant worry of Max breaking his heart again was too heavy to hold. Derek decided to do the only thing he could.

He let it go.

And without reservation, Derek said, "I'd like that."

The grin that bloomed on Max's face when Derek glanced over his shoulder made everything worth it—the lack of sleep, the swollen face, the uncertainty of what would happen next. He'd go through it all again to have Max smile at him like that.

A shout came from the other side of the door, and someone started working the padlock. Derek and Max scrambled to their feet, Max muttering a string of curses as he hugged his rib cage and tried to straighten.

Derek snuck a glance at the bucket, his bladder lodging a string of vile complaints. Max was right. That cursed bucket was looking more like a friend.

"Get ready," Max said as if he was going to rush the door as soon as it opened. Derek didn't argue. He braced himself, ready to fight.

18

THE DOOR FLEW OPEN. THE FIRST GUY INTO THE ROOM CAME armed with an AR-15 strapped to his barrel chest, his finger on the trigger. Any heroic thoughts of overpowering and escaping their captors vanished.

The man motioned with the gun barrel, and Max and Derek shifted over to the corner as directed. Another man came in and dropped a brown paper bag on the floor before leaving again.

The gunman backed out of the room, and the padlocks clicked on the door again.

Max stepped up to the door and pounded on it. "Let us out, motherfuckers!"

A shot rang out, and a bullet ripped through the door just above Max's head, lodging in the opposite wall.

"*Jesus fucking Christ*," Max said. "He could have fucking killed me."

"I guess that was their polite way of saying 'no.'"

Max turned around. "You okay?"

"Yeah. Didn't even come close."

Max picked up the bag at his feet. He reached in and tossed

Derek a bottle of water. It was warm, but it was better than nothing.

He reached in the bag for his bottle of water and the stack of corn tortillas. The edges were stale. But they were still edible.

Max took a tortilla and held one out to Derek. "I guess this is the Mexican version of bread and water."

"At least they're feeding us, which means they don't want us dead yet—bullet through the door aside."

They sat back down, their backs to the wall facing the door. Though this time, they settled in the corner in case some other asshole decided to take potshots through the door.

With the sun rising, the temperature in the airless room rose. Sweat beaded on Max's forehead and ran in rivulets down his back as they ate. He wanted to down all of his water, but not knowing when or if they would get any more, he decided to save the rest for later.

Even after drinking half the bottle, it felt like his throat had only gotten drier. "You ever thought how desperate someone would have to be to drink their own piss?"

"Don't tell me you're going to go all Bear Grills on me."

"I'm just saying I can understand it now."

The day passed. It involved a lot of pacing and even more sweating. Sometime in the middle of the day, three men came and replaced their bucket, making the stench in the room a tad more bearable.

After dark, they were given more water and a sort of stew with bits of mystery meat. At that point, Max didn't care what the meat was, only that it was marginally edible.

Every second, minute, and hour that passed dragged on longer than the last.

As the first streaks of dawn lightened the window, Max asked, "What do you think they're waiting for?"

"Maybe Marco is coming here. I don't know if he wants to see if we're legit or if he just wants to see what all the fuss is about."

"I wish he'd hurry up and get here. The wait is worse thinking about what he might do to us."

Someone fumbled with the lock, and they scrambled to their feet. Max's ribs bitched at him, but after a day, the pain wasn't as severe.

"I guess we might get our wish," Derek said, his gallows humor holding more grimness than it had before.

Their good friend with the AR came through the door barrel first, followed by a couple of guys with lengths of cut rope in their hands. Derek translated when one of the guys spoke. "He wants us to put our hands behind our backs."

Max was already turning around. "Yeah, I got that much."

One of the men wrenched Max's arms behind him, and it took all of Max's will to stifle the grunt of pain. Not only did he not want them to know how much he hurt, but he also didn't want to give them the satisfaction of knowing they'd caused him additional pain.

They bound his hands too tight, and he immediately started feeling the pulse in his fingers. He'd be lucky to come out of this without gangrene.

"Not so fucking tight," Derek groused as he struggled with the man tying him up. "What the fuck is wrong with you."

Max assumed the list was long, but he didn't think spouting off would help their situation. The man shoved Derek face-first into the wall, his hand in the middle of Derek's back. He said something, and the gunman came over and put the gun's barrel to the back of Derek's head.

Jesusfuckingchrist. Max's heart gave him one swift kick before climbing up into his throat. A strangled noise ripped up the back of Max's throat, but he couldn't have said anything if he'd wanted to.

Max caught Derek's eye and gave him an almost imperceptible shake of his head. They didn't need to give these assholes a reason to shoot them where they stood. If they wanted out of this mess without any extra holes in them, they had to wait for an opportunity to escape or overpower their captors. Pissing them off wouldn't help their situation.

And here Derek had been worried Max would be the loose cannon.

Taking them by the arms, the men perp-walked Max and Derek through the old warehouse. It must have been an old textiles factory because there were busted-up sewing tables and sewing machines in a pile by the front wall.

By one of the doors, the men had established a sort of camp. There were sleeping bags and thin, worn mattresses on the floor. A single propane burner served as a cooktop, and a couple of cases of bottled water sat near a steel roof support.

High above, early morning light streamed through broken blacked-out windows. Water rained down at a steady rate from a broken pipe somewhere above. The water pooled and ran off into a crack in the concrete slab.

Max couldn't tell where the stench of fresh-cut marijuana came from, but he suspected a grow wasn't far away.

They were marched up a set of steel stairs to the office overlooking the factory floor and shoved into a couple of bent-legged industrial grade chairs. The back and seat cushions had been stripped down to their frame. Only the back and solid metal seat remained.

Derek leaned toward Max, bumping his chin toward the inner office wall. It had an intact one-way glass. The only thing in the entire place that looked like it had been upgraded since the factory had been built. "Do you think he's back there?"

One of the men kicked Derek's chair and said something that Max assumed amounted to 'shut the fuck up.'

Then came the reverberation of footsteps on the stairs. Derek raised his brows at Max, kind of a 'Get ready. Here it comes.'

A man walked through the door dressed in military fatigues, but that was where all resemblance to the military ended. On his feet, he wore a pair of tattered sneakers instead of boots. His shirt was untucked, and he hadn't seen a barber or a razor in several long months.

The man hooked a leg over the corner of a rusty metal desk and glanced between the two of them. By the inflection in his voice, it sounded like he'd asked a question.

Instead of answering, Derek said, "In English, so we can both understand you."

"You Americans complain about us coming to your country and not speaking the language. And then here you are."

"Next time I'm beaten and kidnapped, I'll be sure I know the language first," Max said.

The man grinned and flicked his hair out of his eyes. "A smart ass."

"What the hell do you want with us?" Derek's chin notched up a fraction. Derek had never easily submitted—at least not outside the bedroom.

"Answers."

"Such as?"

"What do you want with Marco?"

Max shifted. The burning and strain in his shoulder muscles made it difficult to form a coherent thought. "I thought we made ourselves clear. We're looking for women. For drugs. For a party down in Cabo. We were very clear about that. We were told that Marco was the man who could make that happen." Max glanced at Derek, then back at the man. "Unless he's not the big fish everyone says he is."

Derek stood. "We'd be happy to go if he can't give us what we want."

The guard behind Derek moved fast. Derek must have caught the movement out of the corner of his good eye. He ducked, catching a glancing blow on the shoulder from the butt of the man's gun. If it had landed on Derek's head with the intended force, it could have been deadly.

Derek's knees buckled, and he landed hard on the chair. Red rushed up to his face as he choked back the cry of pain. *Fuck*. What Max wouldn't do to get them out of this mess. He felt responsible in so many ways. He'd never be able to pay Derek back if they made it out of there alive.

But that was the kind of man Derek was. He'd have done no less for a stranger. And fuck if Max didn't admire the hell out of him for that.

"You want answers?" Derek finally said, his voice steady but tight from the blow.

"That's what I said."

Derek leaned to the side, giving him a clear view of the one-way glass around the man. "If Marco wants answers, he needs to come out and ask us. Or is he too much of a coward to talk to us himself?"

Max squinted, waiting for the inevitable shot to ring out. In front of him, the man turned a peculiar shade of purple as a vein pulsed at his temple. Before he could say anything, the door to the inner office opened.

DEREK HAD TO HOLD BACK THE SELF-SATISFIED SMILE. HE DIDN'T think it would go over well with his captors. His shoulder throbbed and ached like a motherfucker. The flash of adrenaline hadn't done much to mask the pain. He had a hard time bringing Marco into focus with one bad eye and tears of pain filling his good one.

"Tio," Marco said to the man with a dismissive wave of his hand.

Tio moved aside and took up a position behind his boss. Derek couldn't tell if more men were in the inner office, but he didn't think so.

Besides Tio and Marco, there were two men behind Derek and Max. Four against two. Not terrible odds, but with their hands bound behind their backs, they didn't stand much of a chance of fighting their way out of their predicament, especially when one of them was heavily armed and not in the least bit shy about using it.

They'd have to bide their time and hope they had an opportunity to overpower the men. The odds didn't look in their favor.

Marco laid out their cell phones and wallets on the desk and leaned back against it, spreading his arms out as if to say, 'Here I am.'

He was younger than Derek had expected. Late twenties, maybe. Young and bold and brash enough to think he held all the power. But hopefully not wise enough to realize when he was being manipulated.

But he had that look in his eyes. The look that told Derek that he'd seen enough in his short years. He didn't look mad or crazy. Just callous and conniving.

A man too used to using violence and force to intimidate others and take what he wanted.

Which really might be the more dangerous combination. Marco knew exactly what he was doing and didn't give a rat's ass who it affected as long as he got what he wanted.

"I don't have a lot of time," Marco said. "Even less patience."

Derek's cell phone buzzed on the desk and lit up. Marco plucked it up and showed him the screen. *Cesar.* "Your partner."

Schooling his face, Derek didn't let the 'oh shit' moment show in his expression. He had to give Marco points for doing his research. Maybe Derek had underestimated him.

"I'm going to let you answer," Marco said. "When I turned it on, you had a bunch of missed calls from him. He won't stop calling. You tell him everything is fine."

The 'or else' didn't have to be said, especially with the man behind Derek stepping up in case he needed the butt of his gun again.

Marco answered the call and put it on speaker, holding it out for Derek to talk.

"Oh, thank fuck," Cesar said. "You finally answered. Where the fuck have you been? You can't go dark on me like that and not expect me to start rounding up a posse. I was going to tell you this Marco dude—"

"Hey," Derek said, not wanting Cesar to spill any information that he didn't want Marco to hear, like exposing any contacts he might have.

"We're good," Derek said, trying to figure a way to let Cesar know there was a problem without alerting Marco. "In fact, we're going to be heading back later today."

"Wait. What? You are? Did you find her?"

Derek inwardly winced, and he saw Max stiffen out of the corner of his good eye. "We think we'll have more resources back in the States. I'll explain it all when I get back."

Derek heard the unmistakable clatter during the long pause as Cesar's fingers flew across his mechanical keyboard's keys. "Yeah, sure," he said at last. "I'll see you first thing in the morning."

Marco ended the call. Before he could turn the phone off,

the phone gave off a beep telling Derek his battery was nearly dead. Marco folded his arms over his chest. "Find who?"

If Marco knew Cesar was Derek's partner, Marco had to know that Derek was a PI. Marco must have done some Googling when Cesar's name popped up on his home screen. He couldn't play Marco as if he were stupid because he wasn't.

Their only hope of getting out of this alive was to tell the truth. Or a version of it. He glanced over at Max.

Max shrugged. He had to understand the predicament they were in as well.

"My sister," Max said, his gaze leveled on Marco. "You were one of the last people to see her alive."

He didn't even pretend to look surprised. "Who was your sister?"

Derek didn't like the fact that Marco had used the past tense when he referred to Max's sister. It didn't bode well.

Max grimaced as he shifted in his seat. Derek's shoulders screamed from the bind they were in. His hands had long ago gone numb. But as badly as he hurt, he knew it had to be doubly worse for Max and his bruised ribs.

"Liberty Huff," Derek said.

Marco shrugged. "The name doesn't mean anything."

"She's one of Pelón's girls. She brought you a bunch of cash from your car-stripping operation in the valley. She crossed the border fifteen days ago. Hasn't been seen or heard from since."

"I have many people bringing me money. I can't keep track of them all."

Max bobbed his chin toward his phone. "Untie me, and I'll show you her picture."

Marco turned on Max's phone, but no one made a move to untie him. "What is your passcode?"

Max gave it to him, and Marco pulled up his photo app. It would be the first photo in his library. Marco's expression shifted as recognition hit. He showed the photo to Tio before dropping the phone back down on the desk. Tio reached over and turned it off.

"I remember her. She demanded more money. I've learned that you have to deal with these small problems before they become big ones. You understand. No?"

Max lurched to his feet.

"Max, no!" Derek hollered. Max would get himself shot if he wasn't careful.

Marco didn't flinch. Tio stepped forward and caught Max with an uppercut to the gut. Max doubled over with a grunt, his knees giving way as the man shoved Max to the ground. He fought for his breath, his chest heaving, the air wheezing in and out. "What—" It took a few more ragged breaths before Max could say, "What the fuck did you do to her?"

Tio looked at Marco. As if to satisfy Marco's curiosity more than Max's, he said. "I took care of the problem like you told me. Trust me. She won't be asking for any more money."

Max quit struggling to get up, his face red, and even with vision in only one eye, Derek saw the unshed tears in Max's eyes.

Marco stood, his expression more bored than anything as if Derek and Max were nothing more than a dying mouse for a feral cat to torment. "Take care of these two."

Marco handed their phones and wallets to Tio. Derek stood and got into Marco's face. "What are you going to do?"

Marco tugged the hem of his shirt down. "Go back into town for an early lunch. Unfortunately, you two won't have that luxury."

The man with the gun took hold of Derek's bicep, his fingers clamping down on his muscle. It should have hurt, but so many things already vied for the top spot in the pain column, the crushing grip barely registered.

Tio opened the office door and shouted down to the men

below. A few seconds later, additional armed men came storming up the steps. With a man on either side of them, Derek and Max were hustled down the stairs.

Fighting would probably end with a bullet to their head, but perhaps by cooperating, Derek and Max were only prolonging the inevitable.

19

ONE OF THE BIG OVERHEAD DOORS ROLLED UP. OUTSIDE, A LIGHT rain shower ended as the panel van rolled in. Their handlers shoved Max and Derek inside. They settled onto their backs.

Max didn't have a whole lot of fight left in him. What was the point if they'd killed Liberty? He'd failed her on so many levels. He didn't think he could live with that guilt eating at him for the next fifty or so years. Maybe it was better to let these guys do whatever they planned to do.

Not that he and Derek had much of a say in the matter.

"Destroy the phones and the wallets," Marco said to Tio. "I don't want anything left behind for his partner to find. Take Carlos and Jesus with you."

Tio held up a hand and switched from English to Spanish. He pointed to the man with the AR-15. Max didn't know the point argued, but in the end, no one climbed into the back of the van before the doors slammed closed.

"What was that all about?" Max asked as the van's motor spun and then caught. They backed out of the warehouse and started bumping down the road, the rain shower starting up again and pounding on the roof, water swishing under the tires.

"Marco wanted a few more guys to go with us, but Tio talked him out of it. It's only him and the bruiser with the AR. Sounds like he doesn't trust any of those guys to keep their mouths shut."

Max struggled with his binding and managed to sit with his back against the side of the van. "We're fucked."

"Maybe. Maybe not."

"Yeah, sure, there are only two of them, but one of them has a rifle. I don't think we have a chance of overpowering them."

"You going to give the fuck up? Is that what you're going to do?"

Max didn't answer. He didn't want to voice the 'yes' that ran through his head.

"Is that what Liberty would want you to do?"

Max narrowed his eyes. "Don't bring her into this."

Derek huffed out a laugh. Somehow he made it sound sarcastic. "Don't bring her into this? She's the whole fucking reason we're here."

Derek was right, but that hole in the middle of Max's chest where his sister used to be made it hard to admit that. And if Liberty were looking down on him, she would be shaking a fist at him for rolling over and letting Marco win.

"Are we going to figure a way out of this mess while we still have a chance? I don't know about you, but I've got a whole lot more living left to do and a guy I'm interested in seeing where things will end up."

It wasn't a promise that they would be able to move away from their past, but he appreciated that Derek hadn't slammed the door on a future together.

Max narrowed his eyes at him. "You mean that?"

"I wouldn't have said it if I didn't."

Max tried not to think about what Marco and his men might have done to his sister. As best he could, he concentrated on the sincerity in Derek's eyes, on the promise of something better awaiting them.

"Let's do this." Max angled his hands into one of the voids in the wall of the panel van meant for running wires in a build-out and started trying to saw his way through his bindings. The van pitched and rolled on the rough road, making the arduous task even more difficult.

Derek did the same, their breaths coming fast with their effort, the sun heating the van's interior like a tinder box as the rain shower ended.

They both worked frantically, having no clue how much time they had left. If they weren't prepared when the van stopped, they had zero chances of surviving.

Even if you get your hands loose, what chance do you have against a guy with an AR?

Slim.

None.

Max let reality set in. But maybe if he rushed the guy with the gun, Derek would have a chance to get away before the guy could turn his gun on Derek. A long shot. But more than likely, the only one Max had. As he decided, a calm overcame him, knowing he couldn't voice it without Derek shooting it down. So he kept it to himself and worked hard to make sure they had other options.

Finally, his bindings gave a fraction, and a newfound hope burned in his chest. Sweat ran in his eyes as he glanced over a Derek—at his red face, his swollen eye. The concentration etching lines into his forehead, the determination flattening his lips.

Derek must have felt Max's eyes on him because he stopped sawing and glanced over at Max. Max opened his mouth to speak, but before he could, Derek said, "Don't you dare try to apologize again."

Realizing he'd almost done just that, Max ducked his head and shielded his face from Derek's uncanny ability to read him before Derek read his other thoughts—the love Max had burning not so deep down.

The bindings gave more, and Max used what strength remained in his bound arms to snap the frayed rope.

"Thank fuck." Derek sank against the side of the van.

Max quickly assessed his hands and wrists. The burning in his shoulder muscles put the pain in his ribs to shame. He numbly fumbled with Derek's binding with swollen hands and abraded, bruised, and bleeding wrists. He willed his fingers to cooperate. Derek had pulled the knots so tight that they were nearly impossible to loosen.

The van drove through a pothole the size of the Grand Canyon. It pitched them against the side of the van and tossed them back on the floor.

"Roll onto your stomach," Max said. Waves of pain and tingling shot through his hands as the circulation started to return. Using his hands and his teeth, he finally pulled the knots loose.

Derek's hands fell to his sides, a groan of relief clawed up the back of his throat. Despite the discomfort, Max put his hands on Derek's shoulders and massaged the sore muscles.

"Fuck," Derek muttered. It was hard to hear him over the drone of the tires on the road. "That might be better than sex."

"The fuck it is." Max leaned in and whispered in Derek's ear even though the men in the cab couldn't overhear. "Give me a chance when we get out of this mess, and I'll prove it to you."

"YOU CAN STOP MASSAGING NOW," DEREK SAID AS HE ROLLED TO his back beneath Max's splayed knees.

Max moved off of him and leaned against the side of the van. Derek pushed himself up to sitting as well. They worked their wrists and hands. The swelling in Max's had already gone down considerably, and the feeling had started to return to Derek's even though it felt like someone had surgically replaced his hands with someone else's.

"We've got to be ready as soon as the van stops," Derek said. "We're not going to get a second chance to surprise them."

"Agreed. We can wait on either side of the double doors, and as soon as they open, we go for the guy closest to us."

"No hesitation."

"Not even a fraction."

The van slowed, and they glanced at each other, each wondering if this was it. But then the van turned onto an even crappier road than the one they'd been on.

"Where the hell are they taking us?" Max asked.

"Not back to Las Rocas. We would have been there already, and I would have remembered if we'd taken this road. At this rate, we'll be lucky if we don't break our backs on one of the ruts."

"I'll take it," Max said. "Every second we drive is a second longer for us to get the feeling back into our hands, work the soreness out of our shoulders, and catch our breath long enough to get our strength back."

"If we don't cook to death in this tin can first."

Max huffed out a laugh. "That would be our fucking luck, right?"

"Come here," Derek said. "We might as well get comfortable."

Max scooted over, and they sat shoulder to shoulder, their heads resting against each other. Derek offered his still swollen hand, and Max linked their fingers together. It felt awkward, their fingers not fitting together as they should, but Max wasn't complaining.

They fell into silence, and the longer they drove and the hotter it got, the more likely Derek's prediction would come true. Max swallowed, the thick saliva stuck in his throat, and he had to swallow a few times to get it down.

From moment to moment, Max vacillated from terror to a resolute calm, from abject grief to sparks of hope. His adrenal glands and heart rate didn't know how to respond—the emotional squeeze on his chest tighter than any binding the men ever could have tied around his wrists.

Considering everything his father and mother had put Max through, he'd escaped believing that nothing that life threw at him could be worse than that.

He'd been dead wrong.

His past paled in comparison to the predicament he and Derek faced now. Clarity washed over Max as his perspective on his childhood changed.

How had he allowed his past to drive him?

Even after he'd been free of his parents, he could see now how they'd affected his life in many unsuspected ways. How what their twisted torment had taught him.

How he'd let the bullshit they made him believe ruin the best thing that had ever come into his life. Max didn't know if he and Derek had a future, but he knew that they'd never have a chance at one if he didn't bury his past once and for all.

And in the light of their current situation, telling Derek the truth didn't seem so terrifying.

Max squeezed Derek's hand, opened his mouth, and let the words flow. "My dad was a right bastard, which you'd probably already guessed. And my mom made Mary Tudor look like Mother Theresa. If they'd ever had any kind of love in their cold hearts, life had stomped it out of them by the time I came along."

Max glanced over at Derek, their hands loosely clasped as Derek absently drew circles on the back of Max's hand with his thumb. "But even that is giving them *waaay* too much credit. Honestly, I think the only reason they were together was because of what the other brought to the relationship. What little money we had, my father brought in. My mom... well, fuck. There goes that theory. I have no clue what she brought to the table." Max thought back. "Drugs. Alcohol. But mainly the drugs would have been her thing."

"Did they use or sell or..."

"All of the above. When I was about twelve, I overheard my parents talking about a small grow operation they had in the hills somewhere. They'd also cook meth in the trailer. Don't know how they managed not to blow us the fuck up."

"Jesus Christ."

"Right? Why do you think I never invited you in those few times that we dropped my sister off? I didn't want to take the chance that they'd left shit out, and you'd be the one to have to arrest my parents."

"You could have called it in. You could have left an anonymous tip with the police department."

"My father would have known I'd called it in. He'd threatened me before when I was younger, you know, after one of those drug programs I sat through in elementary school. He just looked at me and said, 'if you tell anyone, the police will never find your body.' I never knew if he was kidding or not."

Max's heart skittered through his chest, that old familiar dread rolling through him. "By the time you and I were dating, they at least cooked their meth somewhere else, and I didn't have to worry about Liberty living in that environment with all the chemicals. But a part of me always believed what my dad had threatened. I should have reported it, or at least told you, but..."

He almost didn't know how to put it all into words, but he reached deep down to yank them out. After all, if he didn't say them now, he might never have the chance.

"You were afraid of what I'd think of you." Derek filled in the blanks that Max found so hard to say.

"I already came from the wrong side of the valley. I didn't want to prove anyone's assumptions correct. Especially yours. And with you being a cop, I didn't want to take a chance that my past, that my shitty parents, would ruin your career by associating with me. I'd do it all different now. But back then, I was so grateful to have you in my life that I couldn't take that chance."

"Cut yourself some slack. From a very young age, your parents threatened and programmed you to ignore what was going on under your nose."

"Maybe." As an adult looking back, it was difficult to give his younger self that grace. "I thought about taking Liberty with me when I first left, but I didn't know how I would survive on the streets myself, much less keep my little sister alive. My dad didn't hit her the way he hit me. I thought she would be safer there than homeless."

"For what it's worth, I think you made the right decision. Liberty may not think so, but you were what sixteen, seventeen when you left?"

Max nodded. "Yeah. I left right before her twelfth birthday. I can see how it would have been madness running with her. But sometimes I still wish I had. And later, though I had started to get my life together and to apprentice at the tattoo shop, I could barely keep a roof over my head and feed myself."

"You've come a long way."

"Others might disagree."

Max laughed and looked around the inside their prison on

wheels. Outside, he heard a car honk, and through the back window, he now spotted a telephone pole instead of only the sky. Maybe they were getting closer to civilization, which didn't make sense. Who killed two people in a more populated area? Wouldn't it have made more sense to take them to the desert and shoot them there?

"But you know what?" It was more of a rhetorical question, and Derek let Max talk without interruption. "The drugs, my dad using me as his personal punching bag, him threatening my life, that wasn't even the worst of it."

"*Jesus, fuck.*" Derek leaned away and locked eyes with Max. Max didn't see the pity he'd feared would be on Derek's face. All Max saw was a fierce protectiveness that made Max's heart melt around the edges. "How can it get any worse? And fuck them. If they weren't already dead, I'd kill them myself."

"That's another reason why I never told you. I didn't want you messing up the rest of your life trying to fix something that was irreparable. The damage had already been done."

Some of the tension left Derek's body, but the compassion in his eyes never wavered. How on earth had Max ever walked away from that?

"You're not damaged."

Max looked away. For the first time in his life, Max almost believed it.

Had Max revealed too much?

Derek squeezed his hand. "Tell me the rest. Tell me all of it."

20

Derek's heart split in half. Hearing Max's story, the old cop in him wanted to bring people to justice, but there was no tangible target for his anger and spite when Max's parents were already rotting in the ground.

And while he'd forgiven Max for running away from him, this grim look into Max's past brought more things into perspective. He could better understand where Max had come from and why he had feared his association with Derek might ruin Derek's career with the department.

He waited to hear what Max considered the worst part, Derek's breath shallow as if his subconscious feared if he breathed too loud, he wouldn't hear what Max had to say.

"I think the worst of it was that from my earliest memory, I knew my father didn't want me. He called me worthless from such an early age that I thought it was a nickname for the longest time. It wasn't until I started elementary school that I learned what the word meant. My father never missed an opportunity to tell me how I'd wrecked his life, how they would be much better off without me. How I was nothing more than a parasite slowly sucking the life out of them every goddamn day."

"What did your mother say?"

While Derek's father had been a narcissistic asshole and selfish as fuck, his cruelty didn't rise to the level of Max's father's by any stretch. Derek hadn't lived every day, wondering if his father would beat the life out of him. His mother, at least, had been on his side. Why the hell she'd stayed with his father as long as she had, he had no clue. But at least he'd had one parent who he knew loved him.

"My mother didn't say much. She didn't tell him to shut the fuck up the way she should have. I don't know if she was too scared of him to stick up for me, or if she didn't give a shit, or if she believed his words. It was all so fucked up. I can see that now. But when you grow up with those lies drilled into you day in and day out, especially from such a young age, it's hard not to internalize everything they said. Impossible not to believe it."

Derek cupped Max's cheek and pressed a kiss to Max's lips.

"That. That right there. That tenderness, that caring... That feeling was so foreign to me when I met you. You were the first person I had ever been with that didn't want me for my dick or a quick fuck. You were the first person to show me what love was. The first to show me that I *was* worthy of love, and it scared the ever-loving fuck out of me."

"I never meant to scare you. I thought we were on the same page. I thought that we wanted to spend our lives together."

"And it terrified me. You have no idea. I knew you loved me. But I had no idea why. Why would you love this guy who came from the shittiest shithole of a home? What made me worth your time and effort? And what the hell would I do when you came to your senses or realized what my parents had always told me—that I was worthless and I'd only drag you down?"

The driver took a sharp corner and must have rolled over a curb because they were catapulted into the air a few inches before crashing back onto the hard metal floor of the truck.

Derek's clothes had long since grown heavy and damp with sweat, but that was the last thing on his mind. Especially after Max had bared his soul. Somewhere a door opened, allowing that darkness in his spirit to spill out and the light to shine in.

"You weren't my anchor, Max. You were my buoy." Derek caught Max's chin with his finger and made him look at him. It was hard bringing him into focus with only one good eye.

He wanted Max the see the truth on his face. Derek knew it would be there. It infused every cell in his battered, sweaty being. "You gave me a reason to get up every morning. You made me strive to be the best version of myself. You're the one who made me see I couldn't hide my true self from the world. That I couldn't go on living my life in the closet, no matter how hard it would be tearing down that door. Because you lived as your true authentic self, you gave me the strength to live mine. I'll always love and appreciate you for that. But more importantly, you had this compassion, this capacity to love and live without judgment that filled the world with light. How could I not be attracted to that?"

Max swiped at his eyes, and it wasn't because of the sweat dripping from his brows. When he spoke, his words came out thick. "When you came home that day, saying you were quitting the department, my insecurities and self-doubt came to a head. All I could hear was my father's words telling me how I'd ruined his life. I was aware enough that I knew I wasn't in good working order emotionally."

Max laughed at himself. It sounded hollow in the van. "Scratch that. I was *broken*, and I thought with time you'd come to realize that and find out what an epic mistake you'd made. So I ran. I'm not proud of that, but I knew I had to work on myself. And I know I'm not all the way fixed now, but I've managed over the years to glue some of the bigger pieces back together."

Derek wrapped his hand around Max's head and pulled him

into his chest. He didn't pity Max. It humbled him that Max had trusted him with his story. "I'm proud of you. It takes a strong man to do the work on the inside. I—"

The driver slammed on the brakes, and the van came to a stop, the tires squealing on the road. The cab doors opened and slammed closed as Derek and Max scrambled to take up their positions on either side of the door. Their eyes met, and Derek wondered if this would be the last time he ever saw Max again.

"Hey," Max said as his chin went up.

"Yeah?" Derek's words came out breathless as his heart drummed erratically in his chest.

"Whatever happens next, remember that I never stopped loving you."

THE SIDE DOORS OPENED, AND MAX DIDN'T HESITATE. HE LEAPED out at the man in front of him. The burly one who'd had the AR. For whatever reason, he didn't have it strapped to his chest. Maybe he hadn't expected any trouble. But that didn't keep Max from going on the offensive.

He barreled into the guy's chest shoulder first. A loud *umpfh* registered as they hit the concrete sidewalk. He knocked the breath out of the guy, but not the fight. Somewhere to Max's left, Derek and Tio landed in a pile of arms and legs and flying fists.

A woman screamed, and it registered that they weren't in a remote location but the middle of a town. Why would these guys bring them to town to kill them?

That momentary distraction was all it took for the big man beneath him to roll Max to his back. Max's head hit the concrete, not hard enough to knock him unconscious, but hard enough to stun him, allowing the man to use his overpowering strength to pin him to the ground.

The man rattled off a string of Spanish that Max had no possibility of understanding, but the other guy, Tio, caught in Derek's chokehold, managed to say, "We're not trying to fucking kill you. We're trying to set you free."

It was then that Max realized that though he had landed a number of body blows to the guy above him, the man hadn't hit him back. "Get the fuck off me."

To his surprise, the guy got up and held out a hand to Max to help him to his feet. With a wary glance, Max took it, rubbing the back of his head as he stood. He'd have a goose egg, but nothing more serious.

Derek loosened the hold he had around Tio's neck, but he didn't let go completely. "Why the fuck would you do that?"

They'd drawn a small crowd, but people started to disperse as if they knew nothing else exciting would happen.

"I've got my reasons," the man said.

"If Marco ever finds out you let us go, you're a dead man."

Tio's derisive laugh skittered along Max's spine. "You don't think I fucking know that? Why the hell do you think I drove you guys so far away?"

A part of Derek must have believed him because he released the hold he had and got up. Tio gathered his feet beneath him and slowly stood, his face still red from the compression Derek had put on his neck. He rubbed at his throat, his lungs working overtime to catch his breath.

Tio glanced behind Max as a diesel bus rumbled around the corner, its pipes belching clouds of black exhaust into the air. "I'm going to tell you the same thing I told his sister," Tio said as he pulled their wallets and cell phones out of the pockets of his military pants and put them into Derek's hands. "Hop on that bus and get as far away from here as you can. And whatever the fuck else you do, don't come back."

Wait. What the fuck? Did Max hear him right? Had Liberty

been there? Max glanced around at the storefronts, half expecting to turn around and find Liberty standing there. The bus braked half-way up the block and threw its doors open.

Max opened his mouth for clarification, but the guy beside him pushed him toward the bus. "*Vamos.*"

Max didn't need a translator or to be told twice, not when a few minutes ago he'd thought he only had seconds to live.

The bus doors closed, but the traffic kept it boxed in.

"Next bus is in two days. I'd be on this one if I were you," Tio said.

Derek bumped his chin at Tio in thanks, and he and Max made a run for the bus. It started to creep into traffic, but they jogged along beside it and pounded on the doors. Just when Max thought the driver would leave them, he stomped on the brakes. The brake lines hissed as the bus came to a stop. Max and Derek climbed in. Derek handed the driver a twenty from his wallet that somehow still had money inside.

It must have been enough to cover their fair wherever the hell the bus was taking them because the driver stuffed the bill into his pocket and jerked his chin toward the back of the bus.

Derek and Max walked down the aisle as the bus lurched, cut off a car, and pulled into traffic. They passed a handful of passengers looking bored and disinterested. Their stopping the bus and climbing on all beat up in dirty, sweat-drenched clothes didn't ping on their radar.

Or maybe they knew that the less they saw, the safer it was for them.

At the very back of the bus, Max and Derek collapsed onto the long bench seat. Max's heartrate downshifted, and he got a chance to catch his breath. "What the hell happened there?"

"I don't get it either. If Marco finds out he let us, Liberty, and who knows who else go, he's going to be dead himself. But I guess he's got his reasons."

Max checked his wallet. His cash, credit cards, and ID were there, though neither one had their passports. They'd left them back in the car in Las Rocas. But he'd rather make a run to the American Embassy than take a chance that Marco's men caught them in the city. He didn't know how they would get Cesar's car back, but all that was just noise.

He stretched his legs into the aisle and tilted his head back. That warmth blooming in his chest was the hope he'd find Liberty... alive.

Derek stretched out his legs beside him, their thighs touching as the bus chugged down the road. The town gave way to the country, scrub, rocky hills, and the occasional house.

Derek bumped Max with his shoulder. "If you want to take back what you said in the van, I won't hold it against you."

Max opened his eyes, squinting at the brightness of the sun and the wind buffeting him through the open window. "Why would I want to take it back?"

"Well, you said it under duress, and—"

"Fine." Max nodded his head. "I get it."

Derek almost seemed a bit disappointed. "Okay."

Right when Derek went to glance away, Max said, "I'm not under duress now."

Derek's gaze landed on Max. Even his swollen eye seemed more open as he waited for what Max would say next.

"And I still fucking love you."

21

"GOOD TO KNOW." DEREK LET MAX'S WORDS—'AND *I STILL fucking love you*'—roll over him, a balm to all the chaotic emotions rolling through his head. He didn't for one second not believe Max's veracity. He just didn't know where that left them.

With a future, maybe?

They'd have to wait and see.

He held back his own 'I love you,' not because he didn't feel it but because he wanted to be sure it had nothing to do with their forced proximity. If they moved forward, he wanted to make sure he knew what he was getting himself into.

Derek changed the subject, wanting to use their time on the bus to strategize, but between the beating, scant food and water, and that prolonged dump of adrenaline, his body was spent, and his brain begged him to take it offline.

He pressed the power button on his phone, but it didn't turn on. "You have any power on your phone?"

Max pulled his phone out of his pocket and hit the power button. "Nothing. I'm surprised you had enough charge for Cesar to get through back at the warehouse."

"We must have used up what little power I had left. When

we get to wherever we're going, we'll find a room, a charging cable, and food."

"And a laundromat," Max said. "Or a match. Not sure I ever want to wear these clothes again."

Derek chuckled, surprised he could find nuggets of humor. He snuggled in closer to Max and laid his head on Max's shoulder. "Agreed."

An hour or so later, the bus pulled into a small town. One person got off, and three teenagers got on. The teens talked and laughed and roughhoused. It helped the knot in Derek's stomach relax another notch. He'd half expected some of Marco's men to meet the bus, which was stupid because Marco had no idea Tio hadn't shot them in the head and left them for dead.

Since it wasn't the end of the line, they stayed on the bus. Derek couldn't be certain if Tio had been serious when he'd said to stay on the bus for as long as they could, but if he'd told Liberty the same thing, she might have stayed on the bus until the bitter end. After all, the more distance they put between them and Marco's men, the better.

At some point, Max elbowed Derek. He groaned, cracking an eye. The sun hung low in the sky, the fresh salt air wafted up to his nose, the sound of rolling surf filled his ears.

"I think this is it," Max said. "Everyone is getting ready to get off."

Derek sat up and scrubbed a hand over his face. They didn't have any possessions to gather, so they sat there until the bus stopped and people inched down the aisle.

If their phones had power, they could have shown the driver Liberty's picture as they left. They stepped off the bus into a quaint seaside town that the tourist industry had forgotten—or at least overlooked.

Max took Derek's hand and pointed down the street.

"There's a market over there. Let's see if we can get what we need there."

Derek's sweat-soaked clothes had dried stiff, and his underwear chaffed with every step. "At this point, I'd walk around in a Speedo if it meant I could get out of this underwear."

Max glanced over and raked his eyes up and down Derek's body. Derek didn't have the strength to do much of anything… but tell that to his dick. "You could totally pull off a Speedo."

"Stop looking at me like that," Derek said. "You're not helping in the chaffing department."

Max threw back his head and laughed. Derek laughed with him, even though there was still so much wrong. But they were alive, which left a whole world of possibilities open. It gave Derek a newfound lightness, and he found himself taking Max's hand and not giving a rat's ass who gave them a look as they walked down the first row of the market.

After finding a stall with a corner changing room, they emerged from the market in swim trunks, T-shirts, and chargers for their phones. They bought a few iced-down water bottles from one of the stalls and drank them all. Derek gave Max the honor of tossing their old clothes into a dumpster in an alley a street or two over.

"I need a shower and a beer," Max said.

"I'm so hungry, I'm willing to fight the stray cats over the garbage scraps."

Max stopped on the corner and looked around. Because it wasn't a tourist town, there wasn't a hotel on every corner. Or *any* corner. But a lady where they'd bought their clothes had given them directions to a bed and breakfast.

"I think she said the house is that way." Max pointed down the street to his right. "Casa Sol, right?"

"Yeah."

A few blocks down, they found the house and rented a room.

They paid for three nights, having no idea how long they'd be in town looking for Liberty.

They climbed the stairs to an air-conditioned room on the second floor with an ensuite bathroom.

"Holy fuck," Max said as he flopped down on the bed face first. "I'm never fucking leaving this spot."

Derek slapped him on the ass. "Get up. As soon as I'm out of the shower, I'm getting food. You'd better get cleaned up if you don't want me to leave you behind."

He may love Max, but after subsisting off of tortillas and a cup of stew for two days, he would ditch him for a steaming hot enchilada and rice and beans in a heartbeat.

Max groaned but got up. They plugged their phones into their chargers and scrubbed off the layers of dirt and sweat.

By the time they got out of the shower, all new missed calls and texts from Cesar popped up on Derek's phone. He hit Cesar's number, and the phone rang on the other end.

"Anything from Liberty?" Derek asked as Max checked his phone.

Max shook his head and flopped down in a cushy chair in the corner of the room. "Just a text from Jordan with an update on the shop."

"What the fuck is going on?" Cesar's voice came over the phone's speaker, the connection a little scratchy but better than Derek had anticipated.

"Where are you?"

"At the fucking border, where the hell do you think I am?"

"At the border?" Max said from across the room.

"I knew something was wrong when you answered. I used the Find My Phone app and got your basic location. You weren't anywhere near where my car's GPS said you were. I knew something had to be up."

Derek smiled. "You have a tracker on your car?"

"I've got a tracker on just about everything. Now, are you going to tell me what the fuck is going on, or are you going to make me guess?"

Derek sat on the arm of Max's chair, and they told Cesar the whole story. When they'd finished, Cesar didn't say anything. Derek checked to make sure the call hadn't dropped, but they were still connected.

"You still there?" Derek asked.

"Yeah. Fucking speechless, but still here. Where are you guys now?"

"Punta Mar. It's a small town way down the coast. I'll send you a pin drop to our location. We think Liberty might have gotten off the bus here, so we're going to look for her here for a few days before we make any other plans."

"I'm in a rental. I'm going to pick up my car, and I'll pick you up in a day or so. Sound good?"

"Yeah. Thanks, Cesar. I'm going to owe you."

"Nope. I'm your partner. It's part of the job description."

They said their goodbyes, and within a few minutes, Derek and Max were back on the street with clean bodies, brushed teeth, and a swipe of deodorant under each arm. They turned left out of the house and headed toward the main drag where most of the stores and restaurants were.

It was already dark, but people walked the streets. They weren't packed by any means, but a light steady stream of people made it feel like it was a safe town to roam around after dark. Even before they hit the main street, they heard mariachi music. As they turned the corner, the source turned out a be a busy restaurant.

"This good enough?" Max asked. "Or do you want to walk around a bit and see if there is something else that catches your eye?"

The restaurant occupied one of those buildings that looked

like it had apartments or offices up above. "Here's fine. A lot of locals here. It must be pretty good. And at this point, I'm not picky."

DEREK PUSHED AWAY HIS PLATE AND DRANK DOWN THE LAST OF HIS second beer. If you had put the plate on the floor and given it to a pack of starving dogs to lick, Max didn't think that the plate could have gotten any cleaner.

"We can order more if you're still hungry," Max said as he glanced over at the bar. He pulled up the photo of Liberty. His phone had only twenty percent charge, but it was enough to show the picture around a bit.

"I'm stuffed." Derek bumped his chin toward Max's phone. "And I know you're itching to show that picture around. Let's go to the bar and see if anyone has seen her."

They paid their tab and worked their way up to the bar, claiming a couple of barstools as they became available. They both ordered another beer. They felt safe enough that going a little heavier on the alcohol wouldn't get them into any undue trouble. Besides, if anyone deserved to go a little heavier on the booze, it was the two of them.

Halfway through their beers, Max showed Liberty's photo to the bartender when there was a lull. "You ever seen this woman? She might have come through here a week or two ago?"

The woman cleaned a bar glass and set it aside to take Max's phone. "No," the woman said. She had a thick accent, but she spoke English well enough that Derek wouldn't have to translate. She glanced from the photo to Max and then to Derek's bruised and beat up face. "Why you want her?"

"It's not like that." Max tried to reassure her, but he wasn't sure he came across as convincing. Even with the alcohol in him, he was having a hard time acting casual about his need to find Liberty, not when the desperation ate away at his belly like a parasite. While he had no reason *not* to believe that Tio had dropped his sister off much the same way he'd dropped him and Derek off, he had no reason *to* believe him either.

And right then, he didn't see any reason not to tell the bartender the truth. He was beyond playing games. "She's my sister. Someone said she might have come through here."

"I haven't seen her. But it's my first day here."

A medium-built man came in from the back, a clean bar towel tossed over one shoulder. He looked like he should be balancing someone's stock portfolio, not taking their drink order. He served a woman at the other end of the bar.

"I could ask my boss," she said, glancing over at the man.

Max nodded. "*Gracias.*"

The woman smiled at him and went to talk to her boss. The man glanced down the bar at them, his brows knit together, and his eyes narrowed. He gave whoever he was serving their change and walked down the length of the bar. Even with the focused scrutiny, the bar owner had one of those faces that Max would have spilled his guts to after a few rounds of drinks.

"I'll look at your photo. I may or may not tell you what you want to hear. We get guys looking for women down here all the time. Not always for the right reasons."

"I can appreciate that," Max said as he reached out with his hand. "I'm Max Huff. I'm looking for my sister, Liberty." It wasn't lost on him that the man didn't give him his name in return. A cautious man. Max didn't have a problem with that.

Derek knocked Max in the ankle with the tip of his shoe. Yeah, Max had seen the momentary flash of recognition in the man's face before he schooled his features. Max's heart rate bumped up a notch even as he warned himself not to get his hopes up. Liberty wasn't the most common name in the world, but it certainly wasn't *that* unique.

Max handed over his phone, holding his breath as he waited for the man's answer. The bartender stared at the photo, and Max finally had to take a breath before he passed out. Either the man recognized her, or he didn't. Derek squeezed Max's shoulder but didn't let his hand linger the way Max wanted, needing that strength to draw on.

The man handed the phone back. "Never seen her."

Derek kicked Max under the bar again. Harder this time, but Max had a feeling they weren't going to get anywhere with this guy if they strong-armed him into giving them the information they needed. Also, it didn't look like slipping a twenty across the counter would get them anything but kicked out.

"What's your name?" Max asked.

After a brief hesitation, the man said, "Antonio Herrera."

Max felt Derek's tension rising. Derek wanted to step in and help but was hanging back and letting Max do the talking. But Max could tell it was killing him. He glanced over and gave Derek a little go-ahead nod.

"Look, Antonio, if you know her and want to protect her, we appreciate that. All we're wanting is verification that she's okay. All this," Derek said, gesturing to his face, "is what happened when the bad guys found out we were looking for her."

"Do you have a sister?" Max asked.

Antonio reluctantly nodded. "Three."

"Then you get where I'm coming from. As Liberty's big brother, I'm just trying to protect her.

"What if she doesn't want your protection?"

"Then, we walk away." The sincerity in Derek's voice almost had Max balking. Derek meant what he'd said. Max agreed, but fuck, it would be so hard to walk away, even if that was what Liberty wanted.

"Give me your number," Antonio said. "You know, in case I ever run into her."

Max scribbled his number on a cocktail napkin and slid it across the bar. Antonio shoved it into his pocket and turned his attention to the customer waiting to place their order.

When the other bartender came by again, Derek flagged her down and ordered them both a whiskey. "Progress. I think we should drink to that."

"He knows her," Max said.

"Without a doubt. But we have to be patient. We press Antonio hard now, and he might never tell Liberty we were here."

When their drinks came, they clinked their glasses together and threw the whiskey to the back of their throats. Max tapped the bar top with the flat of his hand. "Let's get out of here."

"You sure? We can stay longer if you'd like."

"No. We're not getting any further with him tonight."

Max needed a bed. A good night's sleep. And if somewhere in there he got to take advantage of the fact he had one hell of a hot man lying beside him all night, that would be fine, too.

2 2

"Come back to bed," Derek said, his voice still thick with sleep even though they'd slept like the dead for almost twelve hours. His stomach rumbled as if it had missed a month of meals instead of only a few.

Max turned away from the window. They had a street view from their room. Max had been staring at all the people passing by for the past twenty minutes. "I can't stop thinking that if I watch long enough, I'm going to see her walk by."

Derek checked the restaurant's website on his phone. The restaurant didn't open for lunch until eleven. Derek pulled back the covers. "We've got an hour before they open. I'm pretty sure I can distract you for a good portion of that. Then we can get cleaned up, go have some lunch there, and pretty much haunt the place until Antonio gets sick of seeing us or he has Liberty call us."

Max took a step toward the bed, his face in shadows, backlit from the light shining through the window. They hadn't found any underwear at the market, so he stood in front of Derek completely nude, his body responding to Derek's suggestion even as he said, "What if he never gives her our number?"

"Then we'll keep looking until we find her. She's close. Someone else is bound to have seen her." But as Derek studied Max's expression, he knew that wasn't Max's only worry.

Max took Derek's outstretched hand and let Derek guide him to the side of the bed. Max sat, and Derek propped his head on his hand. "You're more worried that he'll give her your number, and she still doesn't call."

"What if she never calls?" The misery on his face nearly tore another hole through Derek's heart. He could see the guilt swimming in Max's eyes, threatening to swamp him and drag him under.

"I wouldn't blame her if she didn't," Max said. "She has a lot to be angry about. I let her down, but I want to make it up to her. If she'll let me."

"She's a grown woman. All you can do is give her the space she needs and hope that she contacts you."

Derek tugged, and Max let him pull him down beside him. He kissed the ball of Max's shoulder and wrapped an arm around his waist. The sex could wait.

Turning to face Derek, Max cupped Derek's cheek and kissed him. It was soft and sappy, and even though it wasn't the kind of kiss meant to turn Derek on, it still had that effect. Blood rushed to Derek's groin, and his growing hard-on brushed against Max's thigh. He shifted away until his cock no longer touched Max. Derek wasn't going to take advantage of Max when he was vulnerable. Despite his comments about distracting Max, he was happy to hold Max in his arms and offer whatever comfort he could.

Max scrubbed his fingers through the scruff on Derek's jaw. They both could use a visit from a razor, but personal grooming had fallen to the bottom of the priority list. Max's gaze hit on every point on Derek's face, from the little scar on his chin to the swollen bridge of his nose to his black and swollen eye.

Max brushed a finger below Derek's eye. "The swelling has gone down a bunch. You're not looking so much like Conor McGregor has used you as a speed bag."

"I can see pretty well out of it again. And I'm getting my sense of smell back now that I can breathe through my nose better."

"Thank fuck for that." Some of the worry fell from Max's face as a grin came to his lips. "I don't know if I could live the rest of my life with you snoring like a bulldog. The walls were sucked in and out every time you breathed last night."

"Were not." Derek went for the ticklish spot under Max's arms. Max laughed and squirmed, and Derek rolled on top of him, pinning his arms above his head. "Take that back."

"I'm pretty sure they're going to have to call in a structural engineer to make sure the house is still sound after we leave."

Derek released Max's wrists now that he had full access to his underarms. Max bucked beneath him, and in a WWE-esque move that Derek hadn't seen coming, Max reversed their positions. Max winced, but he didn't let his sore ribs stop him from straddling Derek's chest with his thighs and catching Derek's wrists this time.

"What are you going to do now, hotshot?"

Max's dick lay in the center of Derek's chest, and Derek ducked his chin, sticking his tongue out and licking the tip of Max's hard cock. Max's head fell forward, and a guttural groan ripped from the back of his throat.

"Do that again." Max stared down at him, his dick jumping on Derek's chest. Precum seeped from the tip and spilled onto Derek's skin. Derek scooted down the bed to get into a better position as Max levered up onto his knees and leaned forward to grab the top of the wrought-iron headboard.

Derek curled his arms around Max's muscular thighs and

brought him down until Max's balls dangled above Derek's mouth.

Derek licked the underside, his own cock bouncing on his belly as another groan ripped through Max's vocal cords. Derek licked and sucked, drawing first one weighty ball into his mouth and then the other. One of Max's hands fisted in Derek's hair, the tension on his roots igniting a series of rolling goosebumps all down his body.

Max's hips flexed, and all Derek wanted was to feel those heavy balls slap against his taint as Max slammed into him again and again and again.

"I want to fuck your mouth," Max said, more plea than order, as his breath became more erratic.

Derek took hold of Max's cock. Their gazes locked, and the heat and desire flamed behind Max's eyes, fueling Derek's own. He'd never had a lover before or since Max who wholly gave into that vulnerability, who wasn't scared to show him exactly what Derek did to him.

Guiding him with his hand, Derek took Max deep to the back of his throat, threatening his gag reflex, but Derek wanted more. When Max started to back out, Derek took even more of him until his breath cut off and his lungs grew tight.

"*Jesusfuckingchrist.* You slay me." Max pulled back a fraction, and this time Derek let him go. He gripped Max's hips and encouraged him to thrust.

Max stared down again, watching his dick disappear into Derek's hot mouth. His thighs trembled beneath Derek's hands, and Max's balls drew up tight. By the harshness of Max's breath and the quake in his belly, Derek knew he was close.

As much as Derek would love Max to come down his throat, he had other, much better plans for that load. He pulled off, drawing a much-anticipated complaint from Max. "I was so fucking close."

Derek pushed Max off of him and got off the bed.

"Where the fuck do you think you're going? You can't leave me like this. It's fucking cruel and unusual punishment."

Derek laughed as he padded into the bathroom. There was a bottle under the sink he'd had his eye on. That didn't stop Max from complaining as he raised his voice so Derek could hear. "There is a statute in the Geneva Convention about this. Article eight, sub-section two: Thou shalt not leave a man with blue balls."

Derek returned to the bedroom and pounced on the bed. He handed Max the bottle and kissed the pout off his lips. Max looked at the label. "This is suntan lotion, not lube."

Derek turned the bottle around in his hand and pointed to the ingredient list. "One hundred percent pure coconut oil." He couldn't help the grin that slid across his face.

"Oh, fuck yeah."

Then Max's smile dimmed. "We still don't have any condoms, though."

"I haven't been with anyone since my last round of negative tests. You?"

"It was a while ago, but yeah. Negative across the board."

"Then I'm game. If you are, that is."

Max caught Derek behind the head and pulled him into a kiss. The expected passion poured into him, but beneath that passion lay an undercurrent of tenderness. Warmth bloomed in Derek's chest, and his breath caught in his lungs. Fuck, he loved that man. And as soon as things settled down, Derek would figure out what the hell he wanted to do about it.

<hr>

MAX POURED ALL HE COULD INTO THE KISS, LETTING HIS insecurities fall away and allowing everything he felt for Derek to come through. The respect, the adoration, the allure. The *love.*

Derek climbed off Max and lay on his stomach, wiggling his ass. Max would have preferred to look into Derek's eyes when he slipped inside, but being able to watch his dick slide between Derek's two magnificent cheeks wouldn't be a hardship either. He dropped the bottle of lotion onto the bed beside his knee, his dick straining for release as he settled between Derek's legs.

He rubbed his hands over the taut muscles, the skin smooth beneath his fingers. He squeezed Derek's ass and ducked his head to get a taste of the man he'd been unable to fuck out of his system. And if Max hadn't managed it yet, he knew he never would.

Derek groaned when Max bit a cheek, arching his back, encouraging Max to go for what they both wanted. Max dragged his tongue from Derek's taint to his hole, and that tight ring of muscles quivered. Derek shifted, his eyes dark with lust as he glanced back at Max with a low throaty growl.

Max licked and prodded with his tongue, probing Derek until he opened up to him. He could eat Derek's ass for breakfast, lunch, and dinner and never want for more. But Max needed relief, and by the way Derek pushed back against his tongue, he did, too.

The sun shined higher in the sky, its warm rays highlighting the curve of Derek's ass. Max rose on his knees and slicked up his dick and Derek's hole with the coconut oil. He would have held the bottle out for Derek to smell if he'd been able to smell much of anything.

The scent took Max back. "This reminds me of that time we found the hidden cove up the California coast."

Derek's grin turned mischievous. "Up near Big Sur."

"I took your ass then as well."

"You don't have to tease me. I'm already close to coming."

Max ran a slick finger down Derek's crease teasing his hole and slipping a finger inside. Derek relaxed around his finger the same way he'd relaxed around his dick before and pushed back against Max's finger. "You were as hungry for my cock then as you are now."

"The only thing different between then and now is I don't have sand in every crack and crevice and—"

Max's finger bumped against Derek's prostate, and whatever else Derek was going to say was lost on a low moan. Max loved Derek's responsiveness. He ran a hand up Derek's back, the long, lean muscles on either side of his spine like high tension wire beneath Max's touch.

"Fuck me already." Derek's throaty demand broke the last shred of Max's will. He lined himself up with Derek's hole, and using gentle, steady pressure, he gave them both what they craved.

Inch by incredible, tight inch, he slid inside until he'd buried himself balls deep. Derek blew out a breath, his tight hole relaxing around Max. He slid out a fraction, then drove back in. Derek got on his hands and knees and started setting a hard, unrelenting pace.

Max's nerves buzzed, his heart raced, his blood whooshed, and his mind soared. *This* was where he belonged—with this man who knew how to give pleasure as well as take it. Max collapsed forward, hugging his arms around Derek's chest as he pumped inside him, the friction, grip, and warm heat taking him ever closer to that remarkable edge.

His balls drew up as he neared that cliff, his toes curling as he did everything possible to hold on as long as he could. Max slowed and reached a hand beneath Derek, taking him in his hand, Derek's precum flowing freely.

Shifting, he stroked Derek's dick as he nearly pulled out, trying to find that bundle of tissue and nerves that he knew would send Derek reeling. Derek huffed out a breath when Max hit his target, his body shaking. Max hit the tight bundle of nerves one last time. Derek stiffened and cried out, his hot cum washing over Max's hand. Beneath him, Derek's arms collapsed, his body shuddering with the aftereffects of his orgasm.

With Derek face first in the sheets, his glorious ass in the air, Max couldn't hold out any longer. With his hands braced on Derek's hips, Max pumped two, three times before he climaxed. Derek's shocks and shivers clamped around Max's cock, milking every last drop of cum out of him.

Ignoring the soreness in his ribs, Max fell forward, his body slick with sweat, a sated and shuddering Derek beneath him. He braced himself on his hands as his lungs worked overtime to catch up on his oxygen debt. But even with shaking arms and an exhausted body, Max hadn't felt that good in a very long time.

Ducking his head between his shoulders, he pressed a kiss to Derek's spine, tasting the salt on his skin before gently pulling out and rolling to his side to face Derek.

Derek's eyes dropped to half-mast as the urge to sleep started to overtake his body.

"That was hot as hell," Max said.

Derek grunted, and his eyes drifted closed.

Max rubbed a hand across Derek's ass, not able to keep his hands off even though he'd just had his fill of it seconds before. "If you want, I can go out and grab us something to eat while you stay here."

Derek opened his good eye, his face all squished up in the soft pillow. "I thought we were camping out at the restaurant all day until Liberty either shows up or Antonio convinces her to call you back."

"That's *if* he knows her. Maybe we imagined that recognition on his face because it was what we wanted to see."

Derek levered up on his arms. "Oh, he knows her. And we didn't imagine anything."

"Well, I can go get food, bring it back here, and head back to the restaurant. It doesn't take two people sitting there all day."

Derek swung his legs over the side of the bed and stood. "I'm not letting you go alone."

Max followed him into the bathroom, loving the play of muscle in Derek's retreating body. "I'm sure I'll be fine. We've got to be way out of Marco's territory by now. No way will he find us unless Tio decides to rat us out. Which he won't do, because that would only implic—"

Derek turned and pressed Max into the wall with a hand in the center of his chest. "I'm going for moral support. I'm here for you. *Always.* You got me?"

Max knew Derek didn't mean *always* always, but his heart skittered in his chest a few beats thinking that Derek might. "Got ya."

They cleaned up, climbed back into the same clothes they'd bought the day before, and headed out onto the street. Derek took Max's hand, their fingers loosely twined. Before Max had left, Derek had never allowed any public displays of affection. That he'd show it here, in a small town in Mexico where they had no clue how tolerant the people were, it meant a lot to Max.

And it gave him hope that things might be different if they got together back in the States.

Don't read too much into it. Back then, Derek had been newly out of the closet. He's had years now to get used to holding a man's hand in public. The simple gesture isn't an unspoken, undying declaration of love, even if it feels that way.

Near the corner, Max tried to drop Derek's hand. He figured Derek might have been okay with handholding on a side street with little traffic, but it might be more problematic for him when the streets got busier.

But Derek didn't let go. He held on tighter and leaned in as they waited for traffic to clear so they could cross the street. "You know what I like?"

Derek's delicious, saucy, sexy grin was contagious, and Max smiled with him as he took the bait. "What's that?"

"I love the thought of running around town with your load still in my ass."

DEREK WATCHED THE HEAT CREEP UP THE BACK OF MAX'S NECK, and the lust seep into his gaze as he swallowed hard. Derek loved watching what his words did to Max.

Even though no one had passed by close enough to hear, Max said, "You need to stop talking like that."

Derek's grin only got wider. "Is that a threat?"

Max laughed. "Baby, that's a promise."

The last car passed, and they stepped into the street. "I'm going to hold you to it."

They opened the restaurant's door and were led to one of the last remaining empty tables as the lunch rush crowded in. Antonio had a pencil behind his ear and a pen in his hand as he took the lunch order of a group of men a few tables away.

Antonio spotted Derek and Max as soon as they walked through the door, his eyes following them until they found their seat. From his intense interest, Derek had expected Antonio to come to their table, but he sent someone else to take their order.

All through their meal, Antonio kept his eye on them. The restaurant quieted down as the lunch crowd turned into the early afternoon lull. Max kept his head on a swivel for signs of Liberty. Derek kept his on a swivel, looking for trouble.

Derek thought they were far enough away from Marco and his men for them to no longer be in any danger, but he refused to drop his guard completely.

By mid-afternoon, Max's nervous knee started bouncing again. The two of them had been nursing beers but didn't think taking up one of the tables was a problem considering all but a handful of them were now empty.

Finally, Antonio left the bar and walked over to their table. "Why are you two still here? My answer is the same as it was yesterday. Haven't seen her."

Derek offered a sage smile. "We don't believe you."

"Believe whatever you want as long as you're paying to sit there."

Max held up his beer, showing Antonio they were paying customers.

"That doesn't count. You've been nursing that for over an hour."

Derek pulled out his wallet and slapped a twenty on the table. "That should buy us another hour."

Antonio cut him a look. "I get two turnovers of the tables in an hour. Which is worth about sixty dollars an hour."

As difficult as it was, Derek managed to hold back his laugh. "There's no one in here."

The man shrugged and continued to stare Derek down.

"Fine," Derek finally said. Paying to sit at the table beat having to stand on the sidewalk all afternoon. He pulled out three crisp one-hundred-dollar bills. It was a *fuck off* without having to say the words. "How much table time does that buy us?"

Antonio didn't answer, but he pocketed the money and walked back to the bar. Above it, a World Cup soccer match from about five years before replayed on a television screen. No one seemed to be watching.

Derek had his back to the sidewall, affording him a decent view of not only the bar but also out the open patio doors to the sidewalk eating area and the entrance. Max sat on his right, his view more toward the bar as if he expected Liberty to stroll out of the back and come sit down at their table.

"How many days are we going to sit here?" Max asked. "You're going to have to get back to real life at some point, and those hundreds aren't going to last forever."

"Max." When Max put down his beer and glanced over, Derek said, "This *is* real life. And there are plenty more bills if we need them."

Max winced, and Derek wanted to kick himself. He didn't mean to point a finger at the fact that Max was low on funds and that Derek wasn't hurting in the money department. It wasn't a problem for Derek, but it seemed a sore point for Max.

"I am going to pay you back. *Sometime.*"

Derek didn't doubt Max's veracity, and he wouldn't insult Max by refusing to let him. Derek nodded. "Suit yourself."

Then the front door opened, and the surprise must have shown on Derek's face because Max turned around to look. Cesar strode over to their table, a huge grin on his face. He dropped down in the chair across from Derek, his eyes bloodshot and his short, black hair messy as if he'd been running his hands through it for hours.

"You two are a fucking sight." Cesar blew out a breath. "I could use a beer about now."

Cesar caught Antonio's eye and ordered a beer and a round of tequila shots for the table.

"What are the shots for?" Max asked. Though, as far as Derek knew, Max had never turned down a shot of tequila.

"We're celebrating." If possible, Cesar's grin only got wider.

"How did you know we were in here?" Max added.

"It's the biggest place in town. I figured I'd check here first before texting."

"We didn't expect you to drive all the way down here. We could have caught a flight home and—"

Except they didn't have their passports. Which nixed their ability to cross the border in a rental car or fly home unless they got replacement passports from the embassy.

Cesar pulled out their passports from his back pocket and tossed them on the table.

Derek swiped his and gave the other one to Max. "Thank you."

"You're welcome."

Max gave Cesar a little salute. Cesar gave him a nod as Antonio came over with their drinks. "So now I'm going to have three of you sitting here all day?"

"Looks like," Max said. "Unless you want to tell Liberty we're here."

Antonio tossed three new coasters down and left. Cesar picked up his tequila shot. Max and Derek followed his lead, clicking the shot glasses together.

"Wait," Max said before they took the shots. "I still don't know what we're celebrating."

Cesar glanced at his watch then turned his attention to the television. "Marco and some of his men have been arrested. I just got the call about an hour ago. The news report should hit right about—"

Someone hollered out, and Antonio turned up the volume on the television. A breaking news report cut off the replay of the soccer match. They tossed back their shots and walked over to the bar to watch.

"You had something to do with this, didn't you?" Derek said

as they sat on the bar stools. The few people in the restaurant gathered around them.

"Maybe," Cesar allowed.

How did Derek luck into a partner like Cesar? He tuned into the report, eager to get the particulars from Cesar later. The video coverage showed the warehouse where he and Max had been held captive.

On screen, Mexican law enforcement led Marco and some of his men away in handcuffs. The reporters talked about the United States' involvement in the takedown but didn't get into the particulars. Marco must have put up a bit of a fight because his face now looked worse than Derek's had.

The agents put Marco, Tio, and the man with the AR-15 into a van.

"We owe our lives to those two," Derek said. "They're the ones who dumped us on the corner. Marco had given them orders to kill us."

Antonio's cautious gaze shifted from the television to Derek and swung over to Max before taking someone's drink order. The news report ended, the soccer match came back on, and Derek, Cesar, and Max returned to their seats.

"Okay," Max said. "Spill all the deets."

MAX COULDN'T COMPREHEND WHAT THE REPORTERS ON THE newscast had said, but watching all the assholes who'd beat them up and held them captive handcuffed and loaded into the back of a paddy wagon brought a smile to his face.

But Cesar had more information, and he couldn't wait to hear it all.

Antonio came by and brought them a round of beers

without being asked. What the hell was up with that? Not that Max would complain. They accepted with a round of thanks.

When Antonio walked out of earshot, Cesar said, "As I said, I'd already had the location services activated on your phone. By the time I'd lost your location, you two were already too far away from my car's GPS location for comfort. I knew something was up before you answered the call at the warehouse. I just didn't know what. But I thought you might need some backup. On the drive down, I was finally able to get in touch with my buddy at the DEA. Turns out, they'd formed a task force with the Mexican authorities. But Marco was wily, and locals were too afraid for their lives and their families lives to roll on him."

"But when Marco turned on Derek's phone, you got our location."

Cesar clinked his beer glass with Max's before taking a swig. "Exactly. Marco's arrest will probably cause a vacuum that some other opportunistic bastard is going to fill. For now, though, it's a blow to Costa's organization and a win for law enforcement."

Thrilled as he was that Marco and his men had been arrested, there was only one thing that Max really wanted. "Now to find Liberty."

A few people started to wander into the restaurant, the early dinner crowd. The woman bartender from the night before arrived and started making drinks for the new customers. Punta Mar wasn't the kind of town with bad rush-hour traffic, though the foot and street traffic continued to increase as it got closer to quitting time.

Antonio walked toward their table with a glass of beer in his hand. He took what looked like a fortifying sip before commandeered the empty chair at the table, turned it around, and sat.

He glanced from Derek to Max. "Were you two really taken by that bastard?"

Max pointed at Derek's face, wondering where Antonio was

going with this. "There's your proof. If you wanna see the size eleven boot print on my ribs, I'll be happy to show you."

Instead of answering, Antonio asked another question, his attention on Max. "You lying to me about being Liberty's brother?"

Blood swirled in Max's ears as his heart rate kicked up. He noticed the knowing grin start to spread on Derek's face. That grin that said they'd been right about Antonio. He couldn't focus on that, though. Max pulled his passport out of his pocket and handed it over to Antonio. Antonio thumbed through to his photo and vital information. He looked at the photo and back at Max with more scrutiny than any TSA or border patrol agent ever had.

Then Max thumbed through the photos on his phone and found the old photo of him with his sister taken shortly before he'd left. She was young there, but she was just as striking then as she was now. He showed Antonio the photo.

The man across from him stared at the photo for so long that Derek reached a hand under the table and gave Max's nervous knee a comforting squeeze. Cesar quietly sipped his beer. Max wanted to press Antonio, but he was too afraid that Antonio would clam up if he added any pressure.

Antonio handed back the phone and pulled his own out of the apron's front pocket around his waist. He punched in a number, and Derek leaned over and pressed a kiss to Max's temple, Derek's hand still on his knee, lending him his strength.

The call connected, and Antonio said, "Hey, Libby, it's me. Can you come down here?"

Antonio disconnected, his expression inscrutable, but he looked a little green around the edges as if he weren't sure he was doing the right thing.

Max was prepared to wait. Fifteen minutes. Twenty. An hour. However long it took. He hadn't been prepared to see Liberty walk down the back stairs of the restaurant, her steps faltering and her smile dropping when she spotted Antonio sitting with him.

Antonio stood when she got to the table. "Hey, baby, I—"

"Don't 'hey, baby' me. What the fuck are they doing here? Did you call them, did—"

"He didn't call us," Max said, wanting to keep Antonio out of the fray. "We've been looking everywhere for you."

She crossed her arms over her chest. "Well, you found me. You can leave now."

Antonio caught her arm as she tried to walk away, the anger and resentment in her eyes melting away when he pulled her into his arms. He kissed her forehead and tucked her hair behind her ears. "Take them upstairs where you can talk. If you never want to see them again after that, I'll throw them out myself. Okay?"

Liberty swiped at her eyes and nodded. Max's heart dropped a beat when she looked at him, tears brimming in her eyes. Sunlight streamed in through the open patio doors and high-lighted the faded bruise on her left cheek. Max had a damn good idea who'd given it to her. Luckily for those men, the authorities had already taken them into custody. Otherwise, Max would have hunted them down for what they'd done to his sister.

"Follow me." She turned on her heel and started walking away. Antonio headed back to the bar.

"I'm gonna go find a room," Cesar said. "Call me later?"

Derek nodded, and to Max said, "Want me to go with you or—"

"No." However, it was an outright lie. Max wanted Derek there but knew this was between him and his sister. "This is something I have to do alone. I'll find you when we're done."

Derek squeezed his hand and kissed him on the lips before

letting him go. That Derek continued to show his affection in public freed a tether on his heart that he hadn't known tied it down. Max had certainly changed since he'd been gone, but it looked like Derek had as well.

"I'll be waiting."

Max walked toward the back of the restaurant, where a sullen Liberty stood at the bottom of the stairs. He followed her to the apartment up above, expecting to find a crowded studio apartment much like his own. Instead, he glanced around, unable to hide his amazement.

"Don't look so surprised," Liberty said, "Antonio is more than a small-town restaurant owner. He's super smart. He's a goddamn graduate from Duke's financial college, and—" Liberty looked at Max then, *really* looked at him. "And he's the only man who's ever treated me like a real person."

Max pulled her into a hug, and, surprisingly, she melted into his chest. She started crying, and it was all Max could do not to cry with her. He held her until her sobs slowed. She sniffed, wiping away the moisture on her face. She leaned back, and Max let her go. A watery laugh escaped as she wiped at the wetness she'd left on his shirt.

"Sorry about that."

"It's okay."

She offered a tremulous smile. "Wanna sit?"

"I'd like that."

Antonio had an open-concept apartment that must have taken up the space over the restaurant and a few of the other shops. But instead of something that harkened back to the building's construction, however long ago, he'd modernized it. It looked more like a sleek New York City loft than an apartment above a restaurant in a tiny Mexican sea village. His eyes caught on a three-screen array attached to the wall above an unclut-tered glass desk, the ticker tape for the New York Stock

Exchange scrolling across one of the screens. Another one had a bunch of graphs on it, while the third had CNN playing on mute.

"Is Antonio some kind of stockbroker?"

"He worked on Wall Street before he gave it all up to start the restaurant. He says Punta Mar is much better for his mental health."

"And you?" Max asked, ready to know more. "What are you doing here?"

Liberty settled into the corner of the leather couch, tucking her legs beneath her. "Healing, mostly."

"I thought you were dead." The words came out without bidding, his voice cracking at the end. His chest tightened, and it took a concentrated effort to breathe through it.

"I thought I was, too. For a minute. Then Tio and his man dumped me in some town. I waited a day for the bus to come and take me wherever it went. I wanted out. Of there, and out of any resemblance of my previous life back in the States, so I took a page out of your book and ran."

Max winced, but he'd deserved it.

"You came looking for me, though." The abject wonder in her voice made the back of his eyes sting.

"I told you that I wanted to make things right with you. I meant it. I don't think I would have survived if I'd stayed. I do regret not taking you with me, though."

"You mean that, don't you?" Again, that utter wonder, that total amazement that she was worthy of being found and of making things right with her. It was part of the fucked-upedness that was their parents. He'd thought she'd escaped the worst of the verbal and mental abuse. After all, his parents' wrath had been focused on him while he'd lived at home. He hadn't thought his parents would have turned on her in his absence.

"With everything I am."

She crumbled in front of his eyes. He scooted across the couch and pulled his little sister into his arms, and they both held on for their dear lives.

When they finally broke apart again, his chest tight, but his heart nearly full, he huffed out a heavy breath. "You got any beer up here?"

She laughed. "In the fridge."

He opened the door of the chef's grade refrigerator and selected a bottle of beer. He held it up. "Want one?"

Liberty shook her head. "I've been sober now for almost two weeks. I even gave up cigarettes."

"Holy shit. I'm proud of you."

She ducked her head when he sat back down beside her, the telltale signs of a blush running up her face. When she glanced up at him, he took her all in. Her hair was clean and cascaded down her shoulders—and dyed a brunette much closer to her natural color. Her clothes were washed and without holes. Her eyes clear, except for the redness from her recent crying.

"You look good, Libs." He squeezed her knee. "You really look good."

She offered a shy smile. Her self-protective 'badass' shield had fallen, and the real Liberty looked good on her. "Thanks."

Then he cut his eyes at her, a smile toying with his lips. "This Antonio guy, how did you end up here with him?"

Liberty put her arm on the back of the couch, resting her head in her hand. "He found me late one night in the alley behind the restaurant digging in the dumpster for food. The bus had dumped me here earlier in the day, and I was starving. He heard the commotion and came down, thinking a bunch of cats had gotten into the garbage. Instead, he found me."

Antonio was protective of her, of that Max had no doubt, but he still had questions. After all, even if Antonio and Liberty were both adults, he'd always be her big brother. "Who takes in a stray woman off the streets?"

"One with a big heart," Liberty said with no hesitation. "He took me in. Fed me. Bought me some clothes and gave me a safe place to stay."

"What is he getting out of it?"

A thick line formed between her brows as she scowled at him. "Stop it. He's not like that. Trust me. I've been around enough of the bad ones to know."

It took effort, but Max tramped down on his protectiveness, knowing he had to trust his sister's instincts. And if he were honest with himself, Antonio came off as an okay dude. "Do you love him?"

"Do you love Derek?" she snapped back.

That she'd recognized Derek after all those years didn't come as a surprise—he was just as handsome and remarkable as he'd been ten years ago. "We're not talking about me."

He raised his brows at her when she didn't immediately answer about her feelings for Antonio.

She raised her hands and let them drop in her lap. "I don't know, okay? It's too early to tell. But there's something special there. Something beyond the gratitude. He treats me like a person, not a means to an end. He listens. He's protective and funny and gives me space yet holds me near. I don't know what that is yet, but I want to hang around and find out what it could become."

Her words hit, not like a punch, but like a round-house kick when he realized what she was saying.

And it fucking hurt.

"You're not coming back, are you?"

She shook her head. "No. There's nothing for me in the valley." Then she glanced up at him. "Besides you. But if you want to visit sometime..."

"We—" Max caught himself before adding Derek where he might not want to be. "I'd like that." And because he couldn't help himself, he added, "If this doesn't work out, if you need money to come home or to stay—"

"I don't want your money, Max."

"What are you going to do then?"

"I'm thinking about going into the family business."

Max couldn't keep the horrified expression off his face. "You want to cook meth and sell drugs?"

Liberty rolled her eyes. "No, dummy. I want to apprentice to become a tattoo artist."

Now she was really confusing him. "But you hate drawing."

"No, I hated that I could never draw as well as you." She leaned forward and picked up one of those black composition notebooks school kids used from the coffee table and handed it to him.

He stared at the first page in the book. The lines on the page made it harder for him to see her drawings, but they couldn't hide her raw talent. Her shading put his to shame, and her three-dimensional game blew him away.

"I have to see what kind of visa I can get to stay here, but there's a tattoo parlor down the street," she said. "I showed the owner my sketches. They're willing to let me apprentice. I'm supposed to start next week."

"If these are any indication, you're going to be sought after."

The grin that grew on her face couldn't have been bigger than if he'd told her she'd won the SuperLotto Plus. "Thanks."

He thumbed through more of the sketches. They heard footsteps on the stairs, and Antonio opened the door with a bag of takeout in each hand and set them on the coffee table. He leaned in and pressed a kiss to the side of Liberty's head before turning his attention to Max. "I brought you guys some dinner to take back to your room."

Max stood. "You didn't have to do that."

"I figured your friend already paid handsomely for it."

Max accepted the bags, recognizing this as Antonio's subtle way of checking on Liberty and telling Max his time was up. "I'm glad you're doing well. That's all I ever wanted for you."

She stood and hugged Max and whispered in his ear. "I'm sorry I put you through all that. Thank you for loving me enough to find me."

And fuck if the backs of his eyes didn't start stinging again. "I'd like to stop by in the morning before we leave, if that's okay?"

Liberty smiled at him. God, she was so beautiful when she was happy. "I'd like that."

Derek and Cesar took turns driving on the way back to the valley. Max slept most of the way, except when they had to show their passports at the border.

It was the middle of the night by the time Derek pulled up to the office to get his car and send Cesar on his way.

Max climbed into the front seat beside Derek, rubbing the sleep from his eyes. "I can drive if you want. You must be beat."

"I'm okay. I caught a nap earlier while Cesar drove."

"You guys should have woken me. I could have done my share."

Derek held his hand out over the Roadster's center console, and Max linked his fingers with his. "You needed that rest more than you realized."

"I guess. I hadn't slept well since Liberty disappeared."

Backing into the street, Derek headed toward his house and Max's tattoo shop. "You worried about leaving her behind?"

"I thought I would be, but she seemed to be in a really good place mentally. I think she needs to be there. At least for now."

Derek squeezed his hand, turning his attention back to the road. His eyes wanted to close, but he didn't have that much farther to drive. Derek couldn't wait to crawl into his bed, hopefully with his arms wrapped around Max. But he didn't want to assume. "Where to? You want to come to my place?"

"I don't know." Derek's stomach tumbled as if he'd lost power to Joss's Otter, and he was about to go into a tailspin as Max spoke. "My appointments start early in the morning."

It wasn't exactly an excuse. As soon as Max had a return date to the valley, his assistant had booked people from his waitlist. But Derek wasn't naïve enough to believe that was all that was going on.

At the next light, instead of turning toward his house, he turned and headed for Max's shop. At the back, a set of stairs led to the studio apartment above. He kissed the back of Max's hand, not wanting to let go but knowing he must.

Max didn't look at him when he unfastened his seatbelt and popped the door. The interior lights kicked on.

"I could come up," Derek offered. He hated the desperation in his voice. Did a part of him think that if he let Max go that he'd never see him again?

Maybe?

After all, they'd done what they'd set out to do. They'd found Liberty.

"I don't think that's such a good idea." Max let go of Derek's hand and stepped out of the car. Derek buzzed down the window so they could still talk when Max closed the door.

"I'll call you tomorrow, okay?" Derek said, searching for any indication that everything wasn't ending at the foot of a set of metal stairs.

Max stood there a moment, then leaned his forearms on the sill of the door and stuck his head back into the car. "You know what? I think we should give ourselves a week. No. Make that two."

Wait. What?

Even though a part of Derek had expected exactly that, the words knocked him back.

That sinking feeling in Derek's stomach reached out for a life ring but couldn't manage to hold on. His voice croaked when he said, "T-Two weeks?" Then anger seeped in. "What the hell for?"

"To give you a chance to take back the things that you said."

"I won't."

"You say that now. But I know this situation with Liberty threw us together. Emotions ran high. And I want to make sure what we're feeling—what *you're* feeling is real. As for me, I'm all in. I just want you to make sure that if we move forward, that we're on the same page."

Derek grunted, not liking what Max had to say, but a part of him begrudgingly understood his point. And it hurt like hell to admit that, even if he didn't believe anything would change. Derek made a point of checking the clock on his dash. "Two weeks. Not a second more."

Max tapped the sill and trudged up the stairs to his apartment. Derek waited long after Max had locked himself inside before shifting into gear and driving to his place.

"Well fuck," he said to no one.

Two weeks.

Only two weeks.

Not that long. Especially compared to ten years. And no matter what Max might think, it wouldn't change how Derek felt about him. If ten years hadn't changed things, thirteen days, twenty-three hours, fifty-five minutes, and twenty seconds wouldn't change them either.

"WHAT THE HELL IS GOING ON IN HERE?" CESAR SAID AS HE CAME

into Derek's office. "I had to end my conference call because you were making so much racket."

Derek stood at his filing cabinet, the flush of frustration burning up the back of his neck. He tugged on the drawer again and gave it another kick.

"Whoa, whoa, whoa." Cesar pushed him aside. "The button slides to the right, not the left."

Derek knew that. "I fucking know that."

He blew out a breath and stuffed the file back in the drawer, then flopped down in his chair.

Cesar hitched a leg over the corner of Derek's desk. He had one of those overly patient looks on his face as if he were dealing with a toddler having a meltdown.

"I take it Max hasn't called or texted yet."

"I didn't expect him to." Though really, Derek had. The two weeks were up at one-thirteen in the morning. And he still didn't know what he was going to do when Max's arbitrary time expired.

Liar.

"Did the two weeks help clarify anything for you?" Cesar sounded more like a therapist than his partner, but considering Cesar had been tip-toeing around Derek's cantankerous mood for the past two weeks, Derek cut him some slack.

Derek rubbed at the scruff on his chin. He'd barely shaved since he'd returned, and he hadn't bothered coming to work in a suit since then either. Luckily, it hadn't put too many of his clients off. "Only that I miss the fuck out of him."

"*Really*?" Cesar dialed up the sarcasm. "I couldn't tell."

"Anyone ever tell you you're an asshole?"

"All the fucking time." Cesar stood and grinned. "I'm going to leave you to your angst then. There's not enough room in here for the three of us. I'll catch you in a little bit."

Cesar left Derek's office, but instead of heading back to his own office, he headed down the hall toward the exit. "Hey, where are you going?"

The retreating footsteps stopped, but when Cesar didn't appear in his doorway, he called out again, "*Cesar?*"

A few seconds later, Cesar stood in the doorway of Derek's office, a shoulder propped on the door jamb as if trying to look casual. He couldn't pull it off.

"Where are you going?"

Cesar's gaze dropped to the floor before he glanced back up at Derek. "I'm going to meet Saxon for coffee."

"*Saxon Grey?* Your ex's boyfriend?"

"That's him."

"Why the hell would you put yourself through that?"

"Because he asked me to."

"You don't owe that guy anything. You had no idea your ex was with someone when you slept with him. That's not on you."

"It's just coffee," Cesar reiterated.

"Okay. Fine." Like Derek had a say in the matter.

Cesar chuckled. "See you later."

The back door opened and closed, and Derek stared out the front window while Cesar's car passed by on the road below.

He glanced down at the time on his computer. It wasn't one-thirteen in the morning, but as far as Derek was concerned, Max's two weeks were up. With renewed energy, Derek did a little research, made a call, and began putting his plan into action.

"I'm back," Cesar said as he stopped by Derek's office.

Derek glanced up from the design program on his computer. Design wasn't his thing, and he'd failed art more than once in elementary school, so it was slow going. "That was quick. Did you change your mind about meeting him?"

Cesar shook his head, an incredulous grin spreading on his

face. "I've been gone for two hours." He moved to come around to Derek's side of the desk.

Derek quickly escaped out of the program he'd been working on.

"What are you doing?" Cesar asked.

"Nothing."

Cesar glanced from the empty desktop view and back to Derek. "Whatever it is, it's *not* nothing. And if it's porn, tell me now so I can make sure our internet security is up to snuff."

"I wasn't looking at porn."

"I'm just saying."

"Don't you have work to do?"

"Yeah, I guess I do."

Cesar left him alone to put the finishing touches on his design project. It came out well if he did say so himself. He hit print, grabbed his keys, and screwed up his courage. He stuck his head into Cesar's office on his way out.

"I'm out for the rest of the day."

Cesar looked at him over the top of his computer with a stupid, knowing grin on his face. "Okay."

Now that he had a solid plan regarding Max, he had a moment to focus on something besides himself. "Two-hour coffee date, huh?"

"It wasn't a date."

Maybe not, but the mega-watt smile on Cesar's face told Derek something was up.

"You kissed him, didn't you? You kissed your ex's boyfriend."

"No. I kissed my ex's *ex*-boyfriend. And you know what?"

"What?"

"I liked it."

Derek barked out a laugh. He hadn't felt like laughing in nearly two weeks. "Good for you."

As Derek walked down the hall, Cesar called out. "Tell Max hello for me."

MAX CLEANED UP HIS STATION AFTER HIS LAST APPOINTMENT OF the day. For the first time in two weeks, he'd not taken any late appointments to catch up on lost work. He'd blocked off the last two slots of the afternoon so he could get off a little early.

He needed the break, and even though he'd done more tattoos in the past couple of weeks than he usually did in a month, it wasn't lost on him what day it was.

Two weeks, and he hadn't heard a peep from Derek.

You're the idiot who told him you didn't want any contact for two weeks.

Yeah, but he'd never really expected Derek to respect his wishes. Every morning he'd checked his phone for messages. He'd done the same thing every night before he crawled into bed, expecting, or hoping, that Derek had sent him *something*. Hell, Max would have even loved one of those kissy emoticons, even though he hated them.

The bell clattered tonelessly against the glass front door, and Max heard the low muttering of his assistant's voice as he spoke with whoever walked in. Max didn't pay him much attention. He was done for the day.

Max stifled a groan as Jordan clomped down the hall in his patent leather platform boots. There was no mistaking that walk. Screwing up some patience, Max did his best not to bite Jordan's head off when he poked his head into the room. "What is it now?"

Jordan had spikey purple hair, cat eye contacts, a Hello Kitty fetish, and enough piercings to set off a metal detector at fifty paces. "Um... your last appointment is here."

"I don't have any more appointments for today."

"He kind of made it at the last minute."

Max closed his eyes and blew out a hot breath. "Please tell me it's not an infinity tattoo. I've tattooed twenty infinities if I tattooed one since I've been back."

"It's not an infinity."

"He can't reschedule?"

"I don't feel comfortable telling him no."

Max liked Jordan. He did, but one of these days, Jordan had to grow a pair. "Fine. But this is the last one."

Jordan disappeared before Max finished his sentence. He sat down on his rolling stool, unpacked his tattoo gun, and pulled out a fresh set of needles. What was one more tattoo?

He had his back turned toward the door, getting out his inks when he heard footsteps behind him. "Have a seat. I'll be right with you."

"Whatever you say, *Maxie*."

Max spun around and caught himself against his tattoo table. "What are you doing here?"

His words came out sounding breathless. A part of him had expected Derek to show up at the shop in that first week, but when he hadn't, a part of Max had given up. In the past two weeks, he'd cursed himself daily for ordering Derek to stay away.

But here he was.

He handed Max a folded piece of paper. "I came to get a tattoo."

"You don't have any tattoos."

"Only because I could never think of something that meant enough to me that I wanted it on my body forever."

Derek stuffed his hands into his pockets. He looked like he hadn't shaved since they'd returned from Mexico, and the bruising under his eyes only seemed worse. Had he not been getting any sleep? And why did that bring a hint of a smile to Max's face?

"Your eye looks good. Looks like you're good as new."

Derek bobbed his chin toward the piece of paper in Max's hand. "I didn't come here to show you how well I healed up."

Max swallowed down the obvious question—*then why are you here?*—and stared down at the folded piece of paper in his hand. Clients brought him samples of work they wanted done all the time. It wasn't anything unusual, but his heart rattled against his chest as he unfolded the piece of printer paper and stared down at the image there.

His breath caught, his eyes stung, and he had to clear his voice before he could speak. "Where do you want it?"

Derek pointed to a spot directly over his heart. "Right here."

Max couldn't look at Derek's face, couldn't see the shine in his eyes without losing his shit, so he avoided eye contact. "Take your shirt off and have a seat. I just need to make a transfer real quick."

Max knew what Derek looked like shirtless, hell he'd seen him naked many times, but that didn't prepare him for how he felt when he saw Derek laid out on his table shirtless. God, he loved that man.

Before his knees gave way, Max sat on his stool. His hands shook as he shaved and cleaned the area. By sheer force of will, he settled his nerves, applied the transfer over Derek's heart, and peeled back the paper.

The words in a bold script read: *All In*.

Derek grabbed Max's wrist before he could put needle to skin. "I mean it."

Max only nodded because he didn't want Jordan to hear him blubbering like a baby.

For the next hour, Max forced the questions out of his mind. He needed all of his concentration as he traced every line and filled in all the shadow work. Leaving Derek with a shitty tattoo wasn't an option.

When he finished, he wiped away the excess ink and thoroughly cleaned the tattoo.

Before bandaging, Derek said, "Can I see it?"

Max stood and held out his hand. Derek took it, and Max helped him to his feet. "Close your eyes."

Even though Derek did as he asked, Max stood behind him and held his hands over Derek's eyes, walking him over to the full-length mirror. He removed his hands. "You can look now."

Derek's lids fluttered open, and their eyes met in the mirror. That one heated, hungry look made Max's chest constrict and his cock hard. Derek tore his gaze away and checked out the tattoo. "Holy fuck."

Derek moved in closer, turning this way and that way, taking the new ink in from all directions, his jaw still dropped open. He turned and wrapped an arm around Max's neck and pulled him into his chest, hugging him tight. "You are so fucking talented."

Derek pulled away enough to see Max's face. "If these last ten years and these last two agonizing weeks have taught me anything, it's that I love you, Maxie. I couldn't get you out of my system then, and I can't now. I know we have things to work out, and we'll need some clear and honest communication to smooth out the bumps, but I'm here, ready to put in the work. And if you'll still have me. I'm all in, too."

Max held Derek's chin and answered Derek's question with a kiss. He didn't go easy on Derek, and Derek didn't give an inch, their tongues dueling, daring.

Max spun and shoved Derek against the wall, careful to avoid the tender skin beneath the fresh tattoo. The fresh tattoo that promised Max the only thing he ever wanted from Derek.

Forever.

ROMANTIC SUSPENSE

Lazy S Ranch Series
Cowgirl, Unexpectedly (Book 1)
Must Love Horses (Book 2)
Hot on the Trail (Book 3)
Cowboy, Undercover (Book 4)
Cowboy, Unbridled (Book 5)
Cowgirl, Unbroken (Book 6)

Wright's Island Series
Don't Look Back (Book 1)
In Her Defense (Book 2)

Steele-Wolfe Securities
Wyoming Confidential (Book 1)
Dealing With the Devil (Book 2 Coming mid 2021)
Swift Justice (Book 3 Coming late 2021)

CONTEMPORARY ROMANCE

Rockin' Rodeo Series
Luck of the Draw (Book 1)
Photo Chute (Book 2)
Reined In (Book 3)
Rockin' Rodeo Series Collection (Books 1-3)

MM ROMANCE

Black Stallion Studios Series
One Shot (Book 1)
Key Grip (Book 2)
Best Boy (Book 3)

Black Stallion Studios Box Set (Books 1-3)

Valley Boys
Art of Love (Book 1)
Flight of Fancy (Book 2)
Den of Thieves (Book 3)

ABOUT THE AUTHOR

Vicki Tharp makes her home on small acreage in south Texas with her husband and an embarrassing number of pets. When she isn't writing, you can usually find her on the back of her horse—avoiding anything that remotely resembles housework—smelling like fly spray and horse sweat.

Join my newsletter at: http://bit.ly/V-W-T
Join my street team and receive free Advance Reader Copies of my upcoming books at: http://bit.ly/S-W-S-T
You can find my website at: www.VickiTharp.com
I love to hear from readers. You can email me at vwtharp@VickiTharp.com

Or you can stalk me at:

facebook.com/VickiTharpAuthor
instagram.com/author_Vicki_Tharp
bookbub.com/authors/vicki-tharp
amazon.com/author/vicki_tharp
twitter.com/vwtharp